'Her characters have the ring of complex truth. These people can aggravate and endear themselves all at the same time. Just like real life.'

—Carol Birch, *The Independent*, on *Kith & Kin*

'She has a special talent for cutting through the apparently ordinary and finding what is remarkable underneath; and, in doing so, reveals deep truths about the extremes of human nature.'

—*Financial Times Magazine*, on *Kith & Kin*

Stevie Davies is a novelist of great skill and this is a brilliantly crafted work...

—Gwyn Griffiths, *Morning Star*, on *Kith & Kin*

'Davies's prose [is] unequivocally superb... She puts many of her contemporaries to shame, with some breath-taking passages and a rendering of place and time so replete with telling and incidental detail that you can taste and smell it...'

—Kathryn Gray, *New Welsh Review*, on *Kith & Kin*

'Davies just writes, very precisely – sometimes wonderfully – sometimes fiction, sometimes non-fiction – and always from the heart. She does what a writer does – making beauty for strangers, passing it on.'

—A.L. Kennedy, *The Guardian*, on *The Eyrie*

'Davies writes with a reflectiveness that finds the drama in the details of lives, following minutely the small steps that amount to growth or decline, and accumulate to trigger rebellion or resignation.'

'Stevie Davies is extremely observant about the micro-processes: the tiny unwritten laws, the daily manoeuvres, the small decisions that make up the texture of daily life…'

Stevie Davies comes from Swansea and spent a nomadic childhood in Egypt, Scotland and Germany. After studying at Manchester University, she went on to lecture there, returning to Swansea in 2001. She is Emeritus Professor of Creative Writing at Swansea University.

Stevie is both a Fellow of the Royal Society of Literature and a Fellow of the Welsh Academy. She has won numerous awards for her fiction, and has been long-listed for the Booker and Orange Prizes. Several of her books have been adapted into radio and screenplays, and she has written for the *Guardian* and *Independent* newspapers.

Parthian
The Old Surgery
Napier Street
Cardigan
SA43 1ED

www.parthianbooks.co.uk

ISBN 978-1-910901-80-9

Cover design by Syncopated Pandemonium
Cover photo by Gabriele Lopez/Millennium Images, UK
Typeset by Syncopated Pandemonium
Printed and bound in Bulgaria by pulsioprint.co.uk

The publisher acknowledges the financial support of the Welsh Books
Council.

British Library Cataloguing in Publication Data
A cataloguing record for this book is available from the British Library.

Arrest Me,
for I Have Run Away

Short Stories

STEVIE DAVIES

liebe Anne
du warst in abgelebten Zeiten / Meine Schwester

Contents

The World When We Abandon It

Up or under — on this ledge or in that vault — the moment comes when you can't hang on and you can't let go. There's nothing for it but to chicken out. Just wail and give up, Violet. Go home. I daren't though, that's the worst of it.

— We guessed you weren't really one of us, they'll say, the alpha males of the Up-and-Unders. — But hey, that's OK, Vi, this extreme stuff isn't for everyone – and, no disrespect, it's a big ask for a lass five foot one in her socks.

But how much more hazardous it would be to settle for living at ground level. There's further to fall and a deeper burial. With the Up-and-Unders, seeing from the perspective of the eagle and the mole, I'm equally mortal, yes, but more alive too. Sasha doesn't seem to like me and Jaxer's a mini Napoleon — but Christie is a poet and Leo's a gentle, mellow guy.

And somehow at altitude my darling lost Jamie seems closer at hand; the membrane between us becomes transparent.

Urban explorers trespass to question the law, to extend citizenship: so Jaxer blogs when we report a stunt and post Sasha's photos on the website. My first Up, my initiation, is St Pancras: the Gothic clock tower of the Grand Hotel. Jaxer, who knows everything and takes a godlike view, pronounces: — It's a doddle, Violet, just a nursery slope.

Day and night the din of renovation throbs on. Access points swarm with builders and security guards. In workmen's hard hats and carrying clip boards, we jump the fence and blag our way, with incredulous ease, past a builder at the front entrance. Jaxer's an inveterate liar and I appear, as librarians do, politely authoritative.

He rushes me up the double spiral staircase: no time to gasp at its Gothic magnificence or admire the vaulted ceiling set with stars. Flight upon dark flight takes us to the Clock Tower steps. A boastful tour. Jaxer, according to Jaxer, can penetrate where others can't and piss in improbable places.

Rotting steps hang at several points clear of the wall. The timber vaulting soars beyond the sphere of my mourning, and in some far-fetched way promises an oblique nearness to Jamie. I've always taken care never to show the Up-and-Unders the state of my heart. I appear quiet and calm and neutral. With every step the staircase flinches. I shoulder open the hatch. We're inside the tower of the Victorian railway cathedral.

— Amazing, I breathe. — Oh, amazing!

Jaxer, who was amazed himself before he became God, plays host. Switching off the clock's backlighting, he grants me a prospect of the city. Pinhead folk in the street will double-take as the giant clock winks. We've time-travelled into the gap between now and then, the world when its Victorian masters abandoned it.

When a security guard crunches his way up the ladder, I huddle in a ball but Jaxer slouches where he is, attitudinising as usual, arms folded. Cursory torchlight sweeps his face but the guard, expecting no one, detects no one. Perhaps he takes Jaxer for a gargoyle.

And then we're outside, high on the balcony, with rainswept London at our feet and the clock face behind us.

— So am I in, Jaxer?

— Course you are, darling.

Christie warned me there'd be an initiation ritual. Scrapy beard. Small, delicate, rather girlie lips. I wait it out. Nobody has tried to kiss me since my husband. They may have smelt on my breath the foulness of the grave. There's only ever one female at a time in the Up-and-Unders and I'm now it. Jaxer can't go back on his word, however corpse-like he finds me.

— Do something for me, Vi?

— What?

— Keep an eye on Leo.

— Why? Leo's a nice guy.

— Sure he is. Just a feeling.

I'm not about to spy for Jaxer. Leo, the environmentalist, is a quiet, modest character and perhaps the only one I could confide in.

★

3

This is the big one, the Up of all Ups — the first of two visits. We're waiting for the Shard-guard to complete his round and retire to his hut. Sasha has been telling Jaxer I'm a liability. — No fuckin balls when it comes to it. Jaxer credits himself with enough balls for two. — She's coming, I heard him hiss at Sasha, — she wants it, she's ready. End of.

Once the guard's settled with Page Three and a pie, five Up-and-Unders swing over icy scaffold-pipes onto the walkway of the nearly-completed, almost-tallest building in Europe. The guard, poor guy, will be fired tomorrow when the photos are published.

Twenty, thirty sets of concrete stairs, we're yomping up and up, forty, fifty, we've slowed down, calves and thighs on fire, oh shit, fifty-five, sixty. Paroxysms of pain set in, I have to keep stopping, I'm yawing like a yacht and Sasha ahead of me is muttering, — Balls of iron, mate, balls of iron!

Metal stairs, then wooden ones. Seventy and still, Jesus Christ, we're not there. One last hatch — and out.

In the icy air your sweat stings like a coat of nettles. The drop sucks at your eyes. Sasha's photographing his foot held out over the parapet. Christie launches into poetry, stating that he's silent upon a peak in Darien.

We haul ourselves up on the crane's counterweight. I'm second to last and my death hangs below me, a thrilling space.

Let go, let go your hold. Go home to Jamie. Pay your dues. Release is offered gratis, the blissful work of a moment. Just vanish, Violet.

Leo, behind me, coughs. A simple, human, understated

cough above the abyss. I'm ashamed to be endangering him; shame pushes me to creep forward, slipping into the crane cabin with the rest.

Light flows across the midnight-blue city in a river-system of silver and golden railway tracks and carriageways.

Scintillations of light, breathtaking coruscations.

The tar-black river.

The puny Barbican, the BT Tower, Centre Point. All dwarfed.

The foundations of the Shard weren't even dug in Jamie's lifetime and that's a strange thought. Somewhere out there beyond Strata is our attic flat: I try to position it within a cityscape that resembles a dream of itself.

They're horsing around pretending to press the green button in the crane cabin. This unhinged behaviour goes on for several minutes. Jaxer acquires my hand and his mollusc mouth angles towards mine. Jesus, here we go. Done. I catch Leo's look of concern. He touches my shoulder gently, as if to warn me. You're too near the edge, his eyes say, and I wonder what else he knows, and I like him.

Our muscles, scalding and convulsing, demand to go down. They ache for the comfort of the steady earth.

We spider past the drowsy guard.

Down here, my eyes clamber the height of the Shard to the red light at the crane's apex, thinking, — I was there and I survived.

— We'll do the Shard again when the spire's going on, Jaxer says. – Don't miss it.

— You'd have to go a long way to see such spendthrift beauty, says Leo.

★

I've never fancied the Under part of the project but if you do Up you have to be ready for Under. I've done the Carlsbad Caverns, I told Jaxer. I didn't mention what I'd done there. Or what I thought I saw.

New Mexico. Ice Age bones were found in the entrance: jaguars and camels and giant sloths. The rocks around the mouth were vulva-pink. I was swallowed in horror, just viewing from a distance the monstrous cavern opening. Jamie hadn't long been gone, I was in no fit state, I was a mad person who'd flown to Texas, driven south, wandered off the beaten track and got sucked down the biggest drain in the world.

While tourists strolled, pointing and exclaiming, I cringed my way down the path, clutching the rail. Each new cavern loomed spectral in the dim light. Millennia back, sulphuric acid had carved out grotesque statuary: the fleshy Witch's Finger; the pinkly anal Devil's Den. A Ku Klux Klansman ruled his own circle of hell.

And all the while he talked, oh how he gabbled, the ghastly old bore who latched on to me, his name was Pogue, a retired professor. — And *this* is America, he bragged. — This is *old,* we don't just have *new,* you folks have nothing like this in England, we have *sublime*, you have *picturesque*. He guided me, the ancient Emeritus, gripping my hand in his bony digits. My right eye whirled migrainous flakes of light.

And in this descent I spied Jamie.

Jamie in his old hooded cardigan that held his scent,

6

Jamie came bounding lightly uphill towards me, Jamie, my oldest and dearest friend, my husband, against the descending crowd. He was wearing his threadbare jeans and old trainers. I snatched my hand from Pogue; reached out. In the half-light Jamie faded, folding sideways, softly launching into the void.

— Don't lean over the rail, the old guy said. — Are you crazy?

I wouldn't have minded falling. Following my hallucination down into the mother of all pits, I might have caught up and in my final instant have seen his face. Instead I laboured back up with croaking lungs, to shuffle out into the smiting sun: the New Mexico desert of red rocks and scrub, cactus and mountain ridges. At the motel I drank iced water and swam up and down the pool, the sun baking my head into a warm loaf, my heart skew-whiff and comforted. Of course it had been a delusion, my sighting. The fact remains, I'd rather have a delusion than no Jamie at all.

★

The Underground's redundant sections preserve traces of our grandparents' world, Leo says. We've arrived early at the all-night café, our meeting place. Jack of all trades, a nomad who works as a seasonal farm labourer, Leo has attended every major eco-protest and lived in a tree house; he's spent a week or two in prison. Leo's arm's tattooed: cupped hands holding an oak tree, the globe suspended in a waterdrop.

— None of my business, he says when Christie's at the

counter. — But don't let anyone take advantage of you, Violet. Really, don't.

— It's OK, Leo. I've got it well in hand. But thanks anyway.

I'm relieved that someone's looking out for me. Maybe that's why Jaxer fears Leo.

Christie reckons there's poetry in chips; wolfs his, then saunters out for a smoke. Leo blurts, — Have you ever lost someone, Violet?

How can he know? What does he read in me? I see him register my recoil.

— Sorry — not prying: I was going to tell you — about Sharon.

I wait. His face works. No words come. I offer my hand.

— But I can't — *can't*. Sorry. Ignore me.

— Leo.

— No, it's fine. Just. Please.

Leo gathers his gear together. Something about him. Very deep, sad, beautiful.

Beneath the manhole is a drain-smelling column of pent air. Hand-over-hand thirty metres into the bowels of Holborn Station we descend and then there's a short walk to the platform. We're counted and ready. Time will loop back on itself. And I'll be ready to squeeze into the gap.

Into my memory as I approach the tunnel comes the epic journey of Neddy the dear old donkey, being led by the nose up Mount Kilimanjaro.

★

Poor Jamie. He'd been dog-sick with altitude sickness, retching and gasping and passing out. An oxygen mask had to be taped to his face, the bottle being carried by his guide, the tube dangling between them. How patient the guide was; how stoical the guided, plodding across the moor beneath Kili like a mule. That was the thing with Jamie, he could laugh at himself, even in extremity. Diffident, rueful, his sweet nature accepted in himself and excused in others a multitude of failings. He'd not make the summit; I would.

Go on, he urged, *don't hang around for me.*

*

The second Underground stage is the sprint through the tunnel. Appetite for danger floods me, though only maintenance trains are running: even so, the track could go live any moment. That's what gives you the buzz. The rails might sing, a train pitch round the bend at forty miles an hour. For a millisecond you'd see your end rushing upon you. Perhaps in that moment I'd see Jamie. My contrition would meet his forgiving face.

The tracks are rusty, the air chill and stale. Rubbish strews the edge — crisp packets, plastic bags, detritus incapable of decay. I'm running flat out, making nil progress. I seem suspended in mid-stride – and there's a blasting draught whose staleness fouls your lungs and seeps into your blood; it starves the heart and muddles the mind. I pause for breath, bend forward. That's better, yes.

Jogging on, I make out the green tiles of disused Aldwych Platform – the Strand, as was. Everyone's looking back along the line and Sasha hisses, — For fucksake Violet keep up, we can't be carrying you.

Cameras flash and torches strobe the walls, picking out decorated tiles, obsolete adverts, a map showing a pre-Heathrow extension of the Piccadilly line. It's our grandparents' world, in a capsule of nostalgia. They did their work, they went to bed. The shuttle train, so it seems, has just left with its passengers; soon the next will arrive, we'll board, the tannoy will sound, the doors close. I'm in the gap's mouth now, the membrane is thinner and my heart's exploding with expectation.

According to Sasha, we're behind schedule. Someone's been persistently slowing us down.

— Don't start on her, *she's* not the problem, Jaxer says.

Leo's camera pans round each face. When the beam of his helmet-lamp finds me, there's a mothy stirring in my heart, I'm drawn, he lingers, I face away into the dark, resisting a force that weakens the tug of my ghost.

It's time to backtrack and explore the 'Hostel' at Holborn and the twin platform, closed long ago. The narrow corridor to Platform 6 is an archaeological gem. Brown plaster flakes from a red brick wall; painted signs label vacated rooms. Cloakroom, Model Railway Club. There's a coat on a peg in the cloakroom. Whoever left that? Now we're exploring arched dormitories where troglodytic office workers slept like larvae, sequestered from the sun, safe through the Blitz. It's as if they'd this minute hatched, to emerge albino, half blind, in the bygone ruins of London.

Voices: — Best turn back. It's getting late.

No way. I'm not turning back yet. An old door has

been laid as a makeshift ramp from platform to track, over a mass of exposed wires. I make out the really alluring tunnel, bricked up, with — at its centre — a small entrance. The blocked tunnel's my magnet. Hundreds of Londoners slept there in the Blitz, beneath dim bulbs strung on wires, in a rich stench of carbon and unwashed human flesh.

A reverberation through the soles of my trainers tells me the day's beginning, trains are running, I should be gone.

★

Here's a ticket stub and an empty cigarette pack — Player's Navy Cut, with a bearded jack tar framed in a miniature lifebelt. Part of a stubbed-out fag is left in the packet — hard, petrified. Could you actually smoke the surviving part?

I need to sit down; can't breathe properly. Out of breath he was, like this, his heart giving out. Jamie had been fatigued for months before Kilimanjaro: I offered scant sympathy, impatient at his weekend lie-ins. It was a general slowing-down, nothing dramatic. When I suggested Tanzania for our summer holiday, Jamie proposed lazy dips in the warm Mediterranean. Full of phlegm his lungs were in the mornings. Quit the fags, I said: you're only thirty but you sound like an old man. He craved sun. Oh but Kilimanjaro, I urged, it would be amazing. And Jamie couldn't begrudge me; he never could. His diary shows what my selfishness cost him. When does neglect become betrayal?

Safety was a priority, the firm's publicity emphasised: we'd enjoy a bespoke trek. For eight days we'd climb through five climate zones, sleeping in tents and carrying three kinds of hat — brimmed sunhat, beanie, balaclava. No special skills were required, just a general level of fitness. The hotel in Moshi would have mosquito nets and offer African cuisine, I read. — Hey, Jamie, we'll be able to brag we climbed the highest mountain in Africa. Thousands of people climb Kili every year: how hard can it be?

Sunrise dazzled us with oceans of scarlet light. Rain forest. Moorlands. Alpine desert. The crater rim: the lunar landscape.

— Slow right down, advised our guide. — As if you were a ninety-year-old walking backwards.

The wind blew right through every layer Jamie wore. His wet clothes never dried. Shira Camp was his last. While I wolfed fried chicken and spaghetti, Jamie managed a dry cracker. — You go on without me tomorrow, sweetheart, he gasped. — I know what this means to you.

— If you're sure, I said.

I was at the crater's edge of Everyman's Everest and you were down there in the toilet tent dying.

★

— What the fuck are you doing? Sasha's helmet lamp skewers my eye. I shield my face; he's caught a weeping coward crouched in a tunnel. — Who were you talking to?

— Nobody.

— Yeah, you were. Jane or something. What are you crying for? There's definitely something not right about you. In the head.

Shepherding me back along the tunnel, Sasha says, as if to a child or half-wit, — You should realise, Vi, that when you endanger yourself, you endanger us all.

Yes, I know, I've done it before. There's nothing you can tell me about how I'm not a team player.

Once we're back in the station corridor, Sasha stalks ahead. Passing the wartime cloakroom, I hesitate, then blunder in. It might have been a shadow but I could have sworn I saw a coat in here. Yes. Lifting it from the peg, I close the door behind me and catch up.

— It's nothing to do with her being female, Sasha's telling Jaxer. — It's that she's a zombie. She'll get us fucking killed.

I don't catch Jaxer's reply. I just want out.

Reaching the surface is like being reborn. There's a three-quarters moon. It's beautiful. Up here in the fresh air you're bathed from head to foot in life.

— Let me take you home, Violet, says Leo.

Straddling the bike, I reach round Leo's waist and rest my cheek against his back. The soft leather of his jacket is far too reassuring: I could nod off, and I mustn't. Leo keeps talking. He seems to know the way without asking. And the address.

★

Everything's altered in the flat this morning but I can't for the life of me think how. It's as if, in the silence of the night, he'd explored my space and handled all the objects, replacing them pretty much as he found them.

— Tea? Coffee? Leo asks. He's padding round in Jamie's dressing gown with the imagined musk of Jamie's mortal body still in its fibres. – Milk, sugar?

Everything's on a tilt; my attic world has rolled and stuck fast and lies becalmed, slightly out of true. I like the way it lists. I want to live on this slant. It's balm to feel cherished: my heart tips and tumbles.

He's back under the duvet and I'm telling him, — Great tea, Leo. Especially as it's coffee.

— Oh no. Let me try again.

— It's fine.

— How's your head?

— Dizzy. In a good way.

He doesn't directly mention Sharon. Instead he describes lambs. He accommodates these lambs in my spellbound head as we lie in one another's arms. Birthing them, you might need to reach right up into the ewe. Don't fumble; be firm. Leo's fingertips caress the small of my back. You hand-feed each by rota, to give the weaklings a chance to suckle. In the barn you feed them bottled colostrum round the clock, you reek of sheep secretions. And you begin to think like a female animal, your mind goes native in that soup of hormones and fatigue. He's got my head in the crook of his elbow; he mouths my forehead. The lambs butt you, Leo says, with their tough skulls to get your milk flowing. Like this. He gives my sternum a push with his knuckles. It's a healing way to live, Leo says.

He's away for the weekend at an eco-meeting in Schleswig-Holstein. If only he could cancel. But wherever he goes now in the world, Leo will keep close to me. He'll ring if there's a signal behind the mountains.

I sit up and stare at the closing door. An aperture opens, a shutter clicks.

In Leo's wake I laze the morning away and get round to opening my backpack, extracting from it the raincoat, a dingy, blighted thing, khaki. There's a tear under the armpit; stained lining; a cigarette hole in the sleeve. One day soon I'm going to start the business of bagging up the remnant of Jamie's things, eight years late, and I'll ditch this relic with the rest.

★

Rosie eyes the cute ginger toy fox on the counter and stretches out her hand. I'm not about to buy that for my niece. — What about a milkshake at Costa's afterwards instead?

It's the exorbitant toy and the window cleaner that jolt me back. Otherwise this feels like a different building altogether, with the bought smiles of uniformed attendants, swanky offices, luxury apartments. Rosie's wildly excited. I haven't told my niece I've been up the Shard twice before. Grey, misty weather: through layers of glass on the seventy-second floor viewing platform, the view is tamed and neutered. We survey model trains and a toy cathedral. Rosie bounces about, courting delicious fear.

A window cleaner abseils down the spire. He rappels from the sky-genie in his harness, in a sequence of deft leaps. His rear end is suspended nearly above my head. It's quite safe, a mother assures her son. It isn't, actually. Nothing's safe up there.

The spire's steel skeleton was almost in place; the glass would come later. That night I was reluctant to go. New love had brought a common or garden kind of sanity. I no longer felt inclined to tempt the gods. Leo came and went, on his own terms, but always bringing a melting tenderness. In the café, Jaxer introduced a new Up-and-Under: Egg she called herself. Sasha, laughing like a drain, mentioned new-laid eggs and Humpty Dumpty. But Egg was a pro, an engineer and veteran of the Willis Tower antenna in America, nearly twice the Shard's height. Jaxer's eyes devoured her with surging appetite. Presumably she was my replacement, for this would be my last excursion. Fine by me.

At the top of the concrete core, Egg hardly seemed out of breath. We earthlings panted, staggered and spat. Elegantly, Egg performed what I can only call a ballet-climb on the spire. Sasha showed how morosely unimpressed he was by perching on the concrete edge, legs dangling. Leo's camera filmed each in turn. It was the human element, he always said, that fascinated him. He came up close and the camera's eye read my face, naked for him.

When Jaxer called for hush, Sasha stayed put, yawning and stretching. Egg landed lightly, next to me. She whispered a query concerning Jaxer's rituals.

— Did he slobber over you, Egg?

— Tried to. Gross.

— He's claiming you. Did it to me.

— Weird little guy.

— No way to break this to you gently, Jaxer was saying.
— Someone we've taken for a friend and brother ... someone you and I have trusted with our lives —

He was outing Sasha at last. The stags would lock horns in a final, frenzied confrontation. The Shard was a scary arena to choose.

— Police infiltrator.

In bed at night waiting for sleep, I'm sometimes prey to the toppling sensation I had then as I turned to observe Sasha — and he wasn't there. A microsecond of lost control. A rush in the ears and the face is gone. Departing to die the death I didn't die. Sasha must have found it. Freefall.

He hadn't fallen, of course. Sasha's taunting voice came from overhead, where, not to be outdone by an American female, he was monkeying about on the spire. — Worked it out finally, did you, Jax? Well done, boy.

I was the woman who'd never borne Jamie's baby: I was the breeder of illusions. Leo lowered his camera and unhurriedly replaced it in its case.

— It's always the one you least expect, isn't it? Jaxer asked. — The guy with the honey tongue – the generous wallet. The quiet bloke who's always volunteering. Comes and goes. Gravitates towards the weak link. Ring any bells?

I knew before he spoke the name.

The Shard oscillated. We are terrestrial creatures. That's how we evolved. A single finger laid on a stable surface can correct your wobble. If you lie prone, the mind is supported. As I dropped to the floor, the tower stabilised on its steel tendons. That's it, belly-crawl forward, I counselled myself: like a soldier, a baby. Towards the trapdoor. Creep, crawl, breathe. Grip the hatch. Descend the ladder.

While the infiltrator was answering to the kangaroo court, I came face to face with a creature.

It stood; I stood. It stank. I stared. The fox had trespassed the same way we did, climbing seventy-one flights and a ladder. It was impossible and he did it. He fed on scraps the builders left. They'd see, hear and sniff him but the fox kept out of reach. He showed himself now, surging past me on the seventy-first and scrambling up the ten foot ladder to the summit.

★

When Leo arrived, he assessed the flat with his practised eye, spotting changes in my space, before dissolving into tears. Real tears. You could have collected the brine in an egg cup. He was still the beautiful man who'd raised me from the dead. Or rather he'd raised me from the dead and had been beautiful. Despite his occasionally imperfect script, Leo, or Michael rather, was a credible actor. He'd defended himself at the summit of the Shard, giving his unit time to mount and make the arrests. Of all but me. Payment for services rendered, presumably. They'd clocked me as they swept past, puffing and blowing their way to the top.

— How's your little girl, Leo ... Michael? I asked.

He looked away. One of the environmentalists whose blood he'd sucked in a former life had borne Mike Machin a child, Sharon Lily. It had all come out in the press. The Met was being sued. He didn't reply.

— Oh and by the way, small point for future reference: there are no real mountains in Schleswig-Holstein.

He blushed to the roots of his hair at his elementary gaffe. — Shit, he said. – So you knew?

— Well, I did and I didn't. In the end it was never you I was looking for. It was someone else.

—Yes, he said with his old gentleness, and his expressive hands lay palms open. – I realised that, Violet. I'm so sorry. For exploiting your hurt.

—What'll you do now, Michael? Direct traffic?

He was leaving the force, he said. How could he ever atone for his betrayal of people he'd grown to love, sincerely love? On his wrist was a tattoo I'd not noticed before. He made sure I saw it. A flower, with my name in it. His body was covered in lies. When I told Egg, she said they were probably fake tattoos anyway. Washable.

As to Jamie, there's little left to see anywhere on earth or under the earth. I've emptied the wardrobe of relics. There's his diary, course.

Jamie sketches his last two days on earth. He treks through the rain forest below Kili. It's like Crewe Station, he writes — swarms of tourists, bearers, guides, cooks. In stifling humidity, he sweats his way along, head down, gasping for breath. Dizzy and nauseous, Jamie's homesick eye dwells on detailed instances of the ordinary and familiar encountered along the way — orchids, violets, moss, impatiens. One step at a time, he counsels himself. Keep going. On the second day, crossing the moorlands, my lonely husband records the bitter conviction that he's a dead weight, a shackle, a disappointment altogether, but he tries not to show me he's 'out of puff and crestfallen and feeling ratty as hell. I've fallen behind before we've properly started and at some stage soon she'll decide to go on without me.'

I spotted Jaxer once, at Euston Station when he'd completed his community service. He was wearing a suit. At least I think it was him. I suppose he was dressed for his day-job.

Christie keeps me abreast of new ventures but I'm rarely tempted. Nowadays I put one foot in front of the other. I dare the harder test. To keep steady at ground level. One could so easily lose one's footing.

Ground-Nester

When Red noses out the mother bird, bloody meat and scrambled eggs is what she'll be, Chris says. But the labrador — speeding down the lawn, nostrils flown with rich scents — lollops past the ground-nester into the poppied wilderness thronged with field mice and hedgehogs, where their garden joins the common.

'Blinded poor Red's nose she has,' Carly says, on tiptoe at the kitchen window. 'Noses are eyes, aren't they, in the doggy world?'

The mother bird has shrunk to a dapple of shadow, hardly visible. The earth's tremor as her enemy swept by must have registered in her belly, jostling the yolks in their shells.

'Red's daft but not that daft,' Chris says. Only a suicidal quirk of nature could have brought the ground-nester to the edge of a Glamorgan housing estate, a tasty come-hither to predators.

'But I've heard about this on the radio. Snipe, was it?

— and quail – they switch off something smelly in their glands and that camouflages them. Nature's so clever.'

The ground-nester's a nondescript sort of bird, dun and puny: no snipe or quail. I can't lose Carly, thinks Chris, even as he sees how naive she is. She has never surrendered that childhood capacity for wonder. What she sees in himself, he'll never know. But whatever it is, he thanks his stars. Not that Chris believes in stars or gods or any powers except Sod's Law. Again, he keeps this to himself. Carly's rooted in a way he'll never be, except through her. It scares him, his dependency, but what can you do?

Chris never names his ex, even to himself. Always two sides? *I don't think so.* Never mind: *she's* history.

Carly doesn't care for his bitter moods. Chris understands that and bites his tongue. She stands at the sink in skinny jeans and long grey sweater, all five foot nothing of her, swaying, arms folded, watching the mother bird, and he'd do anything for her. He folds his arms about his partner's slight body; they rock gently, observing the scene in the garden. Red, lolloping back, again misses the scent of prey, the dope.

'I'm off,' he says. 'When's Mel dropping Jarvis off?'

He tries not to see *her* in their daughter's slutty clothes and slovenly walk and her willingness to dump his grandson on them. On benefits, nil ambition, going nowhere. Cheap rings crowd Mel's fingers, looking as if they'd dropped out of Christmas crackers. Clogs to clogs in three generations.

'She didn't say.'

Though not Jarvis's biological grandmother, Carly dotes on the toddler. She cooks him healthy food, worrying about the takeaways Mel feeds him. You can't broach this without Mel exploding — stomping around in her skimpy clothes, thong showing when she bends, teeth nicotine-stained. Older than her years Mel looks and somehow bewildered in a way that gnaws at Chris: crap dad he was. Carly tries to support Mel. She insists there's good in her; it's just that Mel conceals this in case it's seen as weakness. And Jarvis is a sweetheart. The way Carly sees it, at least he gets a couple of decent meals in the week and perhaps he'll ask his mam for broccoli of his own accord. Doesn't Chris think so?

In — your — dreams, darling! But Chris admires his partner's caring ways and is grateful. More of a mam and nan to his family than *her*, that's for sure.

★

Nobody's in when Chris gets home. Carly's on the lawn with Jarvis straddling one hip. Hallo, you! Chris taps on the window and she beckons him out. *Bampi's coming, Jarvis! Look!* Jarvis in a rapture of welcome leans out, calling Chris close. *Here he is! Give Bampi a lovely cwtch!* Securing his grandfather with the free arm, Jarvis locks the two adults to one another and himself. Kisses all round.

They're keeping a distance from the bird, so as not to alarm her. Carly plants one foot in front of Red, whose baffled nose twitches. She takes the foreign body for a toy perhaps: but not her toy. The ground-nester, sunk into herself, is motionless, oily secretions shut down, glands closed. Nothing helps Red identify prey.

'What I don't get,' says Carly, 'is how she can feed while she's stuck here. And when the chicks are born, how'll she cope then?'

'Maybe they don't feed when they're brooding, maybe they've laid down fat or something?'

'Could be. Watch this space.'

A force-field surrounds the creature in a bubble of safety. Red, bored, slopes off to track foreign urine in the wilderness.

★

Jarvis is staying the weekend. Mel's estranged partner, Taylor, that sordid waste of space, comes round — egging Jarvis on to play rugby in the house. It takes time to calm the lad after all the excitement: cheeks flaring with eczema, Jarvis grizzles as Carly washes his hair in the bath, singing *Row, row, row your boat*. He's gone blond overnight, she exclaims — look, Chris. *Gently down the stream*. Were you blond as a child? *Merrily merrily merrily merrily*. Perched on the toilet seat with a can, Chris watches his grandson melt into the loving kindness of Carly. *Life is but a dream*. She hoists him out to be cuddled in a warmed towel. Her face then: there's something so beautiful in its expression. Jarvis, calmed, slips his thumb in his mouth.

'Can I ask you something, Chris?'

'Course you can.'

'It's a big ask.'

'Ask.'

'Could Jarvie stay more of the time, Chris? Pretty much

24

live with us even? I love him as my own. I know she has her problems and I do sympathise ... but honest-to-god Mel can be neglectful, there's no other word for it. Take your time, don't answer now.'

'Well, *cariad* ...'

'No, love, don't answer now ...'

'It's not that I ...'

'Don't, please. Just think about it.'

Chris defers the answer.

'Oh and by the way,' Carly adds. 'I rang the RSPB. A young guy came round — eyes on stalks. He reckons it looks like a common sparrow but sparrows don't act like this. The area boss'll be round tomorrow. Meanwhile, we've to give the bird space — and see off cats. Red's doing a great job at that.'

★

He's working on the loft conversion when his mobile rings. 'Come home, Chris, will you? If you can.'

She's been crying. 'What, love? Tell me.' He rushes to her, his arms wrap round her.

'It's Mel.'

'What about Mel?'

'The way she *was* today when she picked him up. Shouldn't have been driving, honest-to-god. Her eyes weren't right. Did you ever take stuff?'

'No way,' Chris says, his heart in his mouth, not wanting to hear about Mel's antics — but your mind charges ahead of itself imagining bad things, the worst. And thinking defensively, *Not my fault, she's grown up now, it's her mam, her scummy pals, not my responsibility.*

But it is his responsibility, with Jarvis in the equation.

'Why — you think —?'

'She wasn't right. That's all I can say.'

'But you let her take him?'

Carly flushes. Hastily Chris backtracks. He knows exactly what Mel's like. The small, sad eyes peeping, alert for ambush. The shrieking laugh when nothing's funny. *Coming with me he is, I'm his mam, ta for having him, say tara, goodboy, and stop that fucken racket.* Something like that.

'I couldn't stop her, Chris.'

'Course not. Sorry.'

'Worst thing was, the poor dab didn't want to go. Howling he was — and it hurts her when he prefers us, how wouldn't it? That's why she smacked him — not hard but still — I told her straight and she flared up. Nothing you can say, is there? I didn't ask straight-out about drugs – didn't want her to go off on one.' Carly rubs away tears with the heels of her hands. 'We need to consider taking him.'

Chris hears himself saying, 'We might still have our own baby, *cariad.*'

There he goes again, foot in mouth, opening up her wound. Unsure he wants a baby at his time of life, mind. Broken sleep and a bellyaching teenager when he's in his sixties. Carly's not forty: she has every right to want children. Whenever they discuss it, her antennae quiver, intuiting his selfish thought: *Been there, done that.* Which is only part of the truth, for another part of Chris would love a child with Carly and would do it differently this time, because she's made — he hopes and trusts — a better man of him.

'That's not going to happen,' Carly says in a businesslike way. 'Anyway, Chris, however is that relevant? It's our *Jarvis* I'm concerned for.'

What can Chris say? Mel rolls round wasted, all bullshit and bluster, and there's no knowing what substances might be found in her flat.

Chris sees not only *her* in his daughter, but himself, and it's harrowing. Meanwhile a perfect, heart-shaped, half submerged face peers out through the flab. Mel's mint-green eyes pierce him. Chris doesn't court that stare. He's been afraid of Mel since she hit her teens. She's had him shit-scared and running.

He looks past Carly into the garden where, after the night's rain, everything's lustrous. He should walk Red.

'And anyway,' Carly bursts out, 'I love Jarvis — I love him! No baby would ever take his place.'

He tightens his arms round her; feels the throb of her yearning. Sod's law: the motherly women are childless.

'So?' she presses.

'We can only try.'

'Without the Social being involved. And, Chris, it could be expensive.'

'How do you mean?'

'We might have to pay her off.' Carly shoots him a straight look.

Spot-on. But Mel would break any agreement whenever she felt like it; keep snatching her boy back. So: offer an allowance. Maybe take out another no-interest card and generate monthly cash that way.

'OK — but try not to worry too much in the meantime, Sweetpea. She does care about him.' Is he pleading for his daughter — or for himself? 'Mel's just — not very together, never has been. Keeps bad company. But she has a good heart,' he urges.

The tumble dryer revolves; Jarvis's colourful outfits sail round. The air's warm with talcum-scented innocence. Chris has a sense of Carly as a load-bearing wall. Tucking her hair behind her ears, she straightens up, a crease between her eyebrows. He knows she's about to deliver a judgment.

Meeting his eyes, she says, 'Get real, Chris. Nobody has a good heart when drugs are involved. Nobody.'

Later they wander round the glowing garden, bathed in late sunlight.

'I meant to say,' says Carly. 'She's still there. Look.'

'Who?'

'The bird.'

'Still alive?'

'I did wonder earlier but yes, hanging in there, still with us.'

The strangest sight: a spider has woven a strand of web over the closed wings of the ground-nester. Its web, quivering in the breeze, attaches to a fern at one side and hollyhocks at another. The spider's patrolling the periphery: big chap, well-fed. Chris hunkers with his camera just beyond the RSPB barrier. His zoom catches thistledown in the web and the corpse of a trussed fly.

She looks distinctly mangy, her plumage lustreless. Dying, is she? Some insect hops near her eye; she's hosting a population of fleas. The ground-nester's eye blinks. Chris videos the spider mending its web, each leg working independently to extract gluey fabric from its glands, attach, build, balance. The tensile strength in that silk, he thinks: phenomenal.

'The RSPB boss-man was round,' says Carly. 'He reckons she's a rare sparrow. Native to Carolina of all places. He says there'll be a male around — obviously — to feed and protect the chicks when the eggs hatch.'

'I've not seen one, have you?'

'No. Jarvis brought her a worm, bless him,' says Carly. 'But she won't feed — all her systems but one have closed down. A magpie came and our bird jabbed with her beak and made this weird hissing sound and, honest-to-god, inflated as if she'd been pumped up. And he scarpered. The BBC might want to film her. And the *Evening Post* rang.'

★

Mel's cramming her mouth with another chocolate brownie. Is the sugar something to do with her addiction? How's he going to broach it? And slapping the child? Pot and kettle: he remembers turning her over his knee and giving her what he called a good hiding. It wasn't good. It was a hiding to nothing. He hasn't mentioned this to Carly, who, down on the playmat with Jarvis, is mooing and bleating as she fits shapes of farmyard animals into a board. The child moos and bleats back, rapturously. Again!

Again! — the same game over and over, with whoops and skirls of laughter.

'Mel, we were thinking,' Chris begins.

Oh no, his daughter's face tells him, don't start.

'Please don't be offended. Hear me out.'

Flushed to the roots of his hair, he studies his daughter's face as he puts the proposition, noting the shadows under her eyes.

'You don't change,' is all Mel says. Quite calmly. She seems to assess and dismiss him as, at best, a form of insect life. 'Not — at — all. Thought you might of. But nah. Like Mam says. You always thought the worst of me. Anything went wrong: *must be fat stupid Mel's fault*. Always.'

'No, Mel.'

Her angry young face peers from the mass of her, a soul sitting in judgment. Your children have this power and this right. Especially if you yourself smacked them, smoked over them, yelled stuff you can't remember but they sure can.

'You do know, don't you, Dad, that I only bring him here to please you.'

'To please *me*?'

Carly, disengaging from Jarvis, joins them on the settee, listening carefully. Chris thinks: all this crap is all down to his ex, pumping Mel up with resentment, telling her about his women, chapter and verse, making up what she doesn't know. What's Carly about to hear?

'And now you've decided I'm a fucking junky, to get Jarvis off of me! The pair of you — bloodsuckers! And I've tried to please *you* and all!' Mel rounds on Carly. 'I know you can't have your own kids. I've been fine with sharing Jarvis, haven't I?'

Carly hesitates. Chris hears her mind whirr. Scrolling back. Revising. Looking pained as honest people will when detected in an error they'll need to own up to.

'You have, Mel,' says Carly, voice shaking. 'You've been lovely and generous. Thank you. I'm so sorry. I made a mistake. I love him is all, I worry about him.'

'All *right*. So what gave you the idea I was using?'

Carly stumbles: 'Mel — I thought you were — out of it somehow yesterday. And a couple of times you've mentioned — recreational drugs.'

'Yeah, I've had the odd spliff, haven't you? *He* has. You don't want to know all the stuff he's done — don't ask, you might find out. And if you'd bothered to ask yesterday, Carly, I'd of told you ... migraine. Every bloody noise Jarvis made felt like gunshots. And I didn't hit him, for your information, I tapped him. I bet *he* doesn't even know I get migraine. Do you?'

Chris says nothing; is unpersuaded; thinks he knows his daughter too well. But hasn't a leg to stand on.

Carly says, trembling, 'Mel. I was wrong. I was concerned for Jarvis. I'm so sorry.'

An odd sort of dignity asserts itself in Mel. 'Fair enough if that's what you thought. You got to put the child first and foremost, *chwarae teg*. But you go sending in the Social, you'll never see Jarvis again. I guarantee.'

'I think your dad would do some things differently if he had his time again, Mel. And as for not loving you —.'

Mel cringes. Her face begs, *Don't say he loves me, don't.*

Tears brim. She opens her arms to Jarvis, who enters them, sucking his comfort sheet, eyes heavy.

'All we want is to support you, Mel,' Carly begs. 'You are Jarvis's mam. Bottom line, darling.'

'Right. I am his mam. End of story.'

His daughter's driven them on to the back foot. Carly has prudently surrendered because she fears losing Jarvis. He sees her paying out the line.

Chris watches Carly coax Mel on to the play mat to build a Lego house. As the day wears on, he admires Carly's swerve. All her tact and sensitivity flow past Jarvis, past Chris, towards his daughter. With delicate antennae, Carly unobtrusively schools Mel in how to play with her son. Chris drops to his knees; joins in.

The hurt in Mel's long lashed eyes snags on his gaze like barbed wire.

★

Twitchers everywhere. It's all getting out of hand. The BBC pitches up, with cameras and microphones, a producer, a famous naturalist and a national RSPB representative. Carly keeps brewing up. Neighbours crane from windows, over fences.

'Sparrow *Wilkinsensis*,' says Iolo Williams. 'Never seen in Europe, *bendigedig iawn!*'

He helps Chris and Carly distinguish the song of the male, way up in the birch. They only leave the ground to sing, he explains. But how the Wilkins pair made it here and why they should nest on a Glamorgan housing estate is beyond him. Climate change may be a factor. Chris, with Jarvis on his shoulders, imagines these two bundles of feather tumbled thousands of miles on tides of Atlantic wind across the warming planet, together.

Red, prowling the perimeter, deters cats and foxes. Iolo reassures them about the mess the mother bird is in, bound up in spider silk. All good, apparently, because it camouflages and protects her. The cobweb's festooned with leaves, moulted feather, scraps of bark. It's like a slum dwelling. And all you see in this cocooning detritus is the mam's vigilant eye and the emerging balls of fluff as the eggs hatch.

And at last his presence can be confirmed: the father, swooping from the birch with a beakful of grubs.

Bead

She relaxes to the train's rhythm, scanning back over her weekend with Tasha, a crime novel open on her lap. A grandchild shines her light into dark places, saturating the mind in cardinal colours and intense emotion. Ellen is fascinated by Tasha's passion for small things, the detail that slips through the mesh of adult memory. For instance, that bead today.

Cross-legged beneath the window, Tasha sat twirling her treasure between finger and thumb. In the morning light she turned it this way and that, and mutely offered it for Ellen's inspection. Ellen oohed and ahed obediently but then gazed with fuller attention. The bead held her. What words could describe the ruby lustre burning in the cheap chip of glass? Tasha, scrambling up onto her knees, entrusted her treasure to her grandmother's palm. When Ellen removed her specs to look closely, Tasha held them for her. You could rely on her to keep them safe in her delicate fingers. Though Tasha spoke few words as yet — late for a two-year-old — she possessed understanding. Ellen felt they spoke to one another, uniquely, through this bead.

She held it to her eye, then Tasha's. The child's mouth fell open and she swivelled her head to study the world's surface through the red filter.

Folk are boarding the train — shoppers, guys in suits with laptops. Best to dive deep into your book: you're often left in peace if you're concentrating. Leave me be, Ellen thinks, in my underwater world, where Tasha's somehow swimming around in company with these invented characters from another mind. It's a German crime novel in which a young woman arbitrarily stabs a fellow sunbather on a beach. But why? Ellen trusts the writer to lead her by devious and delicious ways to the answer.

When the bead vanished, Tasha didn't cry. She made signs to show how empty her hands were, raising her eyebrows and wrinkling her forehead so that, with a qualm, Ellen saw Tasha as she might be in age. *Cwtch*ing the child up close, she said, – Oh no, sweetpea, have you lost your bead?

Tasha nodded. They knelt, peering into the dusty void beneath the settee. No bead. Alexander rummaged round in the toy box to find a substitute bead for his daughter. — It's just as nice, it's purple, look, show this to Gran! Alex coaxed. Shaking her head, Tasha pursued her quest for the real thing.

Ellen can comprehend the attachment. It tickles some sensitive memory of her own, one of childhood's many mislayings, the litter of losses that flake away, layer upon layer. How black it is out there beyond the train window.

They're approaching ... she can't think of the name of the station.

The time came when all efforts to divert Tasha had failed. Ellen's taxi was due, an unlucky coincidence. Tasha stood still at the centre of the room in the abject bitterness of her loss. Tears welled. The last Ellen saw of Tasha was the back of her head, arms and legs clamped to her dad's body, face burrowed into his neck, howling.

— It's all right, Mum, you go, don't miss your train, she'll soon forget it, Alex said, kissing Ellen's cheek.

Down, down, Ellen slides, pleasurably, into the story's strange equivocations. At the same time she's pondering Tasha. Who could claim the bead was trivial? Alex at a similar age doted on, of all things, an egg carton; wouldn't sleep without it, sniffing it and running his fingers around the stippled cardboard until it disintegrated.

The train draws in at, yes, of course, Bristol Parkway; people disembark and others board. Ellen takes little notice: the murderer has just fabricated a story about her motive for stabbing the sunbather. But why lie, since from the word go the woman acknowledged her crime? What is she keeping to herself — or from herself, perhaps, a buried self, hoarding unspeakable knowledge? A violent crash shoots Ellen out of this puzzle.

Collision? Bomb? No, just the advent of an oaf. Eyes down. Ignore.

The oaf bursts into the carriage, shouting, — German! Fucking rude Kraut!

— Never mind, darling. His female companion soothingly sits the guy down in the seat ahead of Ellen. Up he bounces and kneels, glaring over Ellen's head, looming so close that she can smell his breath: peppermint and agitation. He looks unexpectedly kempt, mid-thirties, with a large, plum-coloured face. Under his jacket is a well ironed pink shirt.

— Fucking German, jumping the fucking queue! he bawls.

— You're right, Freddie, soothes the girlfriend. — The lady was rude — but don't keep saying German, darling, not all Germans are rude.

— They fucking are. It's well known. Don't look like that. They're a nation of queue-jumpers. *Raus! Achtung!*

— Not every single German, Freddie. Shush.

— I won't shush.

But he subsides into his seat, a snarling hound straining on an invisible leash. Shifting from buttock to buttock, he scratches the overheated back of his neck. The guy's testosterone is restless, Ellen thinks. Something in her swirls in black alarm, deep down. She refocuses on the book.

Woman on the beach, confessing. Bead under the couch, lost. Oaf fighting the Second World War in his pea-brain, amok.

When he shoots up the aisle towards his prey, the hectic rush seems to suck Ellen along in his wake.

What am I doing?

She comes up sharp behind him as he towers over the alleged German — a middle-aged woman with cropped white-blonde hair and a look of anxious surprise. Jabbing a forefinger, the oaf barks: — Kraut, hey I'm talking to you!

— English people queue decently, why don't you?

His victim neither cowers nor raises her voice but suggests, in impeccable English, that he calm right down and adds, 'just as a matter of fact', that she is Norwegian.

Ellen's arm reaches out and, grabbing the guy's shoulder, catches him off guard; swings him round.

— You pathetic little twerp, grow up! are the words she hears herself blurt. But nausea sweeps over her. Because she knows. Knows what's coming.

The puce face looms so close that she again smells his breath. No alcohol: peppermint and a whiff of raw meat. The guy quivers with unslaked violence. His hands bunch into fists. Heat flows off his body.

And Ellen doubles over although he hasn't hit her.

★

Something has hit her. A punch thrown a quarter of a century ago has slammed into her belly.

She was standing in the doorway of the kitchen they'd had then, with its chequerboard floor. And she was pregnant with Alex — suffering endless sickness: *hyperemesis gravidarum* the doctor called it, she'd been in hospital to be rehydrated and was just home — and he couldn't abide sickness, he hated women to be ill, his stepmother had been ill, he'd explained before they married, and neglected him, he'd felt deserted, abandoned. Ellen had reassured him that she'd never desert him, no, never, put it out of your mind. — Yes you will, he predicted. It is most certain, you will forsake me. — No, she insisted, — though of course I may be ill occasionally, I suppose, but that won't mean you're

abandoned, obviously. And she added, after they were married and this conversation recurred, as it increasingly did:
— You know, your poor stepmother didn't mean to be ill.

Ellen suggested this only the once though.

She tried to be ill as infrequently and mildly as possible, and to throw up furtively while pregnant, since it wasn't nice anyway to overhear someone vomit, even if you were a normal person. And she gratefully sipped the peppermint oil 'for your queasy old tum' that he brought from the chemist, and she often improved by lunchtime — but today, though far from settled, she came downstairs anyway and, arriving at the kitchen, scented bloody meat and retched, and unluckily he came in from the garden with a bunch of daffodils and was revolted that some female was retching in his clean kitchen and strode over with dead eyes and threw that punch. He swung his fist into her belly with her baby inside. She doubled up and dropped, she lay curled and foetal

— and oh how sorry he was, immediately, oh Christ he'd never been more sorry in his life, and was she hurt, let him stroke it better (— No? you don't want me to stroke it better?) and she thought she'd better let him stroke it better, just briefly, in case resistance triggered more delirium. And he wept, he mourned, he sank on the floor, reproaching himself extravagantly, he'd never hurt her again, never, and he ran upstairs to write a long letter denouncing himself and lamenting 'your poor punched tummy'.

All the while, gripped in his left hand, he'd held the bunch of daffodils which at some stage he dumped in the bin and later retrieved and brought in a vase to her bedside, along with his contrition and a cup of camomile tea and she made sure to thank him with a weak smile — not too forgivingly for it was prudent to eke out her advantage and his remorse, ensuring a zone of relative safety and a chance to counsel him. All the while thinking: is the baby injured, has he killed it, will I miscarry?

★

— What the hell have you done to her? Pull the cord, someone, call the guard!

He is manhandled into a seat, face down. Someone has his knee in the guy's back. The soles of immaculate black shoes stick out into the gangway for he's a tall man.

— Did he hit you, love? Are you OK?

— I didn't see him strike her. But he must have, surely? says the Norwegian woman, who kneels and tries to take Ellen's head in her lap but there isn't room in the aisle. – She was so brave though. She came to my aid. Is she all right?

— Did anyone else see?

— I saw. Racist thug, scum of the earth. He was definitely punching her, says another passenger.

An empty cardboard coffee mug rolls around. There's a discarded sandwich with a bite taken out of it — ham or perhaps beef. The pain is extreme. Sobs burst from Ellen. For he struck her. He brought his fist slamming into her belly. He had no mercy, no pity whatsoever. He was a man possessed by the terror of abandonment and the urge to punish it. His character was pulped and corrupted by childhood sorrow. And to strike their unborn baby: an impiety. How, how could he, could anybody, do such a thing? Gentle hands raise Ellen to her feet, still clutching her belly, and support her, bent double, to her seat. She can do nothing for herself. In a cold sweat, she gasps and pants. The guard has opened a notebook; his pen is poised.

— What did he do to you? Where did he hit you?

Ellen pauses. What is the truth and is it safe to confess it? Then she nods. Yes. He hit her. At the same moment her fingers close round a pill-like object in her jacket pocket. Here it was all the time: had Tasha secretly stowed it there and then forgotten? Ellen brings the bead out and shakily examines it in the dim light. She fingers its angles and surfaces.

— Excuse *me*, says the girlfriend. — Freddie didn't touch her. This lady came charging down the aisle and grabbed him from behind. What was he supposed to do? There's a right of self-defence in this country: reasonable force or something. He'd never strike a woman. Would you, Freddie?

— No, comes the muffled voice. — Never do that.

— He was just remonstrating with this very rude German person who'd pushed in. He's a gentleman, law-abiding, he's teetotal, aren't you, Freddie?

— Be quiet, madam, says the guard. — Sit down.

— Never drink, wouldn't hurt a fly, comes the martyred voice.

Passengers shout in outrage. They're all on their feet or kneeling on their seats. This foul-mouthed fellow threatened the German lady. The Welsh lady intervened and was punched. Obviously. Look at her.

— Excuse me, but as it happens I'm from Norway.

— Norwegian lady, the girlfriend corrects herself. — That was a mistake. Freddie may have sounded a bit upset. His grandpa fought in the War, you see, he was permanently traumatised by the Nazis. You provoked Freddie, you know, by pushing in to the queue on the platform. Fair play, he shouldn't have lost his temper. He's usually such a lamb. He only wanted to teach you manners.

— Manners, echoes the lamb. — That's all I wanted.

The need to check that Alexander is safe overwhelms Ellen, as when her beautiful son was new to the world, her all-in-all — and if anything happened to Alex, how could Ellen go on living? She takes her mobile from her pocket to call him but — she'd forgotten its presence all over again — the bead comes too. She replaces the phone. The bead sits at the centre of her sweating palm. This time she decides to stow it for safe-keeping in the thumb of her glove and, folding the soft leather like a pouch, restores it to her pocket.

— Excuse me, says Ellen to the guard. — I'm all right now. I won't press charges.

She turns to the girlfriend and clears her conscience. — Cut your losses, I should. If he can behave like that to passengers on a train, do you honestly believe he won't attack you? Think about it.

The young woman, scarlet in the face, hesitates. — But he didn't actually hit you, she murmurs, baffled. — The surveillance camera would show that.

— As I say, cut your losses. I did.

★

For a while the reverberations of the punch ring round Ellen's skull though the pain in her belly — a real pain and not a phantom — has faded. It's good to be home, brewing tea, padding around barefoot. She extracts the bead from the glove and strings it round her neck for safe-keeping. How strange that the full force of an act of violence might fail to connect immediately; that it could rebound and wander off into space. In the end it would find you. Twenty-five, twenty-six years later the arrow homes to its target, but the target it sought has changed beyond recognition from that craven, creeping, self-righteous creature hefting round the stinking burden of someone else's bad conscience.

Of course this Freddie fellow didn't hit her. He was escorted off the train by the guard, head low, the hood of his Parka up, rendering him faceless. They let him loose at the gate. He was innocent as charged. But he would strike. One day he'd crash his fist into the collusive girlfriend.

That earlier life of mine, Ellen thinks, it seems inauthentic. Like a fantasy — someone else's fantasy. He can't help it, she told herself then. She bleated excuses for him every time, grateful for the balm of his fulsome apologies. His childhood had been so appalling.

One night during one of his tantrums she rang their GP, an elderly man, dead now. Alexander was not six weeks old. He didn't feed well and Ellen would often spend the night with him in the nursery. Oh the bliss of marital separation. It was a guilty luxury, almost sensual, to stretch out in the single bed and feel the cool sheets flow around her limbs. Her husband welcomed the chance of a sound night's sleep, so his sense of desertion expressed itself in a minor key or was tongue-tied until the night Ellen rang the doctor. She explained that the baby's father was running amok — he was upset, he'd had a dreadful childhood, but she feared for her baby, not that he'd ever hurt the baby, not voluntarily, or directly, but he hadn't full control of his temper — and the doctor, cutting off the slurry of psychobabble, snorted, — Dreadful childhood, fiddle-dee-dee. Put your husband on the phone please.

He listened respectfully to what the doctor said and thanked him and put the phone down, turning to look at her thoughtfully.

— What did he say?

— He told me to start behaving like a rational adult.

Nice as ninepence he was for over a month. Nice? No, he was lovely. Nothing was too much trouble. It was the longest he'd ever lasted. That gave Ellen a breathing space to make plans and execute them.

It occurs to her that — how odd — ever since her escape she has avoided referring to him by name: it was always 'he' or 'my son's father', never John who committed the crime. There has been a hole where John's name should be, a void over which she has stepped, not looking down.

But as Ellen formulates this truth, the whole palaver feels tediously far-fetched. And the episode on the train is frankly mortifying. She turns the imitation coal fire up high; the flames flap and roar like the real thing. Not much on TV: the fag-end of an old black and white war film.

Muting the sound, Ellen waits for the news. As she settles on the couch with tea and cake and the novel she was glued to on the train, Ellen can't really be bothered to find her place and the plot is a complete blur; it slips off her lap and she makes no effort to retrieve it. She yawns and her fingers twiddling the bead strung around her neck recognise it as plastic rather than glass.

Red Earth, Cyrenaica

After the veterans' reunion, David dreams, awakening in the old anguish. Margie sleeps soundly beside him. I brought *that* into our bed, he thinks, and here it has remained for half a century. There's a self that leaps free of the pieties of married love — a quicksilver, erotic spirit, young through all the years.

Archaic desires resurface. They were born and should have died in wartime Libya, with Colonel Pitway headless in the desert and the red cave's secret mouth above Derna. The desert brimmed and gushed, in a fortnight's torrential rainfall that engulfed one village after another — Giovanni Berta and Slonta, Tocra and Benghazi. The world turned to a mud-slick.

Demobbed at the end of it all, the men gratefully resumed the customs and certainties of Civvie Street: marriage, kiddies, regular work. What they'd known of carnage and carnality they abandoned in the desert. It was filth, you burned it like the troops' stinking underwear at Derna. With hindsight David came to see the episode with Clem as vagrancy, an aberration. The boy in the dream said to him last night: *When all this is over, darling, we'll make a better world of it.* How wrong he'd been.

The pair came slithering hand in hand down the wadi.

Coupled men with ground-sheets over their heads foraged for firewood through gutted Arab houses. Vehicles sank in a universal bog while engineers and road gangs stained red to the thighs laboured to bridge the floods; planes ditched in sudden ponds; corpses oozed in septic water; radios failed. Such rains had rarely been known in Cyrenaica.

Clem, coming close, breathes freshly on David's face.

— 2 —

In the desert, icy night fell in the blink of an eye. Murder paused in the slaughterhouse of northern Africa. In the tank's shelter David lay wrapped in some dead Arab's reeking sheepskin, in a trench dug by retreating Germans. Stars, like jewels on velvet, lit the pallid sands for miles. Craving for his girl Margie, back home, grasped David's heart, a fist thrusting into his tenderest place. An enormous silence surrounded him. The sleep of the world, as it had been before and would be after he was gone and she was gone and the ruined cities were forgotten.

— 3 —

White dust misted the desert, up to the height of a man's chest. Into this murk, tanks and lorries belched blue smoke as stagnant oil burned off. Their Colonel had — outrageously — slept in, wearing silk pyjamas. Suede boots scented with pomade like an Italian's stood at the foot of Colonel Pitway's opulent sleeping bag. David's driver, Private Clement Kazarian, said that when he'd delivered the message to the Colonel's tent, the batman shushed him: 'Not until my Colonel has taken his morning tea.' The men chafed, having long since stowed their bedrolls and brewed strong, sweet chai in petrol cans. The line was ready to move. Heat got up and a dreary wind. The Colonel slumbered on.

Later that day Colonel Pitway was dead and already stinking. The desert drank his patrician blood into its colossal thirst. The column moved past through a graveyard of dead tanks, already half buried in drifting sand. Droves of exuberant Spaghettis cheered their own surrender.

The khaki Padre appeared at the head of Colonel Pitway's hastily dug grave, with five or six men of all ranks. Tears streamed down the batman's face from eyes swollen with weeping. *They shall grow not old.* The Colonel had seemed to the boys already an old man, though he could only have been forty. He'd not been popular. Huntin' shootin' Jew-hatin' type. His head was smashed clear off his body. *As we that are left grow old.* There was no particular sense of horror. A wooden cross cast a shadow. *Age shall not weary them …*

The sequel was a Greek drama all its own. As the funeral party began dispersing, the batman hurled himself on the mound, keening in a voice audible above the din of artillery, the screaming of planes: 'I loved him! I worshipped him! What shall I do now? Where shall I go?'

There were some thoroughly good eggs among the upper officers, men of culture and human feeling. One gentle Major took charge. 'Come along now, my son. You've done all you can for him.' Nobody mocked.

The battalion pushed west. Mussolini's troops ran for it. The pursuers had an open road; their spirits soared. 'To Derna!' Cyrenaica lay on a plateau, with towering cliffs above the dazzling Mediterranean. The Wadi Derna was famed for a waterfall and caves, once the sanctuary of Christians fleeing persecution. The Pass looped down in a series of breathtaking hairpins. A jubilant convoy entered an oasis of pomegranate groves, white colonnaded houses in the Fascist style with neat vegetable gardens.

David translated at interrogations of captured Spaghettis who obligingly blabbed wild, invented secrets. Later he wandered the town, marvelling at its colonial luxury. Officers' beds were laid out with clean linen; gold-laced Fascist uniforms hung on padded hangers. On a white marble mantelpiece a lewd Cupid exposed himself to a naked nymph. Collapsing on a plump mattress, David passed out. For an hour perhaps. Awakening in a state of uncomfortable arousal, he became aware of Clem Kazarian sprawled beside him, dark curls tumbling over the pillow, like David's eight-year-old brother Ned tucked up at home in Truro.

Clem hardly budged as David clambered over him. A Spaghetti officer had bequeathed the luxury of a tooth-brush. Swilling from the ornate brass taps — oh, the ecstasy of running water — David spat red mud. He thought of blood on the sheets in Cardiff. For Margie, against all her principles and upbringing, had given herself to him the night before embarkation. With tears. It had not been a huge success. He lay back down beside the boy.

A bird called harrowingly from eucalyptus beyond the glassless window. Bullet holes pitted walls and ceilings; a smashed piano splayed its keys.

He shook Kazarian's shoulder. No response. Wakey wakey! The statuette of Cupid was scarcely more softly suggestive than Clem's full lips, the flush of his face with its dark eyebrows and lashes. On his cheek was a scar like a pair of wings, the relic of a childhood fall from a tree. David's fingertips brushed his driver's forehead; Clem awoke and smiled into his eyes. The cool room held its breath.

— 4 —

Lower ranks under canvas, officers in commandeered quarters, they'd been granted twenty-four hours for shut-eye: bliss for an army that had spent weeks catnapping in trenches. Clean underwear replaced stinking KDs, which were burned. A musical Lieutenant had reassembled the piano in *that* villa. Strains of Schumann's 'Scenes from Childhood' sparked homesickness as David waited outside for his driver.

Clem said, 'Crime to miss the historic caves, sir, don't you think? The chance might never come again.'

'All right but don't *sir* me, for God's sake.'

'Sorry, sir.'

'Give it a rest, Clem.'

'I will, sir, when we're high and dry.'

They climbed a narrow path up the wadi. David, fuddled with fatigue, stumbled along in the rear, his mind full of longing for his mother, brother and sweetheart. Below, lads played cricket on a green sward, a wooden board for a bat. David's heart wobbled wildly.

The sound of hissing and foaming filled the air. The famous waterfall pitched from a salmon-pink ridge into a turquoise pool fouled by debris, the refuse of centuries of trippers. Semi-literate graffiti, ancient and modern, were carved in many languages: tokens of serial pointless conquests by Greeks, Egyptians, Arabs, Ottomans, Axis and Allies.

David must lie down or he'd fall down.

A decaying mouth: the cave's sour breath hit them a yard in. The putrefying carcase of a goat drove them back to the cavernous opening, where they sat above a sheer drop and drank from water bottles. Rain clouds massed. A plane screamed overhead like chalk on a blackboard. Whether this loosened the knot, David couldn't tell. He went to mush. He began, to his shame, to blub, sobs convulsing him, a string of snot dangling from his nostrils.

The eighteen year old private says to the nineteen year old captain — and David at seventy hears it from his Truro home, quite clearly, *After this lot's over, there'll be a fairer world, a place of greater gentleness, don't you think so? A Socialist republic. It's all I care about. Well, that and you. We'll make it happen, won't we, darling?*

Clem cupped David's face in both palms, a gesture of boundless tenderness.

When they returned to Derna, the rain was torrential. There'd been a raid: two Stukas brought down. Men fell away before them. For Captain Tremain and Private Kazarian had lost all of twenty four hours. Nobody said a word. Old Pitway's batman quietly offered chai.

Later, in the Spaghetti billet, David met himself in the shaving mirror, face raw from the boy's stubble. Now he knew. He knew now. There was no quenching a radiant smile at the beauty of his own anointed body, the kindness of Clem's.

— 5 —

That was 1941. The Desert Army lost Derna. The Eighth Army took it again in 1942. The length of northern Africa the Allies fought the Axis, east to west, west to east, east to west again. Two years of sun stained their faces to teak. The desert stink became their own smell. Clem had swiftly been reassigned after the Caves episode.

Nothing said.

Fraternising with Other Ranks was the sin against the Holy Ghost. Even a newly promoted young Captain was forbidden to consort with a private soldier. After the separation, David demanded demotion to the ranks but his punishment was to remain stranded in the élite, with his soiled reputation. 'Bits of brown', the Tommies called the pansies. But the phase was spoken with wry fellowship: nobody openly leered or mocked. David wrote to Clem, via his home address. No reply. He wrote again. Nothing.

The censors — his bastard fellow officers — were doubtless primed to destroy their correspondence.

By the time David returned to Cyrenaica, Derna was unrecognisable. A bomb site. *That* villa no longer existed. He stood in its ruins. There was no time to revisit the caves, nor in truth was he particularly tempted. Already he was attuning himself to the norms of home and later it was to Margie that he attached a gradually fading ache of intimate loss.

— 6 —

'Poor chap — never made it home. I heard he was ambushed in Palestine at the end of the British Mandate. I'm sorry,' said Colonel Pitway's batman at the reunion, dapper in his decay, a retired insurance clerk. 'You and he were such great pals. Clem was a one-off job, that's for sure.'

He put out a brotherly hand as David turned away, striving to master the decades-deferred sob that burst up from his guts.

Of course the batman had known from the off: who should sniff them out more surely than the unit Fairy Queen? *I loved him!* he'd cried at the Colonel's grave, for all to hear. Throughout his military career Jones would have been joshed, camping it up for all he was worth, giving value. David squirms from the man's complicitous pity, thinking: we were not not like you.

Were we? And does it matter? Who cares these days anyway?

In Cyrenaica a match was struck in the dark: some intense but fugitive illumination threw light on nothing beyond itself. No sequel. Or so he grew to feel at the time. Sundered from his friend, David marched through the meadows of Sicily, into the carnage of Italy.

— 7 —

Downpour: the River Truro in spate, the soil awash. Luke, their grandson, who earns a few bob doing the heavier garden work, has left a spade leaning on a tree. David wanders out, bare-headed, in his slippers; finds himself standing ankle-deep in mud.

Snaring his hand, Margie leads her husband indoors. She seats him at the kitchen table with a mug of tea and chats about this and that, keeping him in her sights, listening, observing. Through the window David ponders the water-logged trench as he hears Margie on the phone to their daughter: 'Soaked to the skin he was and coated with mud. Seems fine now, bless him. He came back from that reunion rather shaken, you know. And I'm not surprised.' Something in her tone makes David's eyes smart. He has lived mantled in this ordinary affection, eating the everyday food of gods, for nearly fifty years.

Later, in bed, she asks, 'What is it, love?'

'Something I should have explained years ago. A pal from army days, Margie.'

'Yes?'

'Oh, nothing. Just a friend.'

'It's Clem, isn't it? Clem Kazarian. You talk to him in your sleep. Only occasionally nowadays.'

David listens, astounded less by his wife's reserve than by her acceptance. Oh yes, Margie minded at first: the bizarrely broken nights, coaxing her sleep-walking husband back to bed. But then, oddly, she got to know Clem: an exceptional young man. She accepted these trysts as a conversation the three of them shared in the night, a reunion of sorts.

'Don't be upset,' Margie says and cups her hands around his face, in that tender gesture David caught from his lover, brought home to his wife and everlastingly receives back from Clem.

Tuner of Llangyfelach

The piano's held together, I explain over the phone, with elastic bands and string: well, in a manner of speaking. It's an heirloom: been in my brother's garage for years and in a ruined farmhouse before that. I've no idea if such a wreck can be salvaged — but perhaps he might just look it over?

Bang on time, Owen Morris stands at the door with his toolkit, a boyish-looking, old-fashioned guy in corduroy, fortyish, his abundant hair side-parted — softly-spoken and courteous. We agree on first names. Leaving him to take stock of the patient, I settle in the attic study. Even here, you can hear the piano's falsity and confusion.

— Tia, calls the tuner, — Never say die.

— Really? You can do something with it?

— Certainly. But what's the history of this piano? Because — this'll sound odd — I may recognise the instrument. I'm almost sure the person who last tuned it was my dad.

Down on his knees, Owen studies the piano's dusty back. — Ah. Here we are. Perhaps. Can you see?

I crouch beside him. What am I supposed to be seeing? The wood's a chaos of score marks. I put it down to Mother Nature running amok while the piano slept. Slept for years, decades, and lost, in the wake of fratricidal family conflict, its mind. The family's unappeasable jealousies built and boiled through time, for reasons no one now recalls. We young-sters, university-educated, got out. I fixed on New Zealand. It's our antipode, I told myself: should be safe enough there. Decades later I've returned, to salvage an inheritance.

There's a mark, apparently, which I'm implored to con-firm, the sign, the tuner says, and his voice cracks, of his lovely dad. — Here look. 'O.M. LLAN. RECREAT'. Latin for 'Owen Morris of Llangyfelach restored this.' See? Can you see it? Clear as day.

When he straightens up, there are alarming tears in the tuner's eyes and he accepts a cup of tea.

— I was apprenticed to Dad, he tells me. — He inden-tured me, binding me for five years. He signed, I signed. It wasn't a legally enforceable document, just a pact between the two of us. It's so moving to see this piano. If it's the one. Yes, it is, you saw his mark. Our firm has been in the business of restoration for a century and there's a pride to it, you know, folk trust us. A rival company had just set up — Kleinkind's — it worried dad, not least because Kleinkind saturated the market with cheap Chinese pianos, a thousand pounds a go. Rubbish pianos.

— But Chinese instruments are the best in the world, aren't they?

Whatever's so special about my piano, I wonder, that has him searching into those underground places of the heart — wells where old tears collect, their salt a barren solace?

— Aye, *nowadays* Chinese pianos are second to none. Different story then. These were all duds. The first we really knew was when we were called out to a piano in Treforys. Dad got to work when — pow! a string snapped — great bang, like a bomb going off. Another string — pow! It lashed him in the face, under the eye, he had the scar the rest of his life.

— Dad told the owner, — Can't do anything with this, boy. You've been sold a pup. Complain, take it back. It's lethal.

— It pained him to see people palmed off with junk. And he saw more and more of it. He made a pretext to visit Kleinkind's workshop. It was attached to a warehouse. Like a hangar it was — relic of the old steelworks, down where the enterprise park is now — packed wall to wall with these clones, as far as the eye could see. Honest-to-God, it was like the terracotta army in the emperor's tomb. You had to see it to believe it. And Dad said it was a vision of the future, of apocalyptic decline. Chapel he was, see. What Kleinkind did was, when customers complained, he just swapped their rubbish piano for a new rubbish piano. Once the three-year guarantee was up, end of.

— I suppose your father confronted him?

Is my piano somehow under suspicion? It couldn't log-ically be. Mine's inherited. I love it anyway. Even if it has to be eviscerated and I'm left with an empty shell. I remove the mugs as a hint that tuning should commence. But

Owen follows me into the kitchen and insists on drying up, still talking. My neighbour but two is a talker like this. When I see her coming I hide in the garage. Nobody's spared.

And yet I like the guy. The gentleness of him, the dark, kindled eyes. The sense of family pieties: who else do I know — aside from myself – who loved their father so profoundly that the rest of life bore the mark of sorrow? And perhaps he intuits this kinship. Although of course mine was a quarreller like the rest of the Francises – emotional, hot tempered, puzzled that the root of love should turn out so cloven. I see in my mind's eye his baffled eyes — and I have to turn away inwardly, softly closing the door on him.

— Kleinkind was a charmer, Owen goes on. — No getting away from that. Where do you hang the tea towel, Tia? Gentlemanly chap, mind — impeccable manners. Instead of defending himself when Dad accused him, he parried with a question: how many working men in the Valleys can afford quality instruments for their kiddies, would you guess, Mr Morris? *Quality?* It was the first time in my life I heard Dad raise his voice. After that he was on a mission, I don't think he was ever quite himself again — or, yes, perhaps just, briefly, once. I'll come to that. He'd tune people's pianos for next to nothing. Thing was, he felt he'd seen the End. But he reasoned that he could in some way arrest this process of ... untuning. Piano entropy. Dad was the boy with his thumb in the dyke. He even undertook to restore rogue imports, more or less rebuilding from scratch. I do believe these pianos killed him. Mam was very bitter.

— But you're not saying, are you, that my piano is —

— Good God no. Venerable instrument is this, Tia. Sorry, I'll stop my chopsing and get down to work. Funny old world though, isn't it? Let's gauge the timbre first.

Owen begins to play: Bach's *Wohltemporierter Klavier*. I realise at once that he's no mean player, despite the reverberations that roar round the instrument's body and explode out in frenzy.

—You may well flinch! Each piano's different, see. Timbre's determined by the harmonics — different harmonics for the same pitch. A little inharmoniousness lends richness to the tone. You didn't know that? Well, your instrument's a challenge — but, Tia, it'll be worth it to you, I promise, if it takes all day. I've got a packed lunch in the van.

— Eat with me. Of course, Owen. I've made soup.

★

—You see, he says, breaking open a warm crusty roll and smothering it in melting butter, — Dad was pious, that's true. Straight-dealing, modest to a fault. But he had a zany sense of humour and plenty of *hwyl*. He'd dance Mam all round the house, singing at the top of his voice. All that went out the window, once he started trying to resurrect pianos. He'd been a tender father — hands-on they'd call it nowadays. One of the old Gower swimmers: he'd swim way out at Pwlldu with me on his back. I never felt afraid. And no matter what comes later, Tia, if you've enjoyed such childhood security, nothing mars it. Even when the rage infected him and he quarrelled with the deacons. And started boasting that nothing was beyond his powers. The real man was still there, behind the rage.

— Thing is, he'd undertaken a labour impossible for one craftsman, stacking the odds against himself. Me he saw as a fellow crusader and successor in the battle against these profane imports. Not easy for an adolescent lad. I had a sober sense of filial duty — but I'd drag my heels and roll my eyes. Dad sued Kleinkind – and lost. And Kleinkind threatened to sue us. That case never came to court. I must admit I was ashamed of Dad, muttering to himself, his face all mottled. He signed the pianos he'd restored so he could make account of himself at the end of time.

— One day we were called to a farm towards Kilvey.

I take a mouthful of water. I know where this is going. Owen has led me to Cae Twmpyn Farm; to my grandmother and her barricades. The livestock sold off and the pyre of fifty pound notes. To the moment when her children came to blows at the farm gate and Uncle John nearly lost an eye and Auntie Gwen went charging like a bull across the cobbles at my mam. To the beginning of the end.

—Yes, I say. — I know the area.

★

We park outside Cae Twmpyn, the tuner and I, in his van which smells of linseed oil and menthol. The farm was once a tenancy of the Kilvey manor, its medieval curtilage defended by towering walls. We grandchildren knew every field by a corruption of its ancient name: they'd been worked by our family for centuries. Owen and I pass the mounds after which the farm was named: twin tumps, a hundred yards apart, where once a Bronze Age cinerary urn was excavated containing fragments of human burial. When the longed-for snow came we'd toboggan down the slopes. On the south-west side the ground slants down to the cliffs above the sea, a grey shining triangle between headlands, with a little beach when the tide's out. Nobody farms there now. There's a caravan site on the lower field.

As we enter the grounds I breast the memory of Gran's barricades. How picturesque ruined houses look when they weather into the earth. Grass carpets her rooms, her walls are yellow and orange with lichen and fireweed thrusts up seven feet tall.

— Yours was the last piano Dad ever restored, Owen says as we perch on a broken wall. — And he died three weeks later. The farmhouse even then looked distinctly seedy. A birch had rooted by the chimney, I remember, and tiles were slipping. When we knocked, no one answered. So we went round the back and tapped on the windows. Eventually an elderly lady appeared. Pale blue eyes, piercing. Rather formidable. I remember her clear as day, I'll explain why in a minute. Indoors it was, well, a mess. The old lady said she was living a student's life and couldn't be bothered to clean. I thought she was a bit — you know. Dad set me to sweep the room, which I did with a poor grace. He snarled that for all he cared I could go and work for Kleinkind in his junk yard if I took that attitude. I said nothing but my expression must have riled him because he told me to get out of his sight and ask the old lady if she wanted any jobs doing.

— So did you?

— I did. And she said, — Yes, young man, I wish to go for a swim.

— A *swim*?

— In the sea. I thought at first she was having me on. Eventually back I traipsed to Dad. Scarlet-faced. *She wants me to go swimming with her.* Well, that tickled him. He burst out laughing and his old, soft self was back — as if it had just been biding time. Mind you, I was hardly in a mood to appreciate that. I drew myself up to my full five foot four and told him it wasn't in my contract that I had to go swimming with old grannies. And I wouldn't, he couldn't make me. He laughed harder and said, *Tell her we'll all go together when this is finished.*

— And did you, Owen?

— Mortifying it was. Yet now it seems a blessed interval. Your gran was quite a woman, Tia, and no mistake. She was an original. Whatever was she like in her heyday if this was how she was at eighty? The embarrassment! — I didn't know where to look. My dad and your gran swam out, way beyond my limit. I saw them basking out there, floating on their backs, water like a millpond, chatting away presumably. And later he played to her. Chopin.

What Owen has tendered me feels like breaking news. I *cwtch* it up in my heart. I can't stop smiling. I want to cry. I remember playing the recorder to my gran and how all the asperity left her as she listened. Driving back, we're both silent, side by side, like shy cousins many times removed. Yes, like distant kin, whose stories mesh at one seam only.

I wish Dad could have heard this. His tales were of bewildered rejection. Of loving too much and being short-changed. Of a taciturn dad with fists. Of a mother who signed off from being a mam once her husband was underground. Greedy bloodsuckers, she called her adult children. After she'd burned her savings, Gran slapped her hands together, as if to say: *Good riddance.* From now on she was just going to be herself. She reverted to her maiden name. Dad described his sister rooting in the bin amongst the ashes of a fortune in twenty- and fifty-pound notes.

My Uncle Bryn took steps to get Gran committed. Nothing doing. She'd got the local doctor in her pocket, so Bryn said. And the social workers were impressed by her intellectual grasp. They said she talked to them about her OU studies and feminism and played for them on her piano. And oh, a lovely cup of coffee she do make, they said, as if that clinched the matter. The family solicitor leaned back in his chair and informed Bryn that it wasn't arson to burn a fortune, though it might be construed as eccentric or subversive. On the other hand, people poured fortunes down the drain every day in bad investments or high living.

— Your mother has left a will, he said. — There'll be enough for her funeral. And just the one small bequest. I cannot divulge that to you.

Meanwhile at Cae Twmpyn the farmhouse descended into senility. Nature ran wild in there. Convolvulus vines overwhelmed the piano, covering it with their white trumpets. Insidious tendrils lifted the lid, clasping the hammers and strings, soundboard and bridges. Year by year as the bindweed rotted, it left a scurf of dry brown dust that began to fill up the cavity. Moths laid eggs on the bindweed and larvae pupated on the keys. Snails festooned the inlay with slime that dried to a map of roadways.

Until the day came to call it home from the dead.

Inside Out

'Are you her mother?'

They would have to operate a second time, said the elegantly suited surgeon; he regretted that there was no option. White coats surrounded me in the midnight ward.

'But,' I objected irrationally, 'she's only fourteen.'

There was no way they could avoid it, he patiently explained. The gangrenous appendix had caused adhesions in the loops of inflamed bowel. She would die if he failed to operate.

Would I sign?

My hand strove to comply. It traced the letters of half my name with great labour; then the pen gave out. Another was supplied. Two separate mothers seemed to have consented.

'I perform this operation, oh, twelve times a year,' he said. 'It generally works fine, don't worry.'

How many didn't work and had to be repeated?

One in twelve.

Oh my ewe lamb, don't be that one.

Lindsay in the side ward lay greenly gowned with her hair drawn up in a complex plait from crown to nape. I waded to her against the drag of a fierce ebb tide, walking against time to where she would soon not be. In the crook of one slender bare arm, rosy with eczema, lay her toy cat disinterred from the childhood she had sought to put behind her.

'The nurse did the plait for me. I've got to have my bowels done.'

'I know.'

'Don't cry,' she said.

'I'm not.'

The child in me wept; but Lindsay and I remained dry-eyed. She neither clung nor offered a token of fear. Her bravery stabbed me with pangs of an obscure remorse.

They lifted her tall, light body on to the trolley and she laughed all the way to theatre, for the hospital in its mercy had provided a clown.

'Way hay, it's cosy in here,' said the grey haired clown. 'Think I'll take a week off portering.'

'It's only for sixteen-year-olds and under, so tough,' retorted the Scots nurse, Margaret.

'Well I am sixteen. I've just had a hard life.'

Lindsay lifted her head and giggled; and all the way through the labyrinth the clown capered; and Lindsay laughed; and Margaret stroked her head; and as I chased alongside the fast-wheeling trolley, my anguish took the form of a remorse more profound than I had yet known;

and she was travelling into regions of remoteness beyond my bounds.

She would not meet my eyes.

Yet still she laughed; and still I smiled; and still we rolled ahead, with the drip and the masked clown, toward blade and blood.

Shod in sterile plastic footgear, we shuffled into the anaesthesia room, with its shimmer of steel and glass.

'Thanks for doing the plait, Margaret,' were her last words. 'It's wicked.'

The needle entered and the blue gaze drowned. They gestured me to leave. I staggered along mazes of twilit corridor. Automatic doors at the main entrance sighed me out. The stars had slipped their moorings and the earth reeled. Metres of bowel would be slithering now through the surgeon's hands as he unpacked her tender body that had burst from my body fourteen years before.

I hurried back to the dim ward, where two young heads murmured cool wisdom in a pool of amber light above the children's notes.

'She's a lovely lass,' Margaret said.

'Both inside and outside.'

'She'll be an hour or two yet. Lie down if you like.'

'When she was born ...', I said. 'When Lindsay was born ....'

'Yes?'

My face worked. I had no idea what I intended to confide: some oblique clutch, at fullest stretch, at the mystery of birth and being and death.

I lay down on my daughter's bed. The wounded

children slept on motionless. This week when Lindsay began vomiting, I'd been less than sympathetic. Last week we'd quarrelled over some petty trespass; she had flounced and fumed.

A toddler startled and bleated in his sleep.

Hours like decades passed but when reveille came, it was too soon, too sudden.

'She's in the recovery room. You can come now.'

'The delivery room?'

'Recovery. Delivery's obstetrics.'

I was afraid to follow Margaret into the lurid light, over yellow-tiled floors to where someone beautiful and mortal lay on her side swathed in grey tubing. Couldn't they hear my deafening shriek at the meat they'd made of her?

'Love,' I breathed. 'My love.'

'She's still under. We got a litre and a half of muck out. Speak to her.'

She opened her eyes and vomited blood.

'Oh my darling,' I poured out. 'Darling beautiful.'

'That's right. Talk to her.'

'Is Margaret there?' she asked, blurred through oxygen mask, nasal tube, swathes of pain.

'I'm here, pal. You're doing great.' The anaesthetist came from eating pizza on the hoof; injected anti-emetic, shouted to Lindsay to press the morphine button when the pain came.

'Nobody can do it but you. You control it yourself. You don't have to feel *any pain*.'

The clown, unmasked, accompanied us back to the ward, his repertoire of jokes and antics laid aside. Now his

voice sang lullaby as we coasted along, slow, slow; Lind
keening at the mildest jolt; Margaret cradling the morph
machine like a precious baby. Tender hands lifted Lind
from the stretcher.

She hangs there still in space, in their hands; those ha
that treated her as their own daughter. Suspended in m
air, she belongs to strangers and is no longer and ne
again to be my own. I surrendered her with gratitude a
grief.

'Your mum's going now, to sleep.'

'*You* won't go, Margaret, will you?'

Speedwell eyes swivelled from me to the nurse; l
hands reached for our hands.

'I could stay,' I faltered.

'Get some kip, go on. You'll need it.'

Dawn was breaking; shifts changing. I lurched past t
people thronging that other world we'd quitted, whe
skins are seamlessly whole; where you read the newspap
go to work. With these people I had nothing to do.

★

Shyly I approached, like a lover who fears rejection; breatl
lessly, like one who comes to judgment without means t
atone. Faint spring petals of blood bloomed on her arr
plastic tubes festooned her.

'How are you?' I whispered.

'I'm fine,' said Lindsay. 'How are you?' Her eyes wer
morphine-glazed.

'I'm fine too.'

'Good.'

We laced fingers; she slipped in and out of a doze.

'Are you still there?' she asked, eyes still closed.

'I'll always be here.'

'Were you there last night?'

'Course I was. Can't you remember?'

'I think so. I did the nurses' heads in by mithering them all night. I've got six tubes, I hate them. I hate this nose-one, it's disgusting. But my plait's still up.'

One by one the tubes were shed, the stitches. Lindsay slid from her high narrow bed, a white-nightgowned wraith; giving herself birth; delivering herself from evil. I followed slightly behind, cheering her silently on her way, turning inside-out-outside-in.

And still I follow; and still she leads. The gap between us widens a little more with every day, and now she is beginning to run.

Waiting Room 1: Pips

I thumb the bell; stalk in, professional face on, but appease-
ment in my eyes and a lip-quiver. I state my name staccato.
Hatchet-face behind the desk sneezes. Criminal to bring
your germs into this disinfected sanctum of oral intimacy.

If you would just take a seat, Mr Williams.

Do I look dessicated? Am I charmless? From the back,
am I ruinously creased? Do the students draw back from
my breath?

A pip from the blackberry jam has lodged in the crevice
between two molars. What else might be there amongst all
that subsidence and crazy paving of amalgam? Clearly it's
an insult to Mrs Roberts to come with imperfectly cleaned
teeth. The pip, tongued free, sits on my tongue a moment.
Then I crunch its tiny rind, from which sparks a purple
taste, the wraith of a taste. Surprising how long such a
minuscule seed can be nibbled, investigatively, ruminatively,
between incisors, before it is pulped and dissolved. Done
in a spirit of archaeological exploration, as one trawls the

menu of meals last taken, working backwards. Certainly a residue of today's meagre breakfast. No sausage, bacon and egg since Frannie went. *Men are hopeless,* Frannie said, with satisfaction, bustling. *Hopeless, they are.*

Cwmrhydyceirw. Cwmrhydyceirw: the bus to Cwmrhydyceirw rattles along in my brain, the ghost-bus.

Just one pip. When they opened up the stomach contents of Grauballe Man (I shift in my seat, gaze slewing to the magazines) they found the whole of the last meal the chap had swallowed, plus his gut wall full of alkaloids. Grain, pulses, pips. Nasty way to go, poor old Grauballe. There he lay, tanning juicily in the peat swamp, for (what was it?) two thousand years.

Hard to eat anything when you've got Mrs Roberts ahead of you. Never mind a sacrificial meal.

Wittgenstein floats unsummoned to the surface of one's mind. Solid Teutonic name to chew on. *Now Wittgenstein,* we're always saying at the Institute, *Wittgenstein this, Wittgenstein that,* but have I got a clue what he meant by what he said?

Have I buggery. Are these trousers beginning to whiff? Frannie would have chivvied me to get them dry-cleaned; always let me know when and how I'd gone out of fashion. Now I'm a codger with dust in my turn-ups. Are turn-ups in? out? The chap over there with the Financial Times also has them. He looks well pressed. Thing is, I know the name of Wittgenstein, whereas he probably doesn't. Estate agent, most like. *Witt — gen — stein* fills the mouth. Solid as bread pud, but with some devious spice added. Something to do with: *language is all we have.* Saussure, yes, and all those abstruse French geezers. I'd like to imagine them all here, sitting round in this oppressive room, sweating like pigs.

Couldn't they open the window? One might ask Hatchet-face but she seems to double as receptionist and nurse, scampering in and out pulling on and off surgical gloves. And she has a snivel. She shouldn't be allowed to spray streptococcus and other ghastliness over us. I covered my mouth with my hand when I confessed my name, pretending to cough. One thing is sure: Hatchet-face knows nothing of Wittgenstein either. What's the point of philosophy and culture if it's down the plughole in emergency? — even to me, no use at all, not the slightest bit of use — let alone to these proles who wouldn't know Kant from ketchup. Ruins a good meal, does ketchup.

Frannie urged, *Don't judge. Don't beetle your brows at folk, you put them off, and anyway your eyebrows and nosehairs need trimming.*

I miss that: Frannie sitting me down with a tea towel round my shoulders, trimming my hair, then my eyebrows and the sproutings in my ears and nose that made her laugh. Dancing around shouting *Nose-hairs!* Now I am just an unkempt bush.

Nobody speaks to anybody. Well, that's understandable. We're all chewing the cud of our own most intimate fears. Moisture in the palms, pricklings in the fingertips, stomachs churning. *We perished, each alone.* Cowper. Yes, that's right, Cowper. A bit of a sweetheart. Dear man. Nobody knows how to pronounce Cowper. But he was on to it, all this perishing alone. Of course they all had rotten teeth in those days. Dentures made of wood, was it, or dog teeth?

That would have to depend on the species, of course. Chihuahuas would be out on the one hand and Great Danes on the other. A golden mean might be a spaniel.

Pain. Scintillations of pain, warnings bugling from far down in the nerves, then a deepening anguish striking up from the heart of the root.

Cwmrhydyceirw. Cwmrhydyceirw.

It's died down: the howling pain has paled. I shouldn't be here amongst these nobodies. I should have gone private, I always thought that, but it was against her principles, and I deferred.

Don't you have a good word for anyone? anyone at all?

Only for you. Why did your shoulders sag then, Frannie, when I said that? You looked so burdened. Wasn't I enough for you or was I too much? You were enough for me.

The pip is gone, I've trawled for its remains. Down the gullet. Down the hole into the vast abyss. Milton. When I see the vast abyss I see Milton looking down into it with milky-blind omniscience. His third wife predeceased him; his daughters led him a caper. I'll just have a ferret around among the women's magazines and see if there are (yes, here's one) any of those men's magazines I wouldn't be seen dead buying. Sex Tips. Wouldn't that be the test? Imagine a pair of boobs like these, while the ship's going down: could you get it up under such circs? Great test that would be of the power of life over morbid preoccupation, Fate, Nemesis, abscess, *les espaces infinis*, how did Pascal put it? *the eternal silence of infinite space makes me afraid.*

Afraid. Oh yes. I back toward my seat, armed with magazines, feigning casualness, exhaling a small sigh to denote the tedium of waiting when one has important duties to perform, in relation to Wittgenstein and Milton. (Here we go, in comes a mother with a horde of children, trust they will not gallop across to me yowling, and children are germ repositories — yes, that's right, go and bother friend Financial Times, who gives them not the expected supercilious grimace but the sweetest of smiles, good God).

Don't I know her? I'm sure I do. I cross my left leg over my right; then right over left. This shows a relaxed bearing or mien.

Abscess. *Les espaces*.

Now I can't share Pascal's footling worries over a large volume of empty space. In fact I find it a positive comfort, an eremitical refuge from the mess and noise, pain in gums and sciatic nerves. Frannie and I inhabited a shared privacy, the inside of a sphere. I imagine now that I'm riding free of the strife, mire, bile of earth, hanging from a balloon-thing: I kite off into the eternal silence. Give me Montaigne if we must have a Frenchman. Now there was a man for you. I could have sat here forever with Montaigne. Place him just where that old biddy's perched like a scared sparrow, bright brown eyes catching a pearl of light as she tries to snare our sympathetic glances. Pearl more probably a cataract. Wants a good gab. Not likely, dear. You're not going to ancient-mariner me. You're on your own, madam. Could do with a drop or two of Coleridge's laudanum. I'm not about to hear the tale of your dental afflictions, those of your husband, alas deceased, and numerous relatives up and down Sketty. That's right, you look at the charming, gap-toothed children in a row. (I'm sure I know the mother from somewhere). Financial Times has been reading the same paragraph for ten minutes, ha! Scared bloody stiff!

Lord God, why isn't it over? Do I appear to Financial Times as Financial Times appears to me? Quailing, quaking, afraid?

Stiffs in a trench. Beasts to the slaughter. You wonder why they didn't just turn round and shoot their officers. Sheep bleating in the pen to be shorn.

But where's Montaigne? Dear, suave, candid, wry Montaigne, who had read so much and credited so little. Who understood you can *imagine* a toothache just by sitting in a dentist's waiting room. And Frannie said, *You imagine things, Michael.* I mean, I am beginning seriously to doubt whether the pain in that molar is real or not. Pain is subjective. Of course he suffered agonies with his stones, did Montaigne. Agonies. Good companion, because he observed them detachedly and discoursed of them so pleasantly.

Try the breast test. Yes. Diagnostic instrument, probably infallible. Erection and toothache cannot coexist in the same body. The sort of aphorism Montaigne would have minted. He dealt with impotence too, though my powers have not all gone, oh no, not by a long chalk. I could still ... well, let's see. But then the magazine text catches my eye, luring it from the pictured bimbo to a list of *Nine Ways* for a woman to attain orgasm. Nine ways? come off it. My god, Frannie never had one such, as far as I knew, let alone nine distinct avenues to pleasure. All my eye really. *Was that good for you, dear? — Very nice, dear, thank you.* And then a cup of tea. I think she enjoyed the tea more than the Act.

Cup of tea this morning nearly shot my teeth into

kingdom come. Pain scalded right through the top of my mouth, through my skull. It rang round my other remaining gnashers like terrible bells. I sat straight up in bed and listened to that pealing pain. Saw my face in the mirror, eyebrows raised, a look of crazed horror.

Nothing stirs. Mind you, how many erections could have taken place in this antechamber to hell? The sound of a drill sings through the door as a brisk nurse calls to Birdie-woman, *Mrs Prys-Rhys?*

Here, dear.

A pang of relief and irritation goes through me at this rhyming litany, a compound pang, for on the one hand, it's *her* going over the top rather than me; on the other, old Rhymy-name, having got in first, will also be first out. And is.

In point of fact, is out.

Already? That was quick.

Sits down. Fingers her cheek.

Numbed you up, have they? Death by lethal injection in these US prisons. Civilised, I call that. Don't feel a thing. Off to sleep in a jiffy. Socrates had much the same luck. Lovely brew of hemlock, comforting as hot chocolate. You may be sure Socrates had something at once edifying and twisty to say about toothache. Socrates was, in his way, a postmodern, pre-Foucault. They think I don't know what Foucault said but I do, or at least I did last week. I could show that by just happening to drop the throw-away remark, off-the-cuff ... *Socrates was in his way a postmodern...* for what, in any case, do we know of Socrates except through Plato?

Nothing.

And we know that we know nothing.

The world's made up of dots. A jitter of dots. Clots of dots. A mindless dodder of dots, like newspaper photos. Mrs Prys-Rhys flexes her numb jaw. It feels massive, bulking out to one side, a tumour. I can see exactly how it feels. That'll be me soon, sitting there waiting for horror, and she'll be free.

Poor Frannie (I mustn't blub), terrible way to go, no justice in it. Up there at Morriston Hospital. Blackberries on the brambles so plentiful last year, I'd see them from the Cwmrhydyceirw bus in the narrow lanes, hanging on to the chrome seat in front, eyes thick with unsheddable tears. And once I couldn't ask for my ticket: no words came out at all. All gone to mush, I was. Noticed the blackberries so plush and pickable. As children we'd go nutting. Often. And pick hips for jam, full of vitamin C, they said on the wireless, highly nutritious for wartime youngsters. But then of course there's Cowper's perishing. Each. Alone. But I. Beneath. A deeper sea & Whelmed in deeper Gulphs than he. Gulfs. I saw gulfs on the bus, plying to and from my girl. *I've had a good innings.* No. You went too soon. Sixty years. What is sixty years? Old Bevan, the sour old bastard, he's still going strong at ninety, and what use is he to anyone? Funny what comes up in your mind. Blackberries taut in their sacs staring like flies' eyes. Burst in your mouth they would, but I thought this fruit was terrible, its flesh hanging from brambles' twisted thorn-crowns. You can't tell anyone about that.

And how the bus rumbled down the hills, myself sole passenger, while I looked out bewildered and thought, *But she was born here. Born in Morriston she was. Born.*

All dots. Pips. Nerves shot to bits.

Who is that woman? Can't she even try to control those kids?

They don't value me at the Institute, that's for sure. Dead wood, am I? me? with a noddleful of Montaigne, Milton *et al* (all nonsense really when it comes down to it, ballast for the balloon). No! It's never nonsense, how could it be nonsense, my Christ she's got boobs on her, I'll show them, there's such a thing as wisdom, wisdom culled from experience (Frannie was culled) but I'll show them, ageist, that's what they are, was that a twinge? Was it? Why is that child looking at me so fixedly, with such grave eyes? But, mind, she's a sweet-looking lass, I smile at her and she pushes her head back into the green breast of her mother's coat and in pops the thumb, suck, suck. Mam put honey on mine, rots the teeth, but at the time it comforted. No doubt of that, it comforted.

'Mr Williams.'

I show no shock. I get up, trying neither to dither nor totter. Dignity, is what we must hang onto in the face of. Of? Replace the magazines neatly, judiciously. In the face of? Raincoat neatly folded on arm. Smile quiveringly. Pass the chatterbox children with their Beano and the wan mother grey under the eyes — and, oh God, yes, I recognise her: well, that was a long time ago. Pass Herr Wittgenstein with his *Financial Times.* Pass Mrs Prys-Rhys who gives a friendly wincing glance of fellow feeling, tran-siently warming me with a wisp of human warmth. *I am getting there, Frannie, I'm reaching the head of the queue. Frannie, my name's been called.*

Waiting Room 2: Pod

Three kids in four years. I suppose it could be worse: four in three years would be biologically feasible, she's murder, is Mother Nature, considering the diameter of the head to come out and the narrowness of the tunnel to be shoved through, all due to our calamitous bipedal status with no regard for ease of parturition, a design fault that ...

Just stop it, Aneurin, stop it now. Put the magazines back. I said ... put them back.

... is nearly as bloody woeful as situating the vagina next-door to the anus, because next to childbirth cystitis has to be the worst pain, doesn't it, the very worst, I slew in my chair just to think of it and my urinary passage winces, flinches, ouch, as if it remembered, but can tissue actually be said to remember, the delicate place where such gross pains come to pass and searing pleasures, such violence, such throes ...

That's right, come and sit here next to Mami, Magdalena, that's right, you snuggle up ... and the dentally immaculate suited guy reading the *Financial Times* flashes us a surprising grin, very nice, very sweet, given the trauma we're subjecting him to, and Dr Up-his-own-Arse Williams from the Institute (he doesn't deign to recognise me, I'm just the ex-academic mother of three human nuisances, well stuff you, Williams, stuff you all) reluctantly simpers at Magdalena, and the ginger biddy grins too, and suddenly everyone's smiling, a festival of sunlight breaks in on us, while Magdalena turns and whispers breathily behind her dimply hand, *Dat man's got hairs up a nose, Mami.*

Shush Magdalena.

She's got an unusually carrying whisper. Oh God, Christ, what a darling she is, what a precious beauty, I ache for her, for her father in her, for those wormy little fingers and her mass of brown soft curls against my face and lips. Treorchy-Gran had seven living children, two stillborn, goodness knows how many miscarriages, shucked like a peapod once a year she was, but what's my excuse, educated with the toffs at Cambridge, criminal casualness, I just love fucking, I love it in the way nature intended: pity ratbag nature pays you back with this excess fecundity, this fat billowingness, and there are times I've felt like a pod, a gourd, a clay pot just abjectly mindless brooding on its own rotundity, so damned conspicuous, not human any more ...

I said, Aneurin, put them down now, stop annoying the people, I won't tell you again.

Oh what's the use? Marie Stopes might as well not have existed for all the notice I've taken and I *don't* like condoms and I *do* like risks, I expect it's something Freudian, I've impaled and imperilled myself and these little loons are the result. Viola wants feeding, my Christ, does her nappy smell ripe, so, Dr Williams, you're going to get a sight of tittie, that'll put the fear of God in you if the dentist doesn't, watch him vanish up his own arse, old poker-face: remember him chairing the library committee and me wandering in from sunbathing with the third year students, and I slid in beside him, what was it he said? *At long last we are quorate!* How solemnly he said it, what reproof for female lecturers gassing with a bunch of lads on the grass, sucking from a Coke bottle, in a strappy sun dress. *At long last we are quorate.* Shuddering with aroused distaste.

And they got rid of me, the wankers. *You have hardly produced at all, Dr Vaughan.* That's a joke: I'm a one-woman Harvest Festival. *A total of one article in five years shows a certain lack of commitment*, said the Dean. *Well, look on the bright side,* I sealed my fate, *I score with the students.*

Pop it in your mouth, Viola, and let sucking commence. She makes such a noise about it too. Little guzzler. All that lip-smacking, slurping, dribbling from the corner of her mouth, her small palm on my breast, Jesus it's still so sensual, the sensations radiating out in a star, ley lines to pleasure, the sweet drag on the womb, I've had many a happy secret orgasm through this, just cross my legs, so, and ...

That's right, Aneurin, you read the nice article ...

Aneurin has a premature interest in Things Sexual and Experimental, especially when someone's having a suck, he'll be fingering his willy or, as now, his little blond head (hair wants cutting but I can't be arsed, my God, three scalps, thirty fingernails and eke toenails, the maths of the thing goes into a dimension that's truly round the bend, and that's without adding in the teeth) and you, you snorting, snotty little brat, you're spoiling my fun, you seem to have needles in your gums, Mother Nature has a lot to answer for.

How old are the little ones, may I ask? enquires the guy with the *Financial Times* sitting nearest to our menagerie. Magdalena is standing with one hand lightly on his knee, the other bunched against her lips, just staring. Is she all right in the head, I sometimes wonder?

Four, three and ten months.

Well, really, they are peautiful children.

Thank you. I think they're peautiful children too, I can't resist mimicking. *It's a pain waiting around with them though. I hope we're not disturbing you?*

Not in the world.

This I like. *Not in the world.* Meanwhile there's a flurry of coming and going: Old Williams and Ginger have had their jabs and been put out to freeze, and the girl on reception is sneezing away over the queue. Give them one, girl, that's the spirit.

Wot you speak for like dat, Old Man? Magdalena is enquiring.

Well, I come from Chermany. In Chermany we speak Cherman. Not Inklish.

Magdalena is fascinated. Then, without warning or seeking permission, she clambers on to the German knee and gazes into the German eyes.

Oh glory. Do you mind?

I am honoured, he says. *Let us read a book together, Magdalena.* Off she trots to fetch one. *Such a charming name. Is she musical?*

Very. On the drum.
The drum is a very robust instrument.
Especially at five in the morning.

I swap Viola to the other breast. By God, I'll be a
saggy woman after all this suckling which I do *not*
please note, Eternal Powers, do *not* do to protect my lit
darlings with my antibodies, no way, though, OK, sure
makes sense and saves them and me a load of hassle, b
because I personally happen to enjoy it, the tender, dra
ging, horny feeling that puts the light on in your boo
even when you're overworked, which by Christ you ar
you're nine tenths dead by bedtime and feel fifty.

Williams is fingering his jaw in bewildered disma
Asks Ginger in an undertone how her injection is taking
Shouldn't she be warned about *being at long last quorate*?

He was on that panel that gave me the push. They al
fiddled with their ties, while Dean Dai Thomas (whose
fingers have been lubriciously active in generations of girls'
knickers, pantihose, jeans, right back to corselettes and
whalebone bras if the truth were known) enquired was
I was a mite overburdened? Not wholly suited tempera-
mentally to ...? *No!* I should have said. *No way mister are
you taking my livelihood!* But Viola chose that moment to
wrench round, grinding her unborn bum on my bladder.
My belly stretched so taut I felt I'd split. Uncharacteris-
tic tears sparked. I fatally crumbled, under bombardment
without and battery within. Lumbered up, said, *Sod the lot
of you, you dessicated load of coconuts. I resign.*

Pure folly. I heard their *basso profundo* murmurings
behind me. Knew it for a catastrophic mistake the moment

I was through the door but at the same time there was an exhilaration, a punching of the air.

I'll reintroduce myself to Colleague Williams. When this little sprog of my loins has sucked me dry — oh for someone to fuck me dry, it's an age since I had a proper shag, by which I mean a shag where you see stars, you can hardly move afterwards and your flesh is so lax that your pee scalds, your legs tremble, oh gorgeous, and the guy is still up for another go — oh for that fuck — anyhow, in the absence (temporary, I trust) of such, when Viola has sucked her fill, I'll introduce myself to old Quorate and watch him squirm. With any luck Viola can do a projectile vomit, I'll aim her at him, she's spectacular at those, I kid you not.

No, Aneurin, you'll just have to hold on I'm afraid.

He's whining for a widdle but you can bet, the moment we reach the loo, our names will be called and we'll miss our turn. When I get home I'll dump them for a nap and have a wank. How pathetic is that? Keeps you going, needs must.

Wow, you are pongy, I tell Viola. *You are one ripe stinky malodorous lass.* And she suddenly and surprisingly topples her head back like a heavy chrysanthemum and falls fast asleep, dead weight on my left arm. With the burp still in her.

Dr Williams has been called. He looks confounded and doesn't respond. As if by some Kafkaesque turn of events, he found himself transformed into a dental emergency in the middle of a seminar pontificating about his favourite, I don't know, *Welsh adverb*, and suddenly all his stained teeth sprayed out, revelatory, over the dozy beery students.

Hi, I buttonhole him as he picks his way past my brat-lings: *Remember me?* He pretends not to hear my *Hi,* not to see my little Peauties. I should have set them on to him while I had the chance. Why keep a weapon of mass destruction to yourself? But he's gone. So that means we've got to wait for him to be drilled before we get our turn. And all we're in for is examinations.

Excuse me, I petition the crazed-looking receptionist. *Can't my kids go in first? Then you'll have a nice quiet place to sneeze and the other patients can rest in peace.*

Not if She says no. What She says, goes. Sorry, Mrs Powell.

Miss, Ms or Dr, I say. *Take your pick. But married I ain't. OK then, never mind about the wait. They might as well run riot here as anywhere. Aneurin, come and sit on Ms, Miss or Dr's lap, you yowling little sod.* I yank him by his dungarees.

The guy next to me who's been used and spurned by Magdalena looks at his watch. He read her something about Janet and John, of which she heard not one word, gazing with forensic curiosity into his face, squirming her behind on his knee until she got tired of it and announced her botty was itching. Now they scramble for my lap. It's a conflict Magdalena's bound to win, since I've strapped Viola into the pushchair and Aneurin, for all his cheek, is a coward. When Magdalena comes at him punchy fists flying, with her stocky body, thick little legs and arms, eyes on fire like Boudicca, he has to bow to superior force. I adore her, I adore her. I see Aaron's face in her face swimming up to the surface as the baby plumpness of her cheeks recedes.

Come here, gorgeous, angelic, peautiful. I kiss her cheeks and she snares my neck with both arms, lovely and solid, kneeling up on my lap. And she kisses back, with rapture, her mouth open and wet on my cheek. How I cried for Aaron, how I drained myself in tears for Aaron, but ah-ha little did Aaron know, he'd leave me with you, my Magdalena.

I have two children pack in Chermany, my neighbour confides. *Two lovely little kirls. Rosa and Gabi. May I show you a picture?*

They're dear.

Yes, aren't they already?

He says no more. I ask no more. Funny, pictures of people's children: what can you say? He restores the two-dimensional girls to his wallet, tucking them into the compartment where they are housed. Nice quiet, paper children who don't require to be fed, potted, washed, hugged, lugged upstairs on your back and lullabied half the night. Got it easy, haven't you, mister. And what a wallet. Fancy, swanky. Any number of pockets and receptacles. Now that we're on benefit our purse is notably light.

So you come to us complaining you're skint, having thrown away all your advantages? Don't you know we scrimped for your education, and what have you done with it?

Given you grandchildren?

Any fool can do that. And Magdalena being, well, coffee-coloured. Aren't you ashamed?

Proud, I said quietly. *Proud. Magdalena is my life.*

I'd hoped for more sense from an educated woman. But I suppose you're after money, is it?

I grabbed the cheque, mortified. Done for myself good and proper. Still there was something mysteriously thrilling about being a pod. Going with my tummy spherical, like Plato's all-round men who rolled around without the need of legs, they were so perfect, and the babe-enclosing skin tight as a drum: well, that doesn't sound too pleasant, but ...

That's the way, Aneurin, you go sleepy-byes, curl up like a kitten ... yes, I know you're hungry, we're all hungry ...

... but it was a feeling of being lusciously ripe, just drifting on a current, thinking of nothing but the next meal because, talk about hungry, I snaffled Mars bars galore, I was a frigging Mars bar, and I said to Aaron that time, *I'll have your child, Aaron. Then I'll be content. You'll not be able to hurt me, no one will hurt me then, I'll be.*

Be what?

Just be.

He made no reply but I could see him chewing it over. Well I got over him. Problem with kids is, you can't put them away in your wallet until convenient. Because I am ravenous for life. For pleasure. So, Dr Powell, why did you not insure against inconvenience by investing in the pill? Haven't a clue. I seem to have lived in a dream.

Wish I hadn't blown it at the Institute. Good feeling, that was, perched on the desk, swinging my legs in the tiniest skirt and the highest heels whilst confiding the obscene habits of Caligula to an agog lecture theatre. Invented novel and ingenious vices on the spur of the moment, on the best scholarly principles. They lapped it up. Gives you a buzz to wow a couple of hundred guys at a sitting. Not wowing anyone much now with my tall tales, my svelte figure. I mean, pods don't, do they? Two a penny in every supermarket. God I could get maudlin if I let myself, I could be hangdog.

Williams reels out. Looks fit to puke. Excellent. So it's our turn? But of course we're all in the land of nod. Some of us are even snoring. We've red cheeks and a sleep-sweat. We're curled up like kittens, we're sucking our thumbs, we're an army that has fallen corporately asleep on the watch. And we are deep under, make no bones about that, the waters have closed over our heads and we are full fadom five. Thus it is, Ms Dentist Roberts, that you have robbed me of my postprandial nap, which these characters would have granted me by toppling asleep en masse after beans on toast. Thus it is that your ears will be assailed by god-awful roaring when you pluck them from dreamland. You have buggered up our day, Ms Roberts, good and proper, and you will suffer.

Williams totters, a pitiful crock, with flecks of blood on his chin. Obviously one tooth lighter than when he went in. Relief suffuses his face at the sight of Ginger. Salvation is nigh. A female person to moan to, lean on, leech from. And oh is she asking for it. *Leech me! Leech me!* You daft bugger.

Mrs Powell, would you all like to come through?

Ms, Miss or Dr.

Oh, yes, right, Mrs Powell.

I'm not married, you see. Powell is my own name. I'm not Mrs.

Well, anyhow, would you like to come through?

Oh yes, that will be very easy, won't it, now that they're all fast asleep.

Well, I'm sorry, Mrs Powell, we've been running late as you know, what with sickness and understaffing, we do our best.

I'm — not — Mrs.

Tell you what, if I take the little one, you could carry the little boy and … we could come back for …

Allow me, says the Teutonic white knight. *Allow me to transport my, if I may so style her, little friend Magdalena.*

So my trinity of young souls trumpet-voluntaries its outraged dolour, its berserk triumph over the forces of fogeyness, bellowing fit to wake the dead, which, as Mrs Roberts jests, is handy, since it serves to pop open everyone's mouth for inspection, without need of coaxing or bribery, and all at once we are out in the street and headed for home, fish fingers and an hour's serious solace under the duvet.

Backpack

He should have been born into the gentry, with acres, a staff of sycophants, a game keeper and several cocker spaniels. Instead of that he's penned in our terrace, snaking up the hill towards the handy cemetery above the limestone quarry. Jerry-builders threw up Bryndu in the sixties, with party walls like plasterboard. Though mine's an end-terrace, I hear twice as much as I want to through the shared wall.

— Wilson. Formerly of The Royal Welsh, is how he introduces himself over the fence.

— Yes, I can see that. Jenkins, ex-teacher.

He seems tickled by my reply, an ironed man in a raglan pullover, chinos and cycle clips, a superior backpack slung over one shoulder.

A sudden snarl. — Hoi! You! Woman! Female person! Trespasser! Private path!

A dog walker is negotiating the low barrier separating the residents' pathway from the Green. She retreats in good order.

— All kinds of roughnecks try it on, he says. — Off to the shops now.

The previous owner of my house, a Quakerly soul, lost all control, according to Trisha, my neighbour the other side. Nobody knew where Marion learned such gutter language — and Marion herself seemed bemused: *It just came out.* She rapidly went downhill and died of a heart inflamed by rage. Trisha bristled as she related her friend's fate. A wonderful person Marion was, she said, a pacifist. Until he took against her.

— What was it all about though?

— He disliked it when her grandchildren tried to romp on the patio.

— There doesn't seem much room for romping, that's true.

— But kiddies need to romp. Who can begrudge them?

— Well, I've no grandchildren. But I've a piano.

— Mind you don't play it, *bach*, that's all.

Determined to keep on my neighbours' right side, I elect to practise only when Wilson is out. I love the house and the wooded green leading down to the sea front, which the Council has always intended to violate with a road and never got round to. It's an avenue of, chiefly, retired couples and widows. The widows observe the decencies by keeping to themselves any excess of grief and arthritic pain. They're — we're — in general pretty feisty, giving the lie to the newsagent who refers to us as Death Row.

— Alive-and-Kicking Row you mean, I tell him, robustly. – Actually.

— Well, I didn't mean you, darling, you're quite young.

— Not for much longer.

My own mourning I carry with me as privately as do my fellow widows. It's nobody's business. There've been a few bumpy moments. Martin's bureau moved in with me. There he'd sit writing letters to the *Guardian*, doing our accounts and jotting poems on the backs of envelopes. Martin needed so little in the form of material possessions: the bureau was the exception. Wedged in the box room, against the party wall, it seemed to muffle the Wilsons' whining.

Its many drawers contained perishing elastic bands, rusted paper clips, a clock that had wound down years ago. The elderly bureau was never an object of beauty. But it was Martin. Martin without Martin. Every time I sidled past, I rocked with grief. Listen, I'm obsolete, the bureau whispered: you'll feel better, Daisy, when I'm gone. I'm only a lump of wood after all.

Off to the tip it sailed on the handyman's roof rack. A bad moment. That week I buried Martin's ashes in the back garden. Turning, I spotted someone in next-door's upstairs window. An addled, recessive face. Was it his or hers? At times the Wilsons seemed to have grown into one another, as they say married couples do: a *folie à deux*.

My neighbour's wife follows him about like a dog. Except when he is following her about like a dog.

Back and forth they cruise in one another's wake, the length and breadth of the house, whining at one another. Not that you can catch the words. The Wilsons converse in voices resembling the song of weeping strimmers on doleful summer afternoons. Sometimes, Wilson bursts out of the French windows, wearing that eternal backpack, to confide in the cat: — Honestly, that *woman*, Pasha, nag nag nag, she'll drive me insane.

I keep water by my window to hurl at Pasha, a dingy cream mat on legs, when he convulses his raised tail in my bushes.

One morning Mrs Wilson comes out alone and shakes a duster for several minutes. Speaking from one corner of her mouth, she passes on the intelligence, — He'll be at the Rotary from half six this evening.

Hard to know what to make of that. Is she hinting that she'd welcome a visit? Or giving the piano all-clear? In the balmy evening she and Pasha loll on their patio enjoying the golden light, sharing a can of sardines, sipping or lapping the drink of choice. I let rip and keep hammering for a couple of hours and she seems to be conducting, out there in the garden, with a fork. The house — possibly our whole terrace — vibrates like the tympanum of a mighty ear.

When I adjourn, Mrs Wilson's still out there: in the gathering twilight she has switched on a lamp. Pasha treats his mistress to a trophy from the wood — a mutilated mouse, still squirming in his jaws. As she bends to receive Pasha's tribute, my neighbour's white-blonde ponytail flicks up and catches the artificial light rather stunningly. It flames out like the tail of a vanishing comet. In the copse the woodpecker has concluded his day's drilling and owls begin to halloo. When I glance out again, it's dark: she and Pasha are still there, milky figures fading into moonlight.

This was the last time I remember seeing her, though

I may be wrong as it was about now that Jasper began to visit. We swanned off to the Costa del Sol, where we lounged beside his nephew's pool — and it seemed life might take more exotic directions than the essentially vegetating concerns of Bryndu.

★

Marriage is a great mystery. I've never been much good at it. Nor was Martin and that's probably why we were so well matched. The idea of being joined at the hip was anathema to him. Who knows what goes on between spouses behind closed doors? They become entangled in bizarre ways outsiders cannot conceive. And who, overhearing the rumbling echoes of others' marriages, can decode the clues?

One day she's there, the next she isn't.

I've unpacked from Spain and bought in provisions. Trisha arrives for tea; invites herself really.

— Gosh, she says. — This house hasn't half changed since Marion's day. Poor soul, she did suffer so. Tea and cake, oh yes please. Thought you'd never ask! I wondered: had you heard what happened to Jean Wilson?

— Did anything happen to her?

— Nobody knows. We thought you might have overheard something through the wall?

— Well, they used to do a lot of conjugal whining but I may have become immune because I don't notice it now.

— Of course you don't: she's gone. Nadine called in the *Heddlu*. She felt it was her civic duty. Two young policewomen came to investigate. They went away satisfied apparently. But, Daisy, you can ask him where she is. He's intimidated by you.

— Really? What makes you think so?

— For a start you're so tall. Were your parents tall? It must be useful when you're in the supermarket and the peas are on the top shelf. Anyway, Wilson looks up to you. And he's got the idea that you're an intellectual. He's in awe of intellectuals. I expect it's your glasses give that impression.

I saunter out, carrying a Complete Works of Shakespeare. Wilson is patrolling for trespassers, stooping under his rucksack. It seems to have grown into one of those massive affairs with sundry pockets and pouches, nets and hooks.

— It's my backpack, he says. — It's killing me.

— Backs are a pest.

— No, Daisy. Keep up. My backpack. It's the devil to get on and off.

— Let me give you a hand. If you just turn round? How's your wife?

Leaning over the fence, I fiddle uselessly with a byzantine system of straps while Wilson flails his arms and heaves his shoulders. I offer to come round and help at closer quarters. Not necessary, he says, but thanks anyway. Neighbourliness, he adds surprisingly, is an old-fashioned virtue these days, like giving up your seat to senior citizens on the bus. Not that he's caught a bus since 1977 but he is aware, as who could fail to be, that standards are slipping. Bring back conscription! Later I hear him barking at some lady wayfarers in raincoats who've wandered along the private path. He's accusing them of being hoodies.

I stick my head out and shout, — It's all right, Mr Wilson, they're my guests.

— Right you are, Daisy, fair play. It's all right, ladies, feel free, he says, motioning them on with a lordly hand. Still wearing the backpack, he has somehow managed to wrestle off his gabardine. I send Jasper round to offer help. He returns looking concussed.

— No luck. He reckons it hurts his shoulders when you lift it. I suggested the fire brigade. Massive weight the thing has. What the fuck's he got in there?

— Cans of beans, I suppose. Was his wife around?

— Didn't see her.

As Jasper and I lie in bed, surrounded by clothes horses festooned with holiday laundry, we hear a kind of braying. You could swear there were donkeys on the Green.

★

The consensus is that she's left him, as we'd all to a woman have done, had he been ours. Or that she's on vacation in Tasmania where she's believed to have relatives. A minority, including Trisha, is convinced she's been murdered. Trish reminds me of what happened to Marion.

— Ah but that was metaphorical.

— Didn't look metaphorical from where I was standing, Daisy. Watch your back. You may be tall, but you're quite spindling — and don't forget he was once a sergeant major and latterly a traffic warden.

Wilson's perched on a patio stool, threading a needle, as I observe from the bedroom window. What a head of hair he boasts, a luminous flaxen mound. Still wearing the backpack, I see. He seems to be slitting and hemming the backs of shirts, a skill perhaps acquired in the military, which equips soldiers with sewing kits when they depart on their manly exercises.

— It's like any affliction, Wilson observes. — A resourceful man adapts. I'm sleeping on my side. New foam mattress. And one can turn over on one's belly.

The way he gazes upon me is bloodcurdlingly tender. He exhorts me to call him Denzil.

— I was wondering – Denzil — about Mrs Wilson? And why you don't just cut the straps?

— Tried that, dear. Obviously. You can't get purchase on a knife or scissors. I'm seeing a consultant next week. By the way you're a real breath of fresh air, Daisy, after the harridan before you. Sociopath, I believe is the technical term. But I never speak ill of the dead.

Wilson gets to his feet, wrenching himself up – gasping – lurching — gripping the wrought iron garden table. Collecting his mending kit, he retreats to the sitting room with a gallant salute. Some tune is coming from the backpack, perhaps from a mobile phone: a whickering as of a puppy penned behind a baby-gate.

But that might be poor old Pasha, who's either sick or has lapsed into feline depression, sprawled on the coal bunker, yowling feebly.

★

While I accompany Wilson to Outpatients, Jasper is deputed to research Mrs Wilson's whereabouts. Happily, as a social worker, he's mastered certain knacks like picking locks with hair-grips to winkle out clients who've shut themselves in the bathroom to snatch essential me-time.

In a malodorous corridor, we sit alongside folk needing replacement hips and knees, stalwarts who refrain from bemoaning the miseries of age. Martin never grumbled either. One evening he just keeled over: everything gave out, lungs, heart, the lot. — It's all right, Daisy, he wheezed. — Live your life, my dearest heart.

This was a blessing on me. This was my inheritance. Memo to self: do not let any sucker-fish feast on your mercy.

Mr Comity's nurse ushers the pair of us into the consulting room for five minutes of his world-famous attention, ignoring my bleating that I'm only a neighbour.

— The MRI results are fascinating! What we're seeing here is an intriguing form of parasitical kyphosis. Yes? No? Got that? Want to write it down? A more superstitious age might have called it an incubus. A demon burrowing into your back, Mr Wilson! Ha! — those quaint old medieval quacks! In layman's terms, you're host to a rare species of parasitism.

To illustrate, Mr Comity cites the taxonomy of ticks: *Ixodidae* that are distinguished from the *Argasidae* by the presence of a *scutum;* in Wilson's case the fortuitous presence of an *alien receptacle* (which will in due course be fully absorbed) has afforded the ever-opportunistic *nymph* an embedding platform. Prognosis: volume will decrease, weight remain stable, as parasite and host fuse in fuller organic union.

— Can't you just cut it off? I put the obvious question, since poor old Wilson, dumbstruck, is humming to himself, away with the fairies.

— It's an irreversible process, regrettably. Palliative care only.

— But where has it come from?

— Ah, Mrs Wilson — dear lady — if we knew that ... But, rest assured, I'll be there every step of the way. Your husband's is a truly historic case.

— I'm not Mrs Wilson, I bleat. — Nobody knows what's become of her.

But Mr Comity has closed Wilson's notes and his nurse ushers us out.

I maximise time for Jasper's inspection by leading Wilson to the Outpatients' Café, The Jolly Eater, and buy him coffee and a bone-dry Welsh cake, which he gnaws bitterly. I remind him of his incipient fame: *Lancet* articles; invitations to exhibit his pathology at international conferences, all meals found, luxury accommodation.

— I know *that,* woman, he snaps, with something of his old asperity. — But did he explain kyphosis?

I google kyphosis on my mobile. — It means hunch-backed. Like Richard III. He was the most famous example.

And again — I cannot seem to help it — I've said the right thing, for Wilson tilts his head and smirks.

★

Under the yellow awning on Nadine's patio, we admire the feast she's laid out: works of miniature sugar-craft for which she's famed throughout Glamorgan. In her time Nadine has sculpted the entire Welsh rugby team in edible form. Her cakes celebrate weddings and divorces, imprisonments, escapes, the funerals of inconvenient family members. Ruthless Thatcherite entrepreneurialism is Nadine's gospel.

Bryndu residents lower down the hill are upwardly mobile: their extensions burst up through the roof or creep out to what lawyers call the curtilage. No need to crane one's neck to view the sea down here: red-sailed yachts tack across our line of vision, mirrored by Nadine's marine-themed cakelets, boats with masts rigged by spun sugar.

— Scoff em fast, she advises. — Before the buggers melt.

We've all got spun sugar beards and sticky fingers, which we suck as unobtrusively as possible. The avenue has united against the Council's revival of its brutalist Soviet-style road building scheme. Discussion centres on whether to invite Swampy, the Newbury eco-activist, either to chain himself to our trees or to train us in tactics.

Wilson is against bringing in Swampy on the grounds of poor hygiene and grooming but his backpack seems to think otherwise. It buzzes and whines and trills whenever he maligns the dreadlocked eco-hero of Newbury.

Iolo Mayo, Nadine's husband, repeats his conviction that we should fight 'em on the beaches.

— But how would we do that, dear? his wife wonders. — In practice? Lure 'em down and spank 'em with seaweed?

Iolo observes that bladderwrack is a natural Gower resource, like blackberries, free at the point of delivery.

He concludes, — And what a photo opportunity for the *Evening Post*! Note it in the minutes please, Daisy.

I write, 'Spank Council with kelp, photo-opp (joke)'. Later I add, 'March on County Hall — mass movement. Heckle dressed in green. Motion carried: email Swampy.'

Wilson's generally mild as milk these days. Of course it's sod's law, I tell Jasper later: just when you need a Rottweiler to see off a vandal like the Council, it turns into a pussycat. Wilson warbles in the shower, with occasional falsetto peaks. He chats to himself over the ironing. I'm no longer nettled. There's an ironic bird in our threatened woodlands that mimics the human voice far more annoyingly than Wilson.

Truth be told, I pity my neighbour and rather admire his fortitude. Pasha sometimes pounces on his master's back in a vicious orgy of cupboard love and is hard to dislodge. One scorching day Wilson removed his vest. And I saw what I was never meant to see. The protruberance had shrunk into a clump or knot: tentacular coils were embedded in its host's back. There's no scarring. The hump cleaves to him, flesh of Wilson's flesh, the frayed backpack long ago sloughed. I saw it rev like a car engine, in spasming paroxysms, as if to dispute a point, whereupon, groaning softly, Wilson reached round a hand to pat and pacify it.

Arrest Me, for I Have Run Away

I was the third: accordingly, they named me Tertia.

She was the fifth: Quinta.

In Venta Silurum slave girls were sexual meat but, transported to Rome, our use and value increased. By then the fifth had flown.

Rome's splendour stupefies me, together with its reek and roar and swelter. If I sleep, I thirst for Quinta; waking, I parch for her. Through the stifling night, my mind quits our quarters, to prowl the house for cool spaces. I imagine sprawling star-shaped on the atrium's marble floor, soaking up cold.

In the moonlight the Empire's gods loom on plinths. Nearby our stone master wears the attributes of Mars. The statue dates from his virile youth: you'd scarcely recognise Marcus Lucius Aelius from it now. His reputation in rags, he'd been sent west to the edge of the known world, the marginal land of the Brythons, where his depravities slackened him and our misery fed him fat as a goose. Boastful scars of wounds won in Iberia criss-cross the trench in his jaw, the famous scar. Or at least it was famous once. Recalled, he fails to prosper. Julia Minor laments with every second breath that Rome is senile, it's losing its memory. It's a city infected by degenerate fads and foreign corruptions where age and wisdom are no longer venerated.

Quinta was, I privately thought, more Roman than the invaders, although to them a girl slave from a barbarian tribe was shit on your sole. They puzzled over why they hadn't erased her at her first offence. The fifth girl must somehow have fascinated our owners, who played with her as cats dandle frogs, mauling her fine skin to see what more could be etched into it.

In Rome graffiti deface every surface. I saw one message that read, 'Can't believe you haven't fallen down, o wall — loaded as you are with this foul scrawl.' Quinta was like that.

Scar for scar, she easily matched Marcus Lucius.

Virgo dura, he called her. Hard girl. Not the least of his threats was that the blacksmith should shoe her like a mare.

★

In Venta Silurum I rapidly saw how the system worked and accommodated to it. I've always had my wits about me; I grasped the value of reason long before Rome taught me the word. Julia Minor once told me I was silver encased in lead ore. Such tributes are counterfeit coins in a scanty purse.

Quinta was in point of fact a foreigner among us

Silurians — a Caledonian, tall, red-blonde. Her silence was clamorous; it called to earth and heaven for redress. The way her freckled skin reddened was not the blush of modesty but the flush of inveterate rage.

Quinta was royalty: to me that was obvious. How she had wandered so far from home was a mystery. Standing a head taller than the women of my dark tribe, Quinta carried herself erect. Decades after Rome's deportation of our last great leader, Caradog, Silurian bands hunkered in the hills and swept down under cover of night to take sheep and garotte the guard. When the legion caught Quinta, she was exhibited around Venta Silurum, a feral, freakish laughingstock with a pelt like a vixen's — and stinking like one too.

Quinta wore a bronze band around her forehead. Those ignoramuses had no clue what that meant.

What is done to a woman is never the measure of the woman. We are standing stones. The roundhouses burn down, our way of life is extinguished, and still we stand. So her silence taught me.

Whenever Julia Minor asks for the headband from her jewel casket, I weigh it in my hands, reverencing its workmanship. There's a pang in my palms as if Quinta's life pulsed through its intricate bronze veins. My mistress preserves such loot as a curiosity. A great hoarder, she likes to refer to herself as an antiquarian. Like the rest of her tribe, she has a habit of unknowingly cursing herself.

Discovering I'd taught myself to read and write, Julia Minor had me catalogue her possessions and their provenance. The Aelius family once kept a pet monkey, she recalled, and there were no end of tricks it was capable of picking up.

— Very like yourself, Tertia.

As to animals, I've seen no end of exotic creatures since coming to Rome, collected from the ends of the earth. They were not entirely new to me. I'd met them first — elephants, lions, tigers — depicted in the mosaics of the stone house Marcus Lucius occupied when the household left Venta Silurum for the east coast of Brythonia. Those mosaics I adored and enjoyed polishing with beeswax to intensify the colours. Adoration is scarcely too strong a word. To me there was something beyond human art in their creation. I fed my eye on designs which now I recognise as altogether rustic and botched.

★

I wing the bird of my mind home.

At Venta Silurum I lived within sight of the ashes of my origins. At first, dumb with shock and grief, we beasts of burden hardly looked one another in the eye. We slept cheek by jowl on the mud and oxblood floor of a lean-to shed, wrapped in cloaks, scavenging food. All around the *civitas* strutted Roman veterans, fawned on by Silurian chiefs who'd switched allegiance, to administer Roman injustice.

One night the wind roared; the timbers rocked. The tempest had the colonists caterwauling at their shrine; they consulted a duck's innards. I have always wondered at their florid superstitions. On the verge of sleep, my mind was visiting the barrow where my ancestors are buried in our

Mother the earth. So I was awake when they pitched the runaway fifth girl into our shed, saturated, quaking with cold, with her lip slashed open. I *cwtched* her down under my cover. We whispered in a mix of northern and western tongues.

— I'm to be inscribed, she said. — What does that mean, Tertia?

I had a good idea but I didn't let on. When I urged Quinta to stop running, all she'd say was that she wasn't a *measchu*, a lapdog, whoever else was.

I tried to reason with her. They'd break her legs and leave her out for the wolves; put her down the mines or crucify her. Why provoke them? The evil-doers would always have the whip hand: they'd slaughtered our invincible fathers and violated our great mothers. Quinta was a runner like no other, fleet of foot, so light she seemed to skim the earth. Had she chosen to bend to the yoke, she could have continued to work as their messenger.

As dawn rose, I watched her sleep. She was a taper burning up too fast.

I wondered what the fifth girl's original, sacred name was. The Aelius household adhered to the rule that human tools cannot be honoured with civilised names: even the famous Silurian warriors gelded by Marcus Lucius for his personal use were renamed Flavus and Glabrio, Blond and Bald.

The master required that everyone attend Quinta's flogging.

— Running away is theft, he said. — Ludicrously, this animal has attempted to steal itself!

On this occasion he proposed merciful tattooing rather than branding.

— What has he written, Tertia?

Whereas previously Quinta had little value, now she possessed nearly none. Who'd want to buy her if Marcus Lucius chose to sell? Some scars might fade but the message on her forehead would be indelible.

There was nowhere now for Quinta to run across the empire. She carried the stigma. It was her own fault. The prudent thing would have been to distance myself. Instead I bathed her bloody welts with brine and honey. We were all orphans in that world. Caring for Quinta relieved some inward pain. I rocked her in my arms, scolding her. We were both about fifteen, but I felt wiser.

— Sleep, you are safe, I hushed her. — You belong to me as a child to its mother.

— Don't, she pleaded, for my tenderness melted her resolution. The fifth girl's tears fell and blood bubbled from the corner of her mouth. – The *Luchd mì-ghnìomh* must be destroyed.

— Let their own iniquity poison the *drwgweithredwyr*. As it will.

While I rocked my friend, I lulled myself. — We're family now. You're tied to me and I to you.

Although she came of royal stock and I was nobody in particular, she assented. I know she did. When I slept, it was against Quinta's comforting warmth; when I woke, it was to her eyes, green-grey, the hue of sage. In time the mud floor yielded to our bodies. I wonder if it's still there, the dint that records us. But having someone to lose brought no peace of mind; rather the reverse. I took to sacrificing to any and every deity, including the Roman Ceres, for hadn't the corn goddess lost a daughter and in her agony cursed the earth?

★

So it was true. We were to leave my native land, to move east. To Rutupiae, one step nearer Rome. On the edge of Brythonia, where Ocean begins. I was to tear my eyes and heart away from the village of my birth. Quinta mothered me then, cradling me in her arms.

You and I walked hand in hand past the yard where roof tiles were being manufactured, for the colonists were planning to build in stone in Venta Silurum.

My left foot.

Your left foot.

We imprinted them side by side in the damp red clay that had been moulded from our Mother the earth. Inside my footprint I wrote my true name. You whispered yours and I wrote that too. Yours is a princely name, meaning 'heather' in your tongue. I shall not betray it here; I shall never betray it in this world. You'd never seen your name written: you knelt in keen joy, drawing a circle around the double inscription with your forefinger. You smiled up at me, gap-toothed like a seven-year-old.

Quitting Venta Silurum in loaded carts, we looked back and saw that this tile — our memorial — had been used to replace a cracked *tegula* on the roof.

★

Marcus Lucius's lady and his Greek slave and secretary awaited him at the stone house in Rutupiae. They'd been sent from Rome as a token of the emperor's renewed favour — and a pledge of return. Our master held the Greek in ambivalent awe as a kind of superior inferior. He'd mockingly address Pelias as 'our pet Pythagoras', with some stale quip that never failed to tickle him.

— Better to be slaughtered by enemies than to trample on beans! – eh, Pythagoras my boy?

The urbane Greek, who did not serve his master solely with the pen, bowed his head in acknowledgment. Pelias rarely lowered his guard. In the end we were all chattel, the equivalent of talking oxen.

At this, to us, luxurious house in Rutupiae, I observed and learned, ingratiating myself with Julia Minor and using all my powers to shield Quinta from the evil-doers and from herself.

— What's-her-name works like a mule, they said of me.
— And she's the next best thing to a mute.

Julia Minor was less deceived. She had time on her hands and grievances on her mind, chiefly concerning life away from Rome, which she said was *not life,* and also her husband's catamites. She would have minded less, or not at all, had he been discreet. In her red and green chamber the birds on the walls were so dextrously painted that you expected them to sing. I would stand and listen to them, sending out the bird of my mind into my native land where larks and thrushes sang to emptied villages.

Julia Minor had taken as handmaidens Cantiacian twins of perhaps five or six. Whenever she tired of petting them, she banished them to the kitchens, summoning me in their place. One day she called for the novelty of a Silurian hair-style and sent for the *virgo dura*'s headband. Julia Minor thought that the circlet was purely decorative. She had no idea of the sacrilege she was committing in usurping it or the penalties that would be exacted.

That day prudence forsook me. I fashioned a mass of outlandish snake-like plaits, braiding into each beads, feathers and silver thread, whatever came to hand, bind-ing the plaits with grease. I added a tassel and a bone ring — and the more of a wanton mess I made, the better she was pleased. For Julia Minor had a yen, she explained, to impersonate an exotic barbarian queen — like Boudicca of old. Twisting her head from side to side, she appraised herself in the mirror.

— Now then, do I look like a savage, Little Runt?

— Never, *Domina*. Impossible. Unthinkable.

— You natives of the west are so dwarfish and woolly: your forefathers must have been half-starved black sheep. We reckon you originally came over from Iberia.

By this time I'd seized every chance to study the colo-nists' written language. It's quite straightforward, compared with the lyrical mutations of *yr hen iaith*. Grasp the rules and you can't go wrong. Pelias was training a boy slave, For-tunatus, to aid his work. The lad practised Latin grammar on a wax slate, chanting aloud. I tested myself by writing in the dust of our Mother the earth. Julia Minor began to use me as a scribe for her correspondence, which sped between Brythonia, Rome and her birthplace of Stabiae. The burden of her letters was: oh mother, oh uncle, I'm so frightfully bored. What's the gossip? Can't you exert your influence to return me to civilisation? This dump is the back end of Hades.

For her delinquency, the fifth girl was assigned to maintain the hypocaust for a month. It was harsh, hot work, generally done by males. She laboured underground, feeding the furnace with timber and coal, to heat the walls and floor and the water of the baths. When she came up from her shift she'd shed weight and her hands and wrists were a blistered mess. All the honey in the world couldn't stop them suppurating. She'd drink and drink and still be thirsty.

★

While I, in my *hiraeth,* looked west and the evil-doers stood tiptoe on the cliff gazing east, you gazed northwards over cornfields that extended to the horizon.

And ran again.

And were taken again. And branded.

And ran. And had the fingers of one hand broken. Your speech was slurred, your skin a memorandum of offences.

I could neither accompany nor hold you.

★

— Home! We've been recalled! the shout went up.

— Now you will see glory! Julia Minor informed the household. — Stupendous wonders. Civilisation.

★

Here in Rome I feel my native language deserting me, although I still dream in Brythonic. When the fifth girl haunts my sleep, asking how I could have abandoned her, I bluster, justifying myself: what choice did I have? All the while I know that a moment of choice did exist.

Seeing my tears, the dream-Quinta sometimes softens, saying, — Never blame yourself, sister. What are we but doves in a net?

In the Roman tales wanderers find their way home, through many vicissitudes. I try to cast my mind into the blue air and wing it to Brythonia. But what place remains for me in my native land, half Romanised as I am, my *rath* and kin long since erased? Bracken and brambles will have overrun the charnel roundhouses of our *mamwlad*.

The best I can hope for now is to be freed — a possibility with which Julia Minor tantalises me. Even then I'd be contracted to the Aelius household for the remainder of my days.

She dotes on me one moment, calling me her *deliciae,* her ugly little pig-pet; the next I'm spurned and she summons her twins, exhibiting them to visitors as trophies. They gambol round *lithping tho thweetly* and completing one another's sentences in their dog-Latin. Soon tiring of their antics, she dismisses them, recalling me.

— Had you ever wondered whether I shall manumit you, Tertia?

I bow my head and murmur that Julia Minor is graciousness itself.

— Well, I might. You never know, do you? But not yet.

There's a consignment of fresh oysters and *garum,* the infamous fish sauce from Pompeii. A stench of death suffuses the house: sea creatures sun-rotted in vast vats. Our owners crave this filth; can never consume enough.

Before tonight's feast, lute music is followed by recitations from the work of Rome's imperial poet. The pious hero carries his ancient father on his back: they turn to witness Troy in flames — a pregnant moment at which female guests dab their eyes and have to be revived with wine. When the declaimer has likewise oiled his voice, he performs a passage depicting the Volscian revolt, led by a warrior maiden, Camilla:

> toughened to endure a fight,
> and, with her quickness of foot, out-strip the winds.
> She might have skimmed the tips of the stalks of
> uncut
> corn, and not bruised their delicate ears with her
> running:
> or, hanging above the swelling waves, taken her path
> through
> the heart of the deep, and not dipped her quick feet
> in the sea.

It's as if my beloved stepped from the painted landscape on the wall into the atrium. Not scarred and defaced, her broken arm hanging limp, as I last saw her hobbling from the dogs of Rutupiae, but hale and whole.

★

The hero of Iberia, rarely sober, has been losing at dice. In a lucid interval he enquires, between mouthfuls, how his lady would like a sumptuous villa in Campania.

Since returning to Rome, she retorts, he has squandered every last morsel of her dowry.

They wrangle: he'll sell her jewels. Or (even better idea!) sell her. Joking aside, put slaves on the market. Obviously. Or mortgage them or something.

Obviously *not*. A villa would require an army of slaves. Is he out of his mind?

Never permit yourself to hope, I remind myself, never. Hope and fear march manacled, a prisoner under escort.

Marcus Lucius proposes breeding from current stock and borrowing on a long-term investment. There's always a lively market for boys and girls. He sorts us into couples. Livestock cannot marry; they bed down as tent-mates. I'm to mate with Pelias: — How'd you care to cosy up as tent-mates? Eh, Pythagoras? — eh, Little Runt?

A voice bursts from my throat.

— What's that? Is the mute talking?

The room rounds on me. A table has uttered; a heifer has lowed with a panic-stricken human voice, like the maiden Io when she fled the cosmic gadfly.

Pelias, quick off the mark, explains that the third girl has claimed in her vulgar vernacular that, unworthy as she is, she's sworn to single life for the sake of Marcus Lucius's lady and hearth. Julia Minor's sentimental eyes brim. Her husband daily humiliates her. She cannot provide an heir.

I've heard him pronounce the word *divorce*. In that event the household would be broken up: I'd be offered on the market to any bargain-hunting brothel-keeper.

Pelias indicates that I should abase myself. I sink to my knees.

– You see? Julia Minor wheedles. – Come here, Little Runt. Our *family* adores us. They worship the ground we stand on.

Mightn't they give – no, *sell* — Pelias and Tertia their freedom? Then marry them. As loyal freedman and freed-woman the couple could be contracted to undertake some lucrative scribal business to ensure the household's pros-perity. It's an idea doubtless minted by her uncle in Stabiae.

— And no more talk of a luxury villa in Campania, husband! Let's enjoy our town house to the full.

★

What's-his-name has forgotten what's-his-name's name. One hand roams, clicking its fingers. He cranes towards the library window, whose cliff top view encompasses miles of glittering sea. He got his way, of course he did, shackling himself with additional debt, and moved the household to Campania. He had the *nous* to act on Julia Minor's advice, freeing Pelias and myself for the task of supporting the household. As we do.

Then fog settled.

His skin no longer fits Marcus Lucius. It sags like an oversize garment. His jowls slump and the war scars have changed their geography, a continent subsiding into the sea.

What's a Roman on an alien cliff top to do, bereft of bearings? One eyelid droops. The other eye queries Pelias's gaze.

— And you are?

— Your freedman, sir. The namesake of Marcus Lucius Aelius.

— And I am?

— Well, sir, you are *the* Marcus Lucius Aelius.

— And this is?

— My wife, sir, your grateful freedwoman.

As ancient custom dictates, we've been saddled with our ex-owners' names, increasing Marcus Lucius's confusion. He generally takes us for his parents. Squeezing our hands, he draws them to his lips to kiss them. Soon he'll jab his thumb towards the door, to rid himself of the illustrious visitor, What's-his-name.

— How tragic, sighs Gaius Plinius, departing for his own villa, — To be exiled from one's own name — and hence from one's immortal reputation. But you, faithful and just retainers, recall the true, erstwhile Marcus Lucius and will piously memorialise him.

I do remember the true, erstwhile Marcus Lucius.

I recall an arm raised to flay the back of an obdurate girl. And how, with the sensitive knowingness of a masseur at the baths, he turned her with his fingertips and palpated her shoulder bones. With succinct movements, the hero of Iberia dislocated the fifth girl's left shoulder and snapped her right arm, tossing her with a quip to the soldiers.

Dusk descends. This is frequently a bad time for Marcus Lucius, who mewls for his wife. It is my duty to remind Marcus Lucius that Julia Minor died nine years ago.

— Oh no! She's run off again, how naughty! Go and fetch her. You! Thingy! Go! Go! Arrest her!

I relate the manner of Julia Minor's death. How, after several months at the villa, she took to visiting the resort of Stabiae, to sample the medicinal spring waters, so she said, residing at her uncle's palatial villa above the bay. And there volcanic smoke found Julia Minor, with the Cantiacian twins, sprawled on the ashy beach.

Marcus Lucius, cowering, shrouds his face in his gown. — No, don't say so, mother! Have some pity!

He has gone the colour of mulberries, blotched with livid patches like oatmeal. Is he suffering a heart attack? I remind Marcus Lucius that Julia Minor was brought here for interment. Would he like to visit the tomb?

— Show me, he begs, for the third time today. — If you will be so kind.

Kneeling at the shrine, he reads his wife's memorial. — But what happened to my sweet dove? However did she die?

Over and over I lash him with the truth. I pity him not one jot. On the contrary, I relish Marcus Lucius's grovelling state. Pelias says a venomous spirit like mine eats its own heart. Such a female consents to become less than human. That is not the case: my heart long ago winged its path west and has never to date returned.

★

I brood in the cool arcade, behind the villa where the breakers' soughing mimics the breathing of a deep sleeper.

Pelias allows the slaves an hour's rest in the midday heat. He is a benevolent master and the best kind of husband: both cerebral and celibate — a respectful stranger, sheathed in silken ironies, not without insight and wry fellow feeling. I sit tapping my lip with a stylus, a gold-rimmed wax tablet on my knee, and muse on the long perspective of rose-trellised walkways, fountains, olives and fig trees, past the shrine, to the wall at the garden's end.

This wall is a window, opening on to another world.

I had Fortunatus depict the scene I dreamed or remembered — or both perhaps: the view west from Rutupiae. Everyone commends the mural as a masterpiece of illusionist perspective. A wheatfield in an expensive arsenic-yellow runs to a dark forest, a panorama so real that you imagine stepping into it. The field of Ceres pulses and glows, dotted with poppies like blisters of blood, packed with seeds of oblivion. If you know where to look, you'll spy a figure forever receding.

— I shall sit with you a little. If it does not disturb you.

It's not what Pelias says that raises gooseflesh but the language in which he chooses to say it. My husband collects barbarian tongues. I reply in Latin, with a face of flint.

— Ah, yes, he continues in Brythonic. — That cold country. You're off visiting again. By the way — I never mentioned this before — I know where you buried the curse tablets — and furthermore I saw what you did with the crown.

— What crown?

— Circlet then. Headband. You know what I mean. The crown of Fraoch.

It seems I speak your secret name in my sleep, my own betrayer and yours.

Pelias has always known. How did I imagine I could cheat the wily child of Odysseus? He watched me bury the curse tablets with the corn dolly at Rutupiae – and years later fling the royal headband to the ocean when Julia Minor was pronounced dead, in fulfilment of my curse and vow. He knew all along of my love for an irreplaceable girl.

— What d'you think of my Brythonic? Pelias asks, preening himself.

I reply, in Latin, — The grammar is adequate; the articulation risible; the idiom frankly crude.

My husband nods and chuckles at my self-possession; folds his arms; yawns; leans back in his seat and falls asleep.

That cold country. Who can paint memory? Or who, having painted it, can resist substituting the artist's enchanting surface for the original scene? I prefer not to think of Quinta plunging into the stubble field at Rutupiae with her shattered arm hanging useless, half naked, her skin a wall scribbled over with obscene graffiti — or of the legionaries choking back the dogs to give her a start. Her mind had gone, pretty well. She didn't know what she was doing. All she knew was the impulse to run.

I elect to remember it otherwise.

It was nearing harvest time. The day of the *drwgwei-thredwyrs'* thanksgiving festival to the corn goddess. When I arrived at the dovecote to collect eggs, the fifth girl was already there, opening cages to free the pigeons. Many birds could not leave, for we'd broken their legs as squabs, to keep them to their nests and tenderise them for the table. And there was no point in freeing the white homing doves, which could only fly in circles.

The weather was clement but you were muffled up in a long-sleeved bodice and over-tunic, fastened with a stolen brooch.

— Come with me, Arianwen, *mo luaidh*.

Nothing that has happened to me in Italy equals the shock when I knew that you — Fraoch — were leaving me. You raised your hood to hide the tattoo on your forehead and the iron collar that promised a gold *solidus* to anyone who returned you.

—You're a dead girl, I said.

— Not yet I'm not. Watch me.

Wheat flowed white-gold to the horizon. Your cloak fell back as you sped through the grain. Your left arm hung limp; your spear-arm was raised, waving me on. You half turned in mid-stride, your copper hair blazed and you beckoned — and I took two steps into the field and halted. You might have skimmed the tips of the stalks of uncut corn and not bruised their delicate ears with your running. My eyes pursued you until you were indistinguishable from the harvest.

The Old Gower Swimmers

August is upon us and our little cove is alive with illusions. Locking my bike to the railing, I look down on the early morning shapes of basking folk — the living and the dead.

The sea's still as a millpond: my body thirsts to be in it. On the curve of the tiered steps sprawl a few couples — perhaps they've been here all night — lying in one another's arms, stretched on the stone like a sacrifice. We flock here to worship, creedlessly.

Are they here yet, Jill and Ray, who basked all last summer on the steps? After his stroke Ray could no longer clamber down the pebble bank to the sand, though once he'd been a swimmer of renown — in the days of the old Gower swimmers who'd freestyle out beyond all limits. Past the point where the seals mate, they swam, past Caswell and Brandy Cove, to emerge through the shallows at, let's say, Pwll Du — padding on to the crescent of pale sand, the oystercatchers' skirl and the silence of the two white houses below the hill. And there they might snooze, the old Gower swimmers, for an hour in the sun, breathing balm of salt and honeysuckle, awakening to power back to our cove for tea. For there's a pathway in the sea, if you can find it. So my father and his brothers told me — and they should have known.

On the grey stone terrace Jill and Ray blended in, the unpretending, loving pair. They spoke with one voice, Jill's, for Ray's tongue had lost its art, his arm its force. — Are you going in, dear? Beautiful, isn't it, irresistible?

I spot them now and wave. And she waves back. Who can measure the gallant courage of the old? Of course Ray isn't really there. So I remind myself. Ray I've reinstated. Even last summer he seemed a fading, intermediate presence. Who knows where the old Gower swimmers go once the last heartbeat is done?

I clamber down the pebble bank. When I turn to wave at Jill and Ray, I double-take: she's not there either.

The sibyls however are real and substantial. They've set up camp beside the cave entrance, observing their customary pieties. On certain rocks they drape towels; on a flat altar they spread picnics. All year round they swim, processing down over the sand in their jewel-bright costumes. Even when waves are high, they rarely wet their hair. You see them bob like silver lamps just beyond the drifting seaweed, chatting away.

— Up early, *bach*! Gwen, a junior sibyl, observes. — You going in? How's your gorgeous daughter?

— Hannah's great, thanks. She's coming down after work. But I'll swim beforehand because she tells me off for tempting the gods.

— Going for a long one then?

And for some reason, I can't stop myself, I begin to brag. I claim to be the daughter of one of the old Gower swimmers, which is true enough, but I allow it to be imagined that I continue the heroic tradition. I speak, hopping on one foot to tug off my jeans, of carrying on round the coast to Brandy Cove. Never mind the Wales Coast Path, I say: there's a pathway in the sea.

— Tidy if you can do it. Nell! Jenny here plans to swim to Brandy Cove this morning, so she says, Gwen tells her friend.

Nell's reply I can't make out but there's general merriment. Nine pairs of sunglasses check me out.

I add lamely, — Well, I might. I'll see.

— What's the world coming to though? Gwen jabs her finger. — See by there, Jenny? Pile of smelly trash! I blame the Council.

She returns to her sun worship. Into my backpack I bundle clothes and towels. The last thing to shed is my specs. With my naked eyes that fuzz every vista, I prepare to launch into the unknown. The heap of rags Gwen deplores rises up into the air: it can't be the wind, there isn't any. Our cove's an odd place. I recently saw a rock get up and manifest itself as a dog. The rock ran barking jubilantly towards its master. I once saw my father and three uncles swim past, performing the butterfly stroke, a decade after the last one died.

— Keep up, slowcoach, they called, as they had in life.

But Dad cried, more woundingly, — Only a girl she is. It's not in her, see. Let her play in the shallows, boys.

I'm irked by the sudden arrival — out of thin air — of George the Kiss and Popeye. Across the glistening plane of water they harry me. They always do: it's beyond a joke. They stride along, one either side. And George the Kiss's mouth is pursed.

— Great day for it, says George.

I'm flying along but they close in. Popeye's outlining his forthcoming trip to Sharm el Sheikh to simmer in the Red Sea — a promise forever suspended for he never actually goes.

— See that pile of rags? I ask, ducking George's mouth. Too late, for the detestable smacker squelches on my cheek.

The heap of clothes is a poet — bearded and dread-locked. He's loping towards us with huge strides, poling along with a staff.

— Busking as a beach bard, boys, he informs George. — I'll recite Dafydd ap Gwilym or Dylan Thomas or invent in either language on request. Which is it to be? Pay me in pints. The Son of Man, he remarks with a certain grandeur, — hath nowhere to lay his head — and would welcome a sandwich and a pint of Speckled Hen.

George taps his shorts as if imagining a pocketful of loose change. I escape into a delirium of icy sensuality.

In this medium there's a swift undoing of your ties to the shore, your pact with the living. Striking out, I'm soon beyond my depth. There's no current to speak of. Oh the green world underwater: the view's unusually clear, down through bent beams of radiance onto stippled rocks, ribbed sand, swirled fronds of wrack. And they are here too, Dad and the uncles, just out of sight. — Catch us if you can, they call.

I'm looking for the sea path: maybe it's this mesmerising trail of rocking light. Hannah calls it my Lorelei feeling. She's beyond weary of begging me to keep well in to shore. I know I ought to defer to her. A wilful mother should be guided by an adult daughter's sober counsel. In this way you maintain your allegiance to the living. In theory I do accept this constraint. But life is out there too in the wild — vitality unlimited.

— I can't always be keeping my eye on you, Mam, she constantly chides. — It's boring. I've things to do.

— Don't worry, sweetpea, I'm a strong swimmer.

— No, you're not, you see. You're a dreamer. What about when you got caught in the rip tide and the lifeguard had to save you? How d'you think I felt then?

She's right to scold. But the waters today are halcyon. A gull takes off with a clamour of wings. Crabs scurry about their business along the bottom, some horizontal, others vertical. I laugh underwater, watching them; the bubbles burst out.

Girls can't! Mothers shouldn't! Oh but we can, we must. One glance back at our homely bay and I'm gone. Off towards Snaple Point, swimming parallel to the coast path.

Easy, take it easy. Rest on the water, relax even the crawling arm, fish-glide forward. Good.

Halfway between beach and point something odious nudges a shoulder: a bluish-brown jellyfish with transparent skirts. A jelly colony is flocking towards the shore. They're not stingers — but, *ych a fi*, what if one slipped between your lips? There's a rushing against my calf: the powerful muscle of bass or mullet. I draw level with the point where walkers shade their eyes against the sun-dazzle. They've come round the coast from Caswell or Brandy Cove, or perhaps they're pilgrims from Rhyl or Rhosneigr or Aber-aeron. I decide against waving from my parallel path in case they mistake me for someone who needs saving. The scents of broom and honeysuckle drift down. And I plough on.

Once I'm round the point, Newton Cliff rears up and the sea is roiling. There's — oh no — a tugging current; surge thrashes the rocks.

Big mistake. You ass, I tell myself. Why did you ever start this caper? What about cramp? I'm not getting cramp. Yes you are, you always do. You've never grown up. What are you trying to prove? Who to? There's no bottom, only endless depth. My mind curdles and a slow, cold estrangement sets in. If I called, who'd answer? Who'd hear above the welter of water? The walkers on the Coast Path are welcome to sling me a life belt — but they've vanished.

Not making progress. At. All.

Bodies barge into mine. Animals trawl my struggling legs with sudden snouts, they pop up to stare with large soft eyes, they dive. When I tread water to clear my misted goggles, one cuff of the sea's paw tosses me towards the rocks.

★

— Oh those pesky seals, the guy on the board says as he paddles me round into Caswell. — That's their nursery, you know, their rookery. They nibble the surfers' toes. Did they have a go at yours?

Never been happier to see a ferryman in all my life. Gavin has sun-bleached hair and no eyebrows and is about seventeen. He sculls us along effortlessly.

— You OK now? he asks as we land. — Don't get me wrong, Jenny, not being rude but are you fit enough for this kind of lark? — I'm not saying you're fat – but at least invest in a wetsuit, my dad runs a surf shop, could do you a tidy discount.

Teeth chattering, mortified, shanks numb and quivering, I thank him for my life. What a weird plum colour I am. When Hannah came safe to shore (I stumble up the sand), she was this kind of colour. (I throw myself down to dry in the scorching sun). The midwife blew into her lungs – and then Hannah cried. She bellowed at the universe — and oh, that blessed hullaballoo.

Waddling and wobbling round the cliff path, bum and thighs trembling, I reel, veering from one side of the path to the other.

— Is that woman drunk?

Down there the sea boils and it would be easy to topple, for the rail seems intermittent and the world a collapsing blur. The rock's hot beneath my soles, I'm stupefied, I've tempted the gods and the gods have sniggered.

— Oi, mind my dog, you ran straight into him.

— He ran into me.

I round the point. At last, Langland. Golf course, green and white bathing huts. How long have I been away? An hour, a day, a year? Soon I'll be limping home, a laughing stock — unless of course I sneak into the sea and freestyle a final lap?

I do.

Carnival's in full flow at our cove now that the sun's high. Buckets and spades, chips and mushy peas, dads cheating at frisbees. Beer bellies precede their daintily stepping bearers like the proudest of pregnancies. My oomph is back. I come stroking in with theatrical brio.

They're processing into the sea, the sibyls: a majestic sight, each in her gem-bright costume. One by one they raise their hands and enquire, — Well, Jenny *bach*, did you make it to Brandy Cove?

I shamelessly nod. And take a bow.

Our beach bard, up to his waist in water, is waving a bottle of cider and toasting Llewelyn ap Gruffydd, the last prince of Wales, betrayed in the belfry at Bangor.

And here at the edge Jill and Ray are dipping their toes, she in her floral sundress, her husband wearing the quiet enigma of last year's smile. And Hannah (wherever did she spring from?) wraps me in a towel and says, — Nice swim? I'll get you some chips and an ice lolly when you're dry.

We sit sucking the melt from our lollies while I brag that I swam with seals.

— Wow, Mam, that's so cool. I'll go in after.

— Yes but take care, I say, and the sun darkens in the cloudless sky. — Don't go beyond your depth.

The sibyls are performing some kind of synchronised swim out there in the green waves and the tide's well on its way out.

★

Walkers on the Wales Path are coated, hatted, mittened and scarved. Nobody's around on the beach. Why would they be on the bleak morning after Guy Fawkes Night? The terrace café has stacked away its tables and sunshades; snow and sleet are forecast.

I cannot quite let go for winter. Imagine being in the sea to welcome the soft fall of flakes on shoulders and hair and tongue and lashes, imagine the white dazzle of snow on sand. Once I pelted across Penmaen with Dad and the uncles. It was New Year's Eve. The sea had frozen into layers like a ruched curtain and beneath our boots the shore clanged iron-hard. In that white world the brothers' eyes showed a mirroring blueness, pale and milky. Shortness of sight seems to run in our family. Those boys were up for anything. — Keep up, Jenny! they called over their shoulders.

Not that their taunts bother me any longer. I've more than proved myself this summer. By daily increments a tall tale becomes – like their yarns — personal legend.

Anyway I'm dying to try out these prescription goggles, though not without qualms: as I strip in the mouth of the sibylline cave, I'm dubious about quitting my old romantic blur. An evil wind balloons my towelling cape. Dead leaves rattle across the stones. Hosts of wavelets pucker the surface and as I quake my way into the water, shouting aloud with icy shock, I decrypt the debris tangled in the rocking drift of seaweed. Cigarette butts, plastic bottles, cylinders of spent fireworks.

George the Kiss lies in a hospital bed, having his tonsils out. Popeye has finally embarked for the Red Sea.

Llewelyn Griffith was last spotted in the ruined and roof-less workshop of Davies the Wrought Iron, prostrate on a bed of sacks, the poems locked in his mouth. I still see Jill and her beloved Ray everywhere. I'm told the sibyls have temporarily abandoned their sanctuary and adjourned to the Wales National Pool Aquacise Club for the winter.

    — Face it, Jenny, enough's enough, said Gwen. — We've held out as long as we can and longer than most. It's up to you now. You're young. Youngish. Well, you're not old. And you've got some blubber on you that should keep you insulated. After all you're the good girl who swam to Brandy Cove.

The Wolf Tone

𝄞

Eva's in the window seat in pyjamas, legs tucked under, the grubby soles of her feet showing. She offers the wraith of a smile. When Aidan stoops to kiss her, she puts up her mouth and passively accepts his early-morning kiss. Aidan takes note. Eva's moods govern the atmosphere in the household; always have, always will. He understands that a world-famous cellist will have a unique constellation of nervous needs. Eva Himmelfarb has always found the lime-light a lonely place to shine. Some darkness, born with her, underlies her brilliance. Their few quarrels have always seemed like the end of the world. Seven years younger than his wife and light-years less gifted, Aidan has pledged himself to support and reassure her.

The cello's still in its case. By this time in the morning

Eva has generally been practising for an hour and still going strong. Better not comment though. Aidan, making toast, squints out at the unseasonably bitter morning; frost whitening the lawn, copper beech buds breaking into their purple, betrayed.

'No kids for nine days, Eva! No bloody Ofsted! Bliss.'

Eva growls, 'There's a wolf tone, Aidy. I can't bear it.'

Whether there's some way to eliminate the wolf tone without damping the resonance of the errant string, Eva is unsure. She doesn't look Aidan in the eyes.

'Oh *no,* love. We had that before, didn't we? I thought it was sorted.' Aidan says *we.* Because certainly the two of them suffered. The aberration drove a wedge between them. That can't be allowed to happen again. The old question surfaces in his mind: what does a famous musician see in a prosaic primary school teacher?

'But it's back, Aidan.' Eva levels this like an accusation. 'It's come back worse. I'm amazed you slept through it.'

'Do you think we should take it to the luthier?' Aidan crouches, taking both Eva's hands in his.

Eva's removes them. Her face is stone. But then her expression is often melancholy, not least when she's absorbed in her music and is, in the deepest way known to her, happy. Eva glances at the Wielkovsky as if something in her world had turned against her. Well, and it has, hasn't it?

'The luthier is dead,' Eva says.

'No, love, no, he isn't: the luthier never dies. Nat has carried on the business. Mr Engelstein the Younger. Well, the Elder now, isn't he?'

Eva shakes her head. 'I don't think Nat will be able to help. It's the end of the road.'

'Don't say that. Ring Nat. Is it the G string again?'

'Mmn.'

Aidan doesn't make the mistake of dismissing the wolf tone as some commonplace affliction like a sore throat. But, hey, he thinks, it did visit before, out of the blue, didn't it, and it did clear off. And we were all right. The first Aidan knew of the wolf was a rasping screech and Eva's shriek of *Aargh! No bloody no!* Old Mr Engelstein resolved it some-how, though not before it brought Eva out in an eczema rash and they rowed so loudly that the next-door neigh-bour banged on the wall.

Upstairs, Aidan showers and shaves. This time I'll keep in close, he thinks. No need to panic. She'll never leave me.

Eva surprises him by bouncing upstairs three at a time and coming in quite cheerfully to dress and brush her hair.

'Have you rung Nat?' Aidan asks. He removes the brush from her hand and begins to draw it through the tangled wilderness of her hair.

'He's away. Sorry for being a pain in the backside.'

'Did that pull? Sorry.'

He lifts Eva's mane in his left hand, bending to kiss the nape of her neck. He looks into Eva's mirrored eyes, meltingly dark. Aidan loves her to lie above him and let the shadowy curtains of hair enclose his face.

'It will be all right. It truly will. You'll see.'

Arms around one another's waists, the two of them drift downstairs. Eva offers to demonstrate the problem. But the wolf turns tail and, retiring to some lair within the instrument's body, cannot be tempted out. Later Eva says, 'Had a thought! If it comes back — and it will come back — I shall compose a divertimento on the wolf tone — why didn't I think of that before?'

Aidan understands what Eva's doing: turning the glass. The blue vase on the sill was picked up from a charity shop. Angle it between your eye and the light: the world, suspended in water, flips upside down, slips out of true, into new kinds of true. Use the flaw. Of course this would have been impossible with the determining events of the Himmelfarbs' lives sixty years before. Revolve the glass of evil and its cracks fork into every curve and plane. For some impieties there's neither forgiveness nor redemption. None would be acceptable. As the late child of a father already elderly, who'd lost his first wife in the camps, Eva has inherited a shadow and carried it through thirty-seven years.

Resting the instrument between spread legs, Eva tunes, her beautiful, broad hands pale against the spruce and maple body.

'You see,' she says. 'Something like this.'

A peculiar, harrowing warble lets rip from the G string. Eva, summoning the predator from its lair, takes it on, taunting and goading. The bad sound bellows through every curve.

The outcry invades the study, reverberating through floor and furniture, entering Aidan through sinuses, soles, spine. No object is proof against its malignity. In the nature of things each strip of two hundred and fifty year old wood vibrates differently. That is always true. But this wildly fluctuating deviance: how does Eva propose to harness it in a viable composition? No audience could bear such barbarity: they'd cringe, snatch up their coats, drop their programmes and flee. What else could they do? The sheer crime of that noise.

And the problem is, the older the cello, the more scintillatingly rich and deep its tones, the more it will be prey to this filthy infection.

Why can't I just enjoy half term in peace? Aidan inwardly grumbles as he registers the paroxysm in Eva's face. Don't I work just as hard as she does? Harder?

𝄢

The bed churns. Love-making fails. The wind plays dirges on the drainpipes; they wrangle.

It's Sunday and neither has slept. Blearily Aidan answers the doorbell to Eva's great-uncle. Something grave is written in Harry's face: presumably he's got wind of the wolf tone. Sensitive and thoughtful, Harry from the first regarded Aidan as family, *goy* though he is. Kissing his cheek, Aidan helps Harry off with his overcoat. He's always so natty though he buys his kit at the charity shop and likes to tot himself up and tell you what he's worth, from hat to shoes. Under a tenner, he's often proud to report.

'I thought best to tell you both face to face. What we feared — well, it has come. No, dears, not liquidation. We've paid all our creditors. But Himmelfarb's is shutting up shop. Not a surprise, we did everything humanly possible. There are worse things by far.'

With the recession, there's no call for antique harpsi-chords, spinets, pianos. It's not as if there were nothing to be salvaged. Prudent and watchful, the Himmelfarbs have eggs in several baskets. But something has come to an end that was full of dignity and virtue — words that belong, Aidan thinks, to another tongue, an earlier world.

In their slender luggage the fleeing Himmelfarbs and Lorenzes brought Harry's fiddle, grimed to fool the border guards. Harry, or Heini as he then was, hadn't a second shirt to his name when he reached Wales. But into the curious shirt he was wearing — a masterpiece of a gar-ment, now legendary — his sister had sewn gold rings; a necklace was concealed in his stiff collar. In Harry's lug-gage crouched the Wielkovsky Stradivarius, a pearl beyond price. Eva's cello had arrived over a decade before, when the Edels claimed asylum, prescient of coming horror. But in 1938 Harry had been exceptionally fortunate to smug-gle out the famous Strad. The whole Himmelfarb family could have survived on the proceeds of shirt and violin, had Harry chosen to sell.

'Eva does not look herself,' he murmurs as he leaves.

'It's the wolf tone, Uncle Harry. What do you think? Is there any hope of curing it?'

Harry shakes his head. 'Nat will know. Let's not give up hope. When is he back from holiday?'

Aidan offers to run Eva's uncle home but, no, Harry enjoys the walk, especially in this brisk weather. Fit as a flea! he says — is that the picturesque phrase? Harry regards himself, even after all these years, as a mere student of English. Aidan watches him set off under the lime trees and marvels at the cavalier spring in his step. Harry makes no allowance for his ninety years. Aidan hopes he'll not slip on the icy puddles. Raising a hand, without glancing round over his shoulder, Harry vanishes.

Aidan imagines passing the defunct shop on the High Street, missing the harpsichords, the racks of scores, CDs and vinyl records, collectors' trove. One day folk will say, *Wasn't that foreign music shop around here once?* He'll miss the scents of glue, resin, oil, varnish, wood shavings; the lathe's purr through the partition of the piano showroom. An immense continuity is to be found there, some spirit of integrity that connects the instruments with the timber they're shaped from.

Eva retreats to the study to nurse the wounded instrument, closing the door on Aidan. If the worst comes to the worst, Aidan thinks, it's insured and can be replaced.

— 2 —

𝄢

What to do with the cello? If Aidan moves house, will it wreak the same havoc there as it has at 'Brechfa'? Because, if so, it will have to go. He'd rather smash it with the axe when he chops wood for the stove than take the wolf tone into a home innocent of damage. And who could you in conscience give or sell the corrupted instrument to, to cleanse yourself of it? Who in his right mind would buy it?

Am I mad then? Have I finally flipped? he asks himself.

The things I have seen and heard, he thinks, that were not really there. I don't think they can have been.

'You're a brave one, Aidan,' say the Himmelfarbs. 'She loved you so much; you were the happiness of Eva's life.'

Aidan knows this is absolutely not the case and that they must be aware of it. For I have always been second-rate, he thinks, looking down at his soiled hands. And latterly a madman.

To relinquish their home would be a turning of his back on their life together. Perhaps there's no realistic alternative.

Bin bags blacken the space beneath the stairs, where he has dumped four years of Eva's presence in his world. Twin spirits, equally crazed, inhabit Aidan: the one that jettisons relics of Eva's existence with an odd, impure sense of exultation, the other who creeps downstairs at night to rescue treasures like Eva's reading glasses, with her thumb print still on the lens and a single hair caught in the joint of the frames.

Twin Aidans silently wrestle, right hand against left, the faithless and the uxorious. One means to live, whatever it costs and the other is pledged to join the diaspora of ashes that swirled beneath the copper beech and went their ways. One afternoon the cruel twin advertises Eva's spinet on Ebay.

How could I have done that? Jesus, what was I thinking?

He has cancelled the advert: no harm is done. Aidan drags himself into the living room, long and high-ceilinged with the most fabulous acoustic. Nobody could explain it. One minute — in the kitchen, the hall — you were in dead air, then, stepping into the living room, you entered a concert chamber. The cello loved it.

I cannot begin to understand or countenance what you did, Aidan thinks, tears coursing down his face. Agent of beauty, Eva chose or was compelled or condemned to look over Aidan's shoulder into eternity.

Same bloody dream every night, boring, boring. He thrusts back the duvet and hefts himself to the edge of the bed. Tedium. Never expected this. Not equipped for it. Days pass into weeks, weeks into months; the doctor has signed him off for six months with stress. He doesn't miss the school or the kids. He crosses the road to avoid them. Nothing changes. At 'Brechfa' there's no time to speak of. It just doesn't pass.

You have left me so intolerably bored.

Mankind is canaille, wrote Goebbels in his diary. *Dreadful knowledge.*

𝄢

Six months after Eva's passing, the strangeness intensifies. There's a stand of evergreens on the Gower road, at a bend between Penmaen and Nicholaston: nothing out of the ordinary. The winds have twisted the firs away from the sea.

Why these trees trigger Aidan's nervous reaction is unclear. For once his mind is not on Eva but on the radio. He's listening to Elin Manahan Thomas singing 'Ravished with Sacred Ecstasies'. The announcer has praised a 'voice of crystalline purity', when the firs come into view. The engine noise magnifies; it assaults the music from every side. Aidan veers, shaking and sweating, off the road.

No obvious damage done. Clambering out, he sits on the grass verge. A lackadaisical breeze scarcely tempers the heat.

Perhaps I've never actually mourned you, Eva? he thinks: I thought I had. If that hell was — is — not mourning, what is it? A vile taste pools in his mouth. He needs to spit himself out. As Eva did. In the end, I was not enough, Aidan thinks. I was nothing to her, I did not weigh in the balance against the power of that negation. Dragging his carcass home, Aidan topples asleep under the copper beech, awakening in stifling heat. The copse at the bottom of the garden has shuffled closer to the house. He retreats indoors.

Eva's cello stands against the study wall. There's a merciful coolness in here; a soft brown patina of age on shelves and panelling and in the antique leather of books and manuscripts. A very particular smell, like coriander. Something Eva said comes back: 'Of all instruments, the cello's is the closest sound to the human voice.'

But it's not a powerful voice, she added. The flute actually exceeds it. The flute produces the power of four cellos, bet you didn't know that, Aidy. Ah, but the resonance. The endpin transmits sound into the floor and through the boards.

Let's see if it's survived her.

What one has witnessed or inherited, Eva once said in her cryptic way, can never be communicated. Language fails us. Music fails us. The Himmelfarbs know that, every last one, to the final generation. It fails over and over, in different ways, the same failure. We are playing games at the seashore, that's about it really.

Well then, good girl, Aidan came back, forcing Eva to smile. Hadn't we better get on and enjoy our game?

Briefly I was able to do that for her, Aidan thinks: divert her from the dark place. But it's monstrous, what you did to me: how could you let me find you hanging?

All this while since finding Eva in the cellar, Aidan has left the cello untouched, encased. He springs the locks and there it lies, Eva's jewel. Lifting it from its casket, Aidan spreads his legs: poor, bungling ass of a player that he is.

Where does Eva keep the rosin? Goodness, what a puny little stub. And it's cracked. It'll do for now. Aidan rubs the sap on the bow: give it a go.

As the bow grabs the strings, the wolf tone snarls, it howls.

It's more harrowing than an ambulance alarm that clears traffic, careering across red lights towards the next casualty. The shriek, once let loose, transfers itself to parquet and panelled walls, it whirls inside the glass bowl of the oil lamp, sears into gums and tongue and anus. Aidan doesn't drop or hurl the cello, no, he's not — apparently — that far gone: it is still, for all its flaws, the most precious thing in his possession, all that's left of Eva. He lays it down by the neck on the floor and abandons it.

Too hot. Too soon. Why am I here and Eva not? Fainting, Aidan makes for the cellar. To outlive Eva is too great a responsibility. How dare he?

With his hand on the cellar doorknob, Aidan pauses. All

quiet. Don't be silly. Call the luthier. The luthier never dies. About–turn.

𝄢

Aidan explains, almost in a whisper, 'It's not just the wolf tone, Nat. If there's a high wind or even a draught, which in these big old houses there often is, the cello seems to pick it up. And then everything reverberates. The stairs, the panelling. Everything.'

Nat shoots him a gravely curious look. There's much Aidan cannot tell him. How he's been getting up in the night to it. As if to a restless infant. Which torments him. There's nothing he can do for it or for himself. He can't locate the source of the infection – whether it's in the cello, the house, the copper beech or in him. He keeps this delirium to himself.

Aidan watches the luthier's hands on the body of the instrument.

'Infinitesimal cracks,' Nat explains. 'You can't detect them with the naked eye. A cello is mortal, you know, Aidan. Bound to change with age for better or worse. Humid weather or not humid enough — knocks and bumps in transit. Time seasons but it can warp — and then you're suddenly landed with these weird structural and tonal anomalies.'

'Can you fix it?'

'Easily. I could completely eradicate it. But I'm not sure if you'd really want me to. And that was Eva's quandary.'

'How do you mean? If you could ... why wouldn't you?'

'I could try restringing with a lighter string — line of least interference. I don't think it would work though. And you'd still be losing something, even if it did. The only thing then would be to fit an eliminator. But it would almost certainly geld the instrument.'

'*Geld* it?'

Well, I'm gelded, Aidan thinks. That's me, a gelding. Anyway who would want me with this suppurating hole in my chest? I wouldn't want me. *She* didn't.

Nat wonders if he'd like to come round for supper one evening. He's catching a nasty echo from Aidan, that's obvious. No, I can't, Aidan thinks as he turns the conversation — I'm unsightly, I'm undergoing some bizarre metamorphosis, some profound disfigurement. He's ashamed of this fouling of himself.

When Nat has gone — *Don't be a stranger, Aidan bach, now don't* — the house settles on its foundations. Aidan takes the cello case by the throat and marches it upstairs. In the attic, he pads it round with an old duvet and locks the attic room where its revolt cannot penetrate his ears.

&

The anniversary isn't a day when Aidan could have expected him, being Podiatrist's Wednesday which, to Uncle Harry's irritation, cuts his day in two useless halves. Well, not *useless* — a poor choice of words — for at Harry's age every moment is a bonus. Not that he wishes to invoke *bonuses*, a word he detests, given the bankers' greed. For Marx, if not correct, was not wrong: capitalism must choke on its own internal contradictions. This is how Eva's uncle talks, crabwise, splitting hairs with himself over the richly imponderable language of Shakespeare, but — just as Aidan suspects he has lost himself in the byways of his idea — Harry finishes his sentence, steps inside and wipes his feet. This Wednesday he has freed himself to be with Aidan.

Harry's advent is only the beginning of a mad symphony of bell-ringing and rapping.

You marry into a family, bone of their bone, heart of their heart. And suddenly here they all are, three generations of Himmelfarbs, Engelsteins, Horowitzes, Lorenzes. To arrive at the door of 'Brechfa', they've wound their way over the course of a century from the *stetls* of Poland, Galicia and Romania; from the cities of Germany, Austria and Czechoslovakia; from long-assimilated communities of Manchester, London and Cardiff.

Aidan has to keep padding to and fro to admit them. Who has summoned all these people? What do they want of him? Whatever it is, he cannot supply it. Such a promising day it had started too: this anniversary of their marriage. A lie-in, snoozing away dreamlessly. Aidan had come down barefoot in shorts and t-shirt; ignored the cellar door; lolled in the window seat watching the pony-tailed lass next door whistling up to the birds in the eaves. For the first time, he'd thought longingly of the classroom. His kids. When Aidan shows guests into the lounge, everyone affects surprise at the presence of all the others.

'Aidan my dear, how are you? I've been baking and I made far too many cakes – so we thought ... I hope you don't mind — '

No sooner has he settled Nat and Molly, with their toddler, than there's another commotion at the door. In the end Aidan leaves it on the latch: they can let themselves in, if they insist on coming. He's exhausted, blitzed. A babble of young voices arises in the hallway: the New Edel Quartet, three of the four young women carrying their instruments; Pearl Lorenz empty-handed and looking expectant.

The wild thought strikes Aidan that they've heard something about the whereabouts of Eva. That she is coming home at last.

Shy: Eva was wincingly shy. Haunted she was and hid her haunting. Her lustrous name on the world stage burned for the darkness of an inviolable privacy. Aidan sees, in his mind's eye, Eva's forehead: a knot of frown lines between the eyebrows. Aidan used, half unconsciously, to smooth it with his thumb. He remembers how the two of them hid in the curtains of her hair. Always it had been there, the mourning apprehension, always. The worst thing has happened; it will happen again. I bless you, Eva, he thinks, for the tenderness you showed me while you were on this earth.

'Shall we fetch it now, Aidan?' asks Pearl.

'Fetch what?'

'The Wielkovsky.'

'Yes, all right. I suppose it's time. You don't need to come up, Pearl.'

Aidan's ready — or as ready as he'll ever be. He runs up two at a time.

For last autumn he began to treat his disease — homeopathically perhaps — by sitting with Eva's cello for a few minutes every day. In its case. Winter light blanched the attic room; snow, slithering down the tiles, flopped to earth with no echo. The body of the instrument was void of resonance. Some tormented spirit, he trusted, was dying in there or already had quit.

The season turned. Aidan took to opening the lid and looking in. All quiet.

In the Easter holidays he lifted Eva's instrument into the golden light of day. He took Eva's bow to the open strings. The creature at bay growled in its throat. But you too are mortal, Aidan told the wolf, you too are capable of sleep. He rang Nat.

When Nat had finished his work — it didn't take long — Aidan carried the cello back up to the loft.

The New Edel Quartet tunes up. Pearl's fingers master the strings; her bow coaxes from the cello's body something softer and more clement than Eva could ever have tolerated. Aidan is amazed at the mellifluousness that carries into the room and seems a sound without ancestry or precedent: it hardly hurts at all.

Auntie & Uncle at the Wedding

A flaunt of bridesmaids whirls down the hotel corridor past Laurie's door: a joyous rolling ball of pink frills. Frills that are fetters; dads giving away daughters like chattel; a small fortune down the drain.

What do you know anyhow, Laurie asks her sour old feminist self. Why begrudge them? What fetters have you not jingled in your time? A pinch of wisdom may have been gleaned along the way in Laurie's rackety life but she can hardly claim to have behaved wisely. Yet. Well, just the once perhaps.

Today is their day — April's and Callum's, of course, but also Laurie's and April's. A niece who's always been more than a niece.

The summer of April's mother's dying they sent the child to Laurie in Gower. She hadn't a clue about kids. But when I cleaned up April's sick, she remembers, surely that was the turning point. The little soul had eaten something that disagreed with her. Up it came in the night, all

153

over the duvet and the cuddlies she'd brought from home. Quiet and compliant, always watchful for expressions on adult faces, April had only woken Laurie after she'd tried and failed to clear up the mess herself.

That haunting face. Those brilliant dark eyes, so like Megan's. — Sorry, Auntie, she said, — I've been a little bit sick. Please don't come too near me, you might catch something.

And then — that was my moment, Laurie thinks, when I became the person I want to be — I took pity. Or pity took me. Changing Megan's daughter's nightgown, she settled April in her own bed, bundled the sheets in the washing machine, brought the bucket, laid a palm on April's clammy forehead and cwtched up with her through the night.

— But Auntie, you'll catch it!

— No way, I've got a cast-iron belly. And anyway, so what if I do, who cares?

— I care, said the girl, wise before her time. It rang in Laurie's mind all down the years.

That night was better than a marriage. That whole summer.

Why am I thinking that? That's mad. It was the season of heartbroken mourning. But still, Laurie turns to the memory with gratitude. So close and tender — and April's hands going slack in hers as, eventually, she slept. It was not that Laurie ever felt broody or unfulfilled. She's a loner, goes her own way, always has done — and her journalism takes her round the world, where no child could go.

Next morning April lay propped, feeble and pale but

calm, against piled pillows. She sipped water and Laurie wove her niece's hair in little plaits — and brought the mirror so she could admire them. April loved that. And then it was Lucozade and triangles of toast smeared with Marmite, to be nibbled, and then it was days on the beach in the sun, with peach juice running down their chins — and Laurie placing her whole self between the shadow of death and this young life. Laurie opens the chamber in her mind where this memory's kept and reminds herself not to ask April if she also remembers, in case she doesn't.

Or in case she does, and the memory opens an abyss of loss. I'd rather die than hurt her, Laurie thinks.

A bridesmaid peers round the door, wanting to know if she'd like a snack before the ceremony? April has asked her specially to take care of her auntie, says the bridesmaid (but which one of April's twenty best friends is it?)

— Lovely, I'll dry my hair and come down.

— No way, we'll do your hair. A bit of pampering won't do you any harm.

Pampering? Like a poodle? Bite your tongue, Laurie tells herself. In dressing gown and slippers she pads towards the pampering place, past a door behind which some kind of riot seems to be in progress. She raises her eyebrows to the bridesmaid, who explains, — Enya's kids. Quite a ceilidh in there.

★

— I'm not wearing it, Stu bawls. — I'm not I'm not I'm not.

— He isn't wearing it, Alasdair remarks. — Is the message I'm getting.

— No — no — no — no! Stu raves. — No.

While her younger son rolls around the floor, Enya's red-haired elder hunches on his camp bed, passing the occasional caustic remark. Alasdair's terse at the best of times but you can't always close your inner ear to what's *not* being said. Enya needs to bring them both into line before Kai's back from his run — because why should Kai, young, free and single, throw in his lot with such a rabble as the Patersons? Last week he seemed about to propose — but was that the drink talking? Time stood still and she waited: nothing. Christ, Enya could do with a drink now although it's not eleven o'clock.

Stu's gone quiet. His head's under his camp bed and what's he doing? Enya crouches to look. Plucking out fluff balls and assembling them in a circle. A hobby! At last!

— My goodness, she says lightly, — they don't clean down here, do they? Are you hungry, Stu?

—Yeah, but I'm not wearing a kilt.

— All the men are though, love. You don't want to be the odd one out.

— He won't be, growls her elder son. — I'm not wearing a skirt either.

— Anyway, why don't we have some cake?

—Yeah. Stu hooks his arm round his mother's neck. His rages seldom last. He plants a juicy kiss on her cheek and his about-turn sparks tears in her eyes. There's always the fear that the boys might be permanently alienated. By their dad's bad-mouthing when they stay over at his. By her own needy and serial mistakes.

— It's OK, Mum, chill, her elder son says, probably anticipating a weeping fit. — It's just we don't wanna wear skirts. That's all. Smily face, Mum?

A charming family scene greets Kai on his return: one loving lad either side of their mother, half throttled but cheerfully sawing wedges of fruitcake with a plastic knife. He'll have a shower, Kai says, he's all sweaty.

—Yeah, murmurs Alasdair. — Sweaty.

Oh a bad mistake to book a family room for the four of them. Not just bad, mad. Irresponsible. However were the lads going to feel sharing a room with this guy they've only met twice? The adults have single beds — but still.

Kai slides the bathroom bolt. Enya thinks of him undressing. They shower together when the lads are with Russ. Kai's hands on Enya's slick belly (slick, not slack), soaping between her legs. She came and came and came.

He's saying something through the bathroom door. Quite annoying when people do that. What's he saying?

— I saw someone I recognised, really surprised.

— Oh? Who was that?

Kai doesn't hear, the shower's thundering and Alasdair's fingering someone's iPhone, oh God, it's Kai's, and now Alasdair's darting for the door, muttering, — Shan't be a mo, just wanna check something out. And he's away before Enya can grab it back.

In the corridor she captures the phone, whereupon Stu comes crashing out, yelling something; the door slams behind him and the Patersons are locked out. They're about to go down to reception when Kai opens up. The boys barge past, informing him that they're not wearing skirts.

— Oh, right, neither's the bride's father, Kai says. — Don't worry, not everyone'll be in kilts. It's quite a brutal fashion. I just saw the best man in the foyer, he's got a real dirk — a war knife — in a sheath.

— Wow! Alasdair can't help but be impressed. Enya replaces the phone. Nothing said.

— Yeah, it's a real knife, apparently. Long blade too, razor-sharp.

★

The guests are killing time in the lounge, Scots to one side, Welsh the other. Someone claims Gaels and Cymrics were once a single tribe and, guess what, they all spoke Welsh. He quotes the poet Aneirin and is trumped by a burst of Burns.

— Oh, I don't drink, Laurie tells the bridesmaids. — Not any more. Well, I can have just a small glass. Her eye snags on her reflection in the glass door: hair arranged in a whirlwind style — she quite likes that. What will Kai think?

For it was Kai Hamilton.

Just outside the pampering room, he brushed past — and Laurie, glancing round, double-took. In shorts and vest, pullover sleeves knotted round his neck, Kai looked a hell of a lot younger than his forty-odd years. Nothing was said. Tottering into the pampering room, Laurie accepted a vegetarian spiced egg and was approached by a pair of curling tongs.

— Wanna cut off his bollocks, says a tall child of perhaps twelve, with the most sombrely charged face Laurie has ever seen. He's wearing a dark kilt and a Bonnie Prince Charlie jacket. He's flicking open a penknife.

— I know the feeling, Laurie says. — But, hey, careful with that.

— Oh, don't worry. It's a cultural artefact.

Do twelve-year-olds do irony? If so, should one be worried? The lad looks up with a smirk. Then his mother looms and the open knife slides up his sleeve. Auburn, green-eyed, like himself, the mother's teetering on towering heels. The kid keeps his arm bent up to conceal the knife.

Laurie introduces herself to the stilts woman, offering a handshake. — Laura James. Bride's auntie.

— Enya Paterson, bridegroom's cousin. My son, Alasdair.

Laurie grasps the kid's hand. — Hi, Alasdair. You look great in your kilt.

She doesn't let go. He holds her gaze and his nerve. Laurie knows the open knife's slipping down his arm: the blade's tip emerges. He flushes. You'll always give yourself away, pal, she thinks, with that transparent skin.

— Amazing shoes, she says to the mother. — However do you fit your toes in?

Laurie yanks Alasdair's hand down. The knife glides into her palm; she closes the blade.

— Go and look after Stu, love. Get him something to

drink. Thanks for chatting to Al, says the mother. — Vulnerable lad: his dad's such a rat. Yeah, you have to lop off your toes to be fashionable these days. We're all foot-binders at heart, aren't we?

— No, says Laurie. She's ready for an argument with someone; her repressed feminism's hissing in her veins.

But here he is. Kai Hamilton slips his arm round Enya Paterson's shoulders. — It's Laura, isn't it? he says with a boyish grin. — Thought so but I couldn't be sure.

— *You*'ve not changed. Transferring the knife from right to left hand, Laurie accepts the handshake. — Well, you have. You've got younger.

—You know each other? Enya looks from Kai to Laurie but triangulates her angle of vision by darting her eye into the corner where her elder son is pouring drink down the younger's gullet.

—Years back, says Kai. — In Lebanon, was it?

The penknife finds safe harbour in Laurie's trouser pocket. No way was she about to wear a skirt, even for April.

★

April's father, twice a widower, delivers his daughter to the bridegroom. No mishaps. Steps back. His head has a Parkinson's shake. The bridesmaids deliver the train. The maid of honour delivers the flower girl to her proud mam. The flower girl delivers her dolly, dressed identically to herself, to her granny.

Callum gazes at April, at her face, her dress. His lip

quivers, he's holding back tears. And then Callum's smile that involves his whole being, his life so far and until his death day, shakes Enya. This generation will be calmer, kinder, more faithful, Enya feels. We made such a hash of things. A wave of emotion sweeps her — like, she can't help feeling, a hot flush. She sees the delicate nape of April's neck, her long dark hair, threaded with mother-of-pearl daisies, brought round over a bare left shoulder: touchingly beautiful.

Her boys are being angels. Alasdair's absorbed and attentive, Stu's half asleep on his feet, so it seems, and, bless him, it's been an exhausting couple of days: the flight from Aberdeen to Hull, the hotel, the strange bed and the boy-friend. She looks up at Kai, all six foot two of him. One day. Maybe. She's torn up the photos of her wedding to Russ. It rained.

Callum will. April will.

They kiss. They sign the register with quills. Now Callum-and-April, two-in-one, are poised for their walk down the aisle.

Whereupon time pauses. Two diversions occur in suc-cession: the bride detaches her arm from the groom's. She approaches the auntie-woman and, handing her the bouquet, kisses her cheek; murmurs something. A ripple of applause. Then the bouquetless bride rejoins her hus-band for the recessional walk. What was that all about, that breach of protocol? What's the bride going to toss over her head at the end?

The second thing that happens is that Stu falls down, dead drunk, striking his temple on the chair edge. These chairs, robed in white gauze like an army of miniature bridesmaids, are not the softest, should you find yourself landing on them.

— No way, says Alasdair the innocent. — It was Lucozade. I'm sure it was. Well, you know, it looked like Lucozade.

He sticks to his story. In any case, Stu has brought up whatever liquid Alasdair fed him in error. He is demanding biscuits. Quite perky. The injury to his head's a scratch; Enya's covered it with a plaster. He doesn't need his stomach pumped, she's sure. I must watch Al like a hawk, she tells herself. Kai may not be all that keen on vomiting kids for he disappeared while she carried Stu to their room.

★

The bride requires the assistance of two bridesmaids to slacken her tight-laced bodice, allowing her to tuck into her meal.

—Ye gods, she says, — I thought I'd break a rib.

During the main course a spider gets loose on the top table, charges down the table cloth, vanishes, is forgotten and emerges on the adjoining table where it appals the maid of honour and isn't caught for hectic minutes, until, snared beneath an upturned glass, it prowls in baffled circles.

Speeches. The best man narrates historic drunken antics of the groom. *Monkeyed* on a veranda. *Rat-arsed* up a Norman tower. *Peelywally* in an aeroplane. Higher and higher soars his yarn. If one tithe were true, April should apply without delay for a decree of nullity.

All Laurie can think about, seated in the absent mother's

place at the bride's right hand, is dearest Meg. And that moment when the bouquet came to herself as the living echo of her sister's mother love. It had been a moment of such silent, tear-brimming rapture that nothing could equal it ever in this life. I'm here in Megan's place, she thinks, and I will live this for her. April, I will.

So sit, she advises herself, and revel in your painful joy. She accepts another glass of champagne — and why not?

Laurie's light-headed already. But Enya Paterson has clearly drunk deeper, cradling a bottle of red wine in the crook of her arm. She's drinking at a well of baleful bitterness, abashed no doubt at the conduct of both sons — especially young Machiavelli, who sits observing Kai Hamilton across the table with a sneer.

Should I feel anything about Kai turning up like this? Laurie wonders. He'll not marry Enya, that's for sure: Kai's the male of a species primed to deposit the sperm bag and scarper. Of course he might have grown up since then, she reminds herself. Probably not though: he looks as if he could be his own son.

Kai didn't hang about. Good, because he was nobody.

The best man's tongue, still going strong, acts independently of his brain evidently; he sways where he stands and is clearly embarrassing his fiancée. There's a rictus on her face and her torso in its red sheath dress twists away. Shoot me now, her posture pleads: don't delay. For he's talking about her, praising her tolerance on lads' evenings when he reels in *mingmong* and *fecked* and *bladdered* and *off his woo*, his lassie is cool with it, the goose obliges the gander, law of nature.

Just shoot me. Now. Because I know where this is going.

Whereupon the best man, after a medley of kilt jests, offers to lay bare a splendid sample of Scottish manhood.

— Quail, you Welsh lassies' blouses!

Down goes his hand to his groin. Pause for mirth. Not much of it.

Out, with a wild whoop, flashes the dirk from its scabbard. The blade glints, keen as Laurie's mam's breadknife. Laurie winces and the best man's fiancée cringes and young Alasdair Paterson shrieks in bloodcurdling arousal, a sugar mouse half way to his mouth. The best man waves the dirk around his head.

But the bride is on her feet. — Pass the knife, Jack, I've a use for that!

Applause as April reaches across to disarm the guy who's clearly been off his woo most of the last thirty years. Surreptitiously Laurie supports her niece's bodice at the back as she stretches. The best man, relinquishing his treasure, subsides.

— How was my speech? he asks his fiancée and takes a swig of whiskey.

— It was just as good as I expected, replies the fiancée.

★

Ceilidh about to begin. Guests have dumped their fascinators on Enya's table: one's black-feathered and looks like a bat; she shreds the feathers for something to do. Ach I'm so fucking plastered, Enya thinks. These days I'm a non-sipper. Just a frigging slurper now. Perhaps the ceilidh'll bring her round. What has she been saying to Kai? God knows. Not needy things, no way, she reassures herself. Not maudlin, pathetic, demanding things. Light-hearted, sexy things. He's slipped out for a smoke. Enya went and called (not in a nagging voice). She thought of ringing his mobile but couldn't find her own.

She hears Kai's old (antique) flame (probably) interrogating the bridesmaids about the difference between vintage and retro fashion in that waspish way she has. What Kai saw in her, who can say?

Strobe lights, blue and red and yellow, whirl round the panelled hall. It makes you fucking dizzy. The ceilidh band's tuning up. It's gonna be deafening. Enya likes deafening. She's ready to dance. Except where's fucking Kai?

There's something Enya should be worrying about — what was it? Oh — the lads. Completely forgot I had sons. Your darlings, your life sentence, your angels. But hey, all's well: there they are, at the next table with some granny-type folk, causing no trouble to anyone, bless them. And here's Kai. Mustn't ask where he's been.

— Hey. Kai brushes her lips with his. — Been looking for you everywhere, babes. Bad news, I had a call from work, I'll have to be off at dawn. Lousy timing, I'm gutted. But, hey. We've got tonight!

Her world is dashed, Enya's crushed. That's that then, she thinks. Nice while it lasted. (Was it?) Well, it was all right. Always carking care beneath the surface. Anyhow fuck all this carking — seize the hour!

— OK, she says. Shrugs. Grins. A surprising bubble of relief rises. Decarking has begun. — I'm cool with that.

Curious to know though, Kai, your tan — can't help wondering — what bottle's it from?

Kai is morally affronted. He colours up. — There's some Italian in my family.

— Yeah, right. That'd explain the blond wig. Only joking. Tell you what, Kai, let's miss the Gay frigging Gordons. It'll be nice and quiet in our room.

— But — your boys?

Kai's expression says: are you really willing to dump your kids for a final chance of a fuck?

At a neighbouring table a Scots solicitor is explaining the difference between divorce law in England and his native land. — Consummation means vera copula or conjunction of two bodies or sexual intercourse between the two — husband and wife. Vera copula consists of erection and intermission or penetration. I think we can agree upon that?

★

She feels *faint*, the boys' lush of a mother whispers, leaning over Laurie's shoulder, mascara smudged, each half of her face contradicting the other. If Laurie could just keep an *eye* on Al and Stu while she lies *down*? Just till she comes *back* to collect them? An *hour*, tops. Thanks *so* much. Be good for Auntie, boys!

Off she sashays. Kai in her wake slaps his pockets as if something's gone missing but he can't think what.

Before the ceilidh gets underway, the newly-weds will cut the cake with the best man's dirk. Covering the bride's hand with his own, Callum offers a photo opportunity. Laurie's struck by the rhyming faces of the Paterson boys returning with slabs of cake. Their mouths turn down, there's a sour taste, they want to spit, they have forgotten how to relieve their pain by crying.

— Nice phone, Alasdair, says Laurie. — Get any good pictures?

— I'm only borrowing it. Show you in a minute.

Alasdair chomps. Stu can't face the cake. He's flushed; his eyelids droop; his head sinks down on to the table.

—Your brother should be in bed, Alasdair.

— He can't go yet though, can he? Because of Uncle.

Too much knowledge, too young. Woman and boy stare into one another's eyes in consternation. Of course Alastair's right. The mother can't be caught *in flagrante*.

— No. I suppose not.

Someone offers to cuddle Stu: Laurie surrenders him gratefully. She has a good mind to go and hammer on Kai's door. Yes, I will, she thinks, and starts getting to her feet.

But the boy begins to speak. His words gush out. Laurie sits and listens: she has the impression of light and honesty.

The boy wonders if Laurie feels, ever, as if she's somehow outside? In a room and out of it at the same time, looking in? They bend inwards to one another like conspirators. Couples spin and clap and yell in an eight-some reel, raising a sweaty draught as they romp past the tables.

—Yes, Laurie says. —Yes, I recognise that, Alasdair. You don't need to feel you're outside though. Your mam has her wings over you. She needs adult company, is all.

Is that a lie? A white one? Or does it contain — at the centre — the truth?

The lad looks grateful. Would Laurie like to see the pictures on the phone, he wonders? It's not his, he explains.

Kai Hamilton and a couple of kids, not the Patersons: girl and boy, quite small, about three and five perhaps, she in a pink frock printed with cherries; he in a blue t-shirt. Unknown youngish woman with the same children on the same settee. Dated last week. Texts too. Leaked information, as Alasdair puts it.

The Paterson brothers didn't like the last uncle either, he informs Laurie. Their mum's the best but *uncle*'s a rat. *She* says their dad's a rat but their dad's a *dad*.

And something breaks inside Laurie at the tender rightness of the boy in the midst of all that's haywire in his world: it's Meg, it's ambush, anguish washes over her as violently as the news did twenty years ago that her sister was gone, she had no sister; April no mother. Her face works. And, intuitive beyond his years (and the worse for him that he is), the boy reaches out to offer comfort.

—Your hair suits you fine, Auntie Laurie, he says. — It's not scruffy, it doesn't make you look a freak, no way. Also, you don't look old. Also your boots, they're cool, don't worry about them.

— Oh, thanks, that's good to know! Laurie roars with laughter. Couples behind their closed doors never suss that kids are loudspeakers of their gossip. — You're great, you know that, Alasdair? Apart from your pilfering. Maybe pass me Kai's phone for safekeeping?

— If I can have my penknife back? I'd like to be a reporter like you, Laurie, how do you get to be one?

They exchange trophies. Stu, awakening in a stranger's arms, bellows surprisingly; topples back to sleep.

When in the early hours they knock on the Paterson door, the unconscious Stu a lead weight in Laurie's arms, Kai opens, not a hair out of place.

— Oh hi, how're you doing, Laurie? I was just coming for them. Their poor mum's spark-out. Here, let me take the wee one. Get your pyjamas on, please, Al. Yeah: now. Had a nice time?

Then he whispers, — Fancy a nightcap, Laurie? For old times' sake? Do say yes.

— Here's your phone, Kai. You dropped it.

— Bar's still open, isn't it?

— I didn't hear that.

— I did, says a contralto voice from inside the room. And as Laurie retreats to her own room, a fresh rumpus arises behind the Paterson door, and something is hurled and breaks.

★

Dawn — and of course you scarcely slept. Firstly you stood at the black window staring at leaves gusting around in lamplight and you thought, *April,* and you thought, *Megan.* The day's events seemed like a film you'd watched. You half-filled the wash basin and plunged the bouquet into water. In the early hours you heard an owl's cry; rumblings in the pipes. Awakening peacocks screeched in the grounds. Later, staff cantered past your door and plates clattered in the hotel's bowels.

Breakfast and the newspaper always come round at last with their reassurance. Laurie's first into the dining room: good. Scrambled egg on toast: good. Pot of powerful coffee: very good.

By and by other guests appear. The Paterson family *sans* Kai looks subdued and bleary, although the wee one livens up and revs a toy car round and round the dining room, quite irritatingly. The elder son, waving briefly to Laurie, dollops marmalade on his mum's plate, his haunted eyes playing over her face. He bends forward and whispers. And perhaps he's just told her a joke for, as Enya leans back in her chair, stretching wearily, her yawn breaks into a convulsive giggle.

The best man's fiancée arrives looking vivacious, without the best man who's still a bit *cabbaged* and *loo-la* and generally *phalanxed*, as she reports, and may have to miss out on sausages. Several bridesmaids turn up and a hubbub of hugging breaks out. The Scots lawyer, still kilted, has much to impart on legal niceties pertaining to his native land. And the bride arrives in jeans and a sweater, her ravishing hairstyle demolished.

Applause. Catcalls. — Where's your husband, April? Lost him already?

— On his way, don't worry. Oh look, there's a peacock out there, isn't he wonderful? I'm just going to sit here with my lovely auntie for a while.

— What are you doing up so early, sweetheart? Laurie asks as April's arms softly circle her. — Have some coffee. How was the bridal suite? It was such a special day.

A Pane of Seeds

If he thinks her odd for hankering after an obsolete chapel in a wasteland of fern and brambles, he doesn't show it. Meredith finds security in Mr James's courteous presence, his practicality, his willowy tallness. She's been warned, and accepts, that he doesn't come cheap. Her uncle bought Penuel and obtained permissions, dying before he could begin the work.

— I attended here as a child, Meredith confides. — With my great-aunts.

The chapel on the common was once the centre of a village long abandoned. It boasts neither cross nor altar, just the Lord's Table at the centre, built of massive dark oak and encircled by benches. It's still in place. The carpenter must have assembled it inside the chapel, Mr James thinks, because how could it possibly have been hefted in? There's no stained glass, just plain arched panes, which somehow have survived the centuries intact. A chapel has stood here since the time of the wooden church of St Idris. Cromwell's soldiers, smashing everything tainted with Popish ritual, left in Penuel a full kind of nothing in which worshippers found — it's hard to say what — a transparency, perhaps, for light to pour into the heart. The windows are boarded now; Mr James sweeps his torch round the dark interior.

Would he understand if she tried to explain what Penuel means to her? Something of dream haunts Meredith's feeling; she shrinks from exposing it. What if the aura vanishes, leaving her with a white elephant and a spiralling bill?

There's a rank smell. The walls bulge. Ferns and grasses are working to dislodge the roof tiles. Meredith could halt everything; keep the flat. Cut her losses or rather learn to live with them like a grown-up person.

Whatever am I doing with our money? What would you say, Eiros, if you were here to counsel? Her husband's absence comes rearing upon Meredith. The dark floor shifts; she steadies herself against the Lord's Table.

— Hey — you OK?

— Can't see, lost my balance.

— I'll let in some daylight.

Mr James levers boards from the windows, speaking of the need for disease-resistant heartwood, the integrity of a building.

— It puts a responsibility on us.

On us, he said. He's fired up with the project; knows what he's talking about. Everything must be tackled as they did it originally, using hand tools and authentic materials.

— Cheap it won't be, Miss Isaacs — we can't betray the building, see.

Eiros, from his ashes, urges caution with savings: *Sweetheart, it's your security I'm planning for.* It preoccupied Eiros: Meredith's far-off old age. He'd transfer money between bonds, drawing her attention to fussy figures in the blue notebook recording capital and interest. Whatever am I doing, proposing to squander these funds, garnered from modest teaching incomes and small sums his flute earned him? *Chwarae teg,* you've spent no money yet, Meredith reassures herself.

The boarding comes down from the eastern window.

Meredith's hand flies to her mouth. She wants to cry, fall to her knees. Light drenches the pews. No going back.

— I won't cut corners — although my means are relatively limited, Mr James.

— Oh please — it's Tim.

— Tim — and do call me Meredith.

— Just look at that light. Look.

It's all decided by *that* light. It's like no other. This is a broken light, skewed by impurities in the glass and mismatings of irregular panes. As board after board comes down, Meredith places herself — just here — in her accustomed seat between her aunts. Light ripples over her grey cardigan sleeve and across Tim's face. The building has opened its eyes. She recalls venerable menfolk who now sleep in the graveyard choked with mallow and sorrel. They wore wing collars and carried fobs in waistcoat pockets. Mrs Rhys would tether her mare to the silver birch. When the preacher paused, you heard the creature shift around. Winking, Auntie Els would pass Meredith a peppermint for the sermon.

— I'll need instalments upfront, Tim advises. — We'll save the original plaster and wood wherever we can. If it's lasted hundreds of years, it can go another century — see us out anyway.

$\oint$

She holds the tape as he measures. How alone I've been, she thinks. They agree, there's a good year's work in it.

— This will get the tax lady off our backs, anyhow. You'll laugh, Tim says. — I told Georgie I was off to chapel — she comes back, quick as a flash: *Seen the error of your ways, have you, goodboy? Bit late for that.*

Tim's a talker. But that's all right, Meredith's a listener. He describes passing chapel after disused chapel all the way from Brynhyfryd: Salem and Bethesda, Zion and Zohar. Normally Tim hardly notices. Now he sees nothing but chapels. Penuel's a baby one, plain and austere. Its Welsh-speaking congregation, faltering between the wars, declined to a devout handful; the pastor died and it was deconsecrated in the nineties.

Appetite quickens in them both. No going back.

$\oint$

That was the decisive moment, when Tim unboarded the eastern window: they both drew back in awe. A wild disorder of molecules, like bugs in amber, cast the light in spangles every which-way. Whatever it costs, Meredith thought, surrendering her will. But am I unhinged or what?

— I'm older than you, dear heart, Eiros pointed out. — And a tad wiser, if you don't mind my saying so. When I'm gone, I want you to be comfortable.

— But don't go, Meredith pleaded, missing or evading the point. — Not ever.

—You might be ill one day and need care. When I'm dead or gaga. The important thing is: a roof over your darling head. Are you paying attention? Do you think you're immortal?

Eiros saw the recklessness in me, thinks Meredith — or do I mean fecklessness? I mustn't let him down. The nest egg mustn't be broken. I'll manage everything without touching it.

She's here at dawn; can't sleep for throbs of expectation. Wearing a parka and gloves, Meredith brews up on a calor gas stove.

Though birds divine the approach of light, the window remains dark to her eyes. Someone's mouth blew this glass through a punty. From a treacle of molten sand and silica and soda and lime, lungfuls of breath streamed into an elongating balloon of glass. Meredith remembers how long, before the emphysema, Eiros could hold his breath on the flute, lips spread for the embouchure; the authority with which he voiced the instrument. She can't bear to listen to his recordings.

I've silenced him, Meredith thinks. Eiros could still be speaking but I can't let him. I'd be destroyed.

The chapel walls, with their patina of age, glow less faintly. Imagine waking daily to this. Penuel is the interior of a camera; Meredith's nothing but an eye. Moment by moment daylight increases.

Move your head and the view alters. Whorls distort trees and clouds. Dreaming colour wanders the walls' lime-washed irregularities as the glass twists and scatters light. Tim has explained that the bubbles are called seeds and the ripples reams, created by fold marks or waves in the glass. A pane of seeds. A slant prism forming on the sill casts an oblique rainbow stain on the opposite wall. The blower wasn't all that competent, Tim has remarked: and that's the beauty of it, in a funny sort of way.

Surprised to see Meredith here so early, he accepts coffee.

— When can we start the proper work then, Tim?

Although he grins at her fizzing excitement, his eyes look tired. Business problems, Tim explains. Never been a great one for paperwork. To put it mildly. Anyway — once Meredith's cheque has cleared, he'll get hold of materials. Or if she can advance another thousand in cash, why not begin today?

Driving to the bank, he asks about her husband. She's so young to lose him.

— Eiros was that much older, Tim. We always knew he'd go first.

Acceptance becomes, as she voices it, a version of the truth. Probably he's thinking: you can start again. You're not bad looking. She flushes as if he'd spoken these words aloud. But he's chatting fondly about his wife now. Meredith feels she's getting to know Tim in a friendly, equal way. He says, honest to God, she'd be shocked at how slow his clients are to settle their bills. It jeopardises cash flow. He keeps the van's engine running while Meredith goes for the cash.

— Penuel, he remarks, on the way to the salvage yard.
— Funny old name. I wonder what it means.

— It means The Face of God.

— I must remember that to tell Georgie. Brought up
chapel, she was. Not sure what she believes now but she
reveres — well, you know, the decencies, the pieties. She
keeps me right.

Meredith's touched. By his genuineness altogether
and the fact that he's open about money and trusts her to
understand.

𝄞

She can't make it to Penuel today. In fact this chapel nonsense will have to stop, it's one of these grandiose illusions
of hers, she lives in story-land, everyone's always told her
that. Switching off her mobile, Meredith lies like a log until
the day's somehow over. Radio voices lament the recession.
Roofs are lifting off people's lives like lids from cans. They
raise their eyes to find nothing between them and heaven.
She forces herself to get up, shower and dress.

Wet hair in a turban, Meredith shrugs on her dressing
gown and shuffles in her slippers to answer the door.

— I was worried about you, Meredith, he says.

His height and the concerned expression on his plain (and
beautiful, sincere) face feel powerfully protective. Meredith
shakes with longing to cross the threshold and take refuge in
his arms. Can't do that. Stop it. Does he read her eyes?

She forces herself to step back. — Oh, sorry, Tim, I
wasn't well. Should've phoned.

— As long as you're OK. Can I do anything?

— Get me a new head?

She grins and he grins, reassured. He must have hung around at Penuel, wondering, and tried her phone. And this is Tim's livelihood, for God's sake. He can't afford to lose a day here, a day there, without reason: whatever were you thinking of? Why hasn't she given him a key before now? She locates a spare and hands it over.

— It will get better, *bach,* he says quietly, just as he's leaving. — Trust me, it will.

$\oint$

In the ruined space they stand and dream together of how it will be when the upper floor's in place and the spiral staircase built. Their partnership is sealed in the shared work: the splendour of the project. Not that they're familiar or intimate. Tim treats Meredith with scrupulous respect.

— I'm going to camp here tomorrow night, she tells him. — To make it mine.

— Rather you than me — I like my creature comforts. Let's rig you up a nest.

Meredith helps shift rubble and cart it to the tip; puts her back into it. Tim's hands tell a story, she thinks. Asymmetrical, spread, the thumb joint swollen and calcified where he bashed it with a hammer.

— My hands know, he has told her, — when my brain doesn't. Like the medieval craftsmen. Or that's what I tell myself.

He checks stuff in Central Library and pumps a retired restorer who dispenses advice in return for pints.

— When we're finished, Meredith says one day — and doesn't end the sentence.

His stricken face tells her how Tim dreads the work's completion. Dreads, more so, Mrs Harrison whose claws — it all comes out — are in his back and who has insisted, *This is the last latitude I can allow you, Mr James, no more second chances.* He hasn't confessed to Georgie the extent of their debts.

That will work out. Always has. His brothers will help, his old mam. Trouble is, he can't find it in him to go round and strong-arm his creditors. But Mrs Harrison's a decent sort and seems to recognise his genuineness.

𝄢

— Damp proof course? Good God, no, Meredith!

Old buildings are porous, Tim explains, they breathe, they're alive — fetched from the earth, see, limestone blocks and timber. The wall whose bulging list has bothered Meredith is perfectly stable, for an ancient building has elasticity. Bulges, bows, sags and lists: bring them on!

She says no more about the persistent smell of damp.

She shows him her dead husband's flute.

— Can you play? he asks.

— Oh, my technique's woeful, it's nothing compared with his.

— I'm sure that's not true.

— I'm not being modest, he was professional.

— Even so — play me something anyway. Please do. I'd love that.

The last hymns ever sung in the chapel, presumably at its deconsecration, remain on the hymn board. She's going to keep them there. Meredith plays *Iesu Mawr*. Then she plays Tim one of Eiros's CDs. A Bach Partita.

— Your husband — your Eiros — he's there in the music. You'll always have that. And, if you don't mind my saying so, many people would envy you.

Meredith takes Tim lightly by the shoulders and he bends as she stretches up on tiptoe to kiss his cheek.

— Thanks, Tim, you're a pal.

A trace of the kiss lingers on her lips like menthol. There's a warm sensation, followed by a prickling chill. Taking herself to the very edge of the graveyard, she scythes a stand of waist-high nettles until she sweats.

To earn the roof over her head, as she puts it to herself, Meredith signs up to teach at summer school.

— Anything you'll need before I'm back? She registers Tim's ashen face. He really doesn't look well. — Listen, take time off while I'm away.

— That's kind. But I can't afford to.

— What is it? What's happened?

— Oh — nothing.

— It's not nothing.

— Well, just Mrs Harrison. Putting the squeeze on. Twenty K. By the end of this month. I told her I can do it. And I can. I asked — I pleaded — for time. I'm owed more than that. I promised I wouldn't let her down.

— Oh Tim. Do I owe you anything?

She searches his face with concern. He shakes his head.

— I do. I'll leave it out for you.

All morning the hypnotic light flows over the envelope she places on the Lord's Table. A hundred in cash. She sees Tim stuff the envelope in his pocket, rasping his palm over his stubbly chin. She can hear his thoughts: whatever's in there will go precisely nowhere.

Before she says goodbye, Meredith visits the filing cabinet. Did she leave it open like this? She allows herself to imagine Tim James's fingers trespassing through Eiros's files:

OUR WILLS
INLAND REVENUE
PENSION
MEREDITH: NEST EGG

Did he come in here burrowing into her privacy, wondering what she's worth?

Tim's in the doorway. — Meant to say: I saw your cabinet was open. Got hold of a small padlock for you. Two keys, keep them safe.

Those were unworthy suspicions. Meredith dismisses them.

9:

When he tells her, she's unprepared. One moment she's admiring the arabesque of the newly installed oak and glass spiral staircase; the next Tim seems to collapse into himself.

Meredith has no idea what to say when he utters that terrible word, *bankruptcy*. He's been forever chasing the rolling debt and discharging it, or most of it, when suddenly it appears that a new sum is payable and his own creditors default or hand over trivial instalments.

— It's a nightmare, I dream about it and the worst of it is, I can't tell Georgie, he confesses.

He looks ready to weep. Probably he has been weeping. Her heart goes out to Tim. Be practical, Meredith tells herself. You had someone to look out for you; now pass it on. What would Eiros have advised?

She takes his hand and sits him down. — Is Georgie in work, Tim?

— Tesco's. Part time. Sorry to burden you with this, Meredith.

— Don't be daft. You can't leave your wife in the dark. What can I do for you? I think I've paid for the staircase, haven't I?

— Oh please. Don't even go there.

He's mortified, she can see, at laying bare his trouble. He'd see it as unmanly. Fifty-two years old, a grandfather, proud, honourable. No pension to look forward to. And now he's citing, with gleaming eyes, some lottery millionaire in Bridgend.

— Do you play the lottery, Tim?

He does, religiously. Twice weekly, hope is nourished and beggared. It's painful to think of Tim going under. After many second chances the tax woman, not a bad sort, has given up on him and set a date to declare Tim a bankrupt. He sees no way of finding the money by that date. It's all up. Is the stoop in Tim's shoulders new or has Meredith failed to notice till now?

— You know what the worst thing is? he asks. — Not to be trusted. I always prided myself on decency, always.

— I trust you, Tim. I'd trust you with my life.

This declaration flies out of her mouth before she can tone it down.

His face lightens. He stands a fraction taller. — Thank you, Meredith, for saying that.

— But, you know, you do have to confide in Georgie.

— I will. Tonight. Thanks. Still got my good right hand and most of my marbles so let's crack on. Oh, by the way, I found a period door — oak — over there. What do you think? Picked it up for three hundred. It pays to keep your eyes skinned.

Penuel is what Tim has made it: she owes him much. Funds are depleted. But breaking into the nest egg, Meredith sternly reminds herself, is taboo. Penuel has absorbed everything from the flat sale. She's been realising she must call a halt. How to broach this now? Not so very much remains to do, not really. But Tim seems able to find things and —

As she swivels her head, the eastern window flashes and winks deliriously, there's a flurry of sparks from the seeds in the pane.

He's deliberately spinning out the job. How much did the door actually cost? Anything? There's never a receipt for his costs: her own fault for not insisting. And what's meant by 'period'?

Eiros would have sussed this long before. He's bleeding

you dry, he'd have said. Blind trust is folly, Meredith. You're too easily swept away: *Oh, so-and-so is marvellous, what an amazing person* — and then you feel betrayed when you detect his feet of clay. And it's true, thinks Meredith, I'm flighty. I seem to extend false promise.

Suddenly, as Tim is leaving, he pins her against the wall.

𝄢

He may not have meant to do it.

— I've grown to think of you as a true friend, Meredith. I hope that's right.

— Oh — yes.

She sees Tim seeing her seeing it coming but he apparently can't stop looming at her.

— Remember what you said? You'd trust me with your life. That really got to me. And I'm wondering — and I hope this won't harm our friendship — in any way — because that is priority as far as I'm concerned — would you trust me with your money?

— How do you mean?

— A loan. I'll repay you within a month. Nine grand — call it ten. I'm sure I could persuade Mrs Harrison to accept it as an instalment. Buy me time. I know I can do it.

She sees Tim register her flinching recoil. But he moves fractionally towards her. Not away.

She can't breathe. There's a foot in height between them. Meredith doesn't stand a chance. It's the first time Tim's ever come too close. He reaches out to rub her shoulder in reassurance. Her head bangs back against the wall.

— Don't. She shields her breast with her arms. — Please, no. She turns her head aside.

— Oh come on now, Meredith. Cut me some slack.

— Cut you *what*?

— Give me a chance. You know I'd never cheat you, ever — we're friends, you'd trust me with your life, you promised.

Meredith finds a low, calm voice to say, — Tim, step back.

He shambles away, mumbling about middle class females being all out for themselves. She does have the wherewithal. He knows it. She knows it. Small fortune in the Principality. Milk you they do — boy, do they see you coming. Ditch you when they've sucked you dry. And then the system comes and crushes you. People top themselves for less.

I'm to blame, Meredith recalls, scarlet-faced, when he's gone. Often and often, I've wanted him to hold me. I kissed him that time at the edge of his mouth. Perhaps I do owe him something and ought to honour the debt.

𝄞

It was one of the last sermons she attended at Penuel. For weeks the flock's expectation mounted. The so-called Saint of Wem was at hand. He was burning, so said the minister. Meredith imagined a human fireball. Was he dangerous? she asked Auntie Vi, who laughed and explained that the Saint of Wem was a Revivalist, alight with the Spirit, on a mission to Wales. The faithful — and even backsliders and the unsaved — flocked to hear him.

The Saint materialised as a short, balding chap in black. Meredith, nursing a cold, drooped in her seat. But then, what a blaze! Chrysanthemums shook in vases. The rafters rang. The Saint flapped his arms, jumped, spun, turned out his pockets. Coins clattered onto the Table. He called for collection plates. *Relieve yourselves of lucre! Hold nothing back!* Weeping folk cried *Selah!* as they lightened pockets and purses. They drummed their heels and Meredith felt the reverberations through her backside.

Duw duw, sighed Auntie Els, exalted, as they emerged into the drizzle. *Such a Vision! Like old times!*

The text for the sermon was: *Sell that thou hast and give to the poor, and thou shalt have treasure in heaven.* It stuck in Meredith's mind because of the spat that broke out between her aunts over tea. Violet condemned the Saint's communistical cant. Els was all for rushing into the street looking for paupers to present with her Post Office book. They both turned rather nasty and began to accuse each other, naming old, incomprehensible grievances.

The Sin against the Holy Ghost was mentioned.

What was that? Nobody specified — but — if you sin it — you're finished.

𝄞

All over the common, the new season's ferns have uncurled from their embryos, in the reliquary of the old year's rusty bracken. Meredith stands barefoot in the doorway of Penuel, tasting the texture of the threshold with her sole. She and Tim left the step just as they found it. Soft stone, abraded by generations of feet, has worn into a shape like a pillow indented by a sleeper's head. In and out they filed, Sabbath by Sabbath, Jesus's prayerful people.

Why this guilt? I've done nothing that should make me squirm, Meredith reminds herself. Have I? He thought I led him on. Just as she's turning to go in, his van draws up. Tim James makes his way up the path and shame greets shame.

Later she spies a dark stain low on the living room wall. The light of the afternoon sun discloses it. Perhaps it's just a misleading shadow cast by a seed in the pane — the biggest of the blemishes, which the blower must have rued. Nowadays these lustrous flaws rarely kindle ecstatic surprise. She knows more or less what to expect as each day tracks round. Meredith runs her palm over the wall and a dirty residue comes away. It's definitely mould or fungus fingering up from the earth.

They breathe, he said, old buildings do. What qualifications has Tim James? How many restorations has he actually done, this jack-of-all-trades? Why did she fail to enquire? And now the Planning Department has rapped her over the knuckles, announcing an inspection.

There's a knot in her guts. For Meredith profited by Tim's advent and has not lost by his departure. He crossed a border, bringing comradeship. When he withdrew, she remained standing. Little by little Eiros has receded until Meredith can think of him without despair. She's learned to carry her pain dipped in honey, to see it in the ordinary light that elucidates the chapel and its mysteries. That's down to Tim.

One morning, through a bubble of glass she spies an autumnal figure at the chapel gate softly latching it behind him, glancing back for a moment before he melts away.

𝄞

Thank Christ the house is in Georgie's name. Tim must have no part in it. Mrs Harrison vetoed a joint bank account. Play by the rules, Mr James: the rules will secure you. Patiently, she guided the couple in completing vast, intimidating forms that made Tim want to weep with insufficiency. He saw that he'd lived like a child, from year to year, never accounting for himself. Mrs Harrison relieved him of some fears, which were rapidly reinstated by invisible clerks in call centres. In theory a bankrupt is permitted to open a business account; in practice, no bank will look at him.

Why would they?

Georgie took it staunchly. Ebay, she said. They listed income and outgoings. But some window closed in his wife. There was no sex, only *cwtches.*

— Cuddles are not nothing, Georgie insisted. — Where would we be without lovely *cwtch*es? You are not to blame. Except you should have told me.

— Keep the van, Mr James, Mrs Harrison decreed. — Your tools also. We can allow you £10 per week for your personal spending.

— Go round. Ask Miss Isaacs again, said Georgie one evening. — She can only say no.

Keeping his distance, he asked again; she refused again,

hot with embarrassment. He recognised that the iron had entered Meredith's soul.

Standing squarely in the doorway, arms folded, Meredith Isaacs said, — The work is finished. I'd been meaning to tell you before you mentioned your situation — which I'm truly sorry for.

— Fine, he replied. — No problem. I'll take my tools and be back for what I can't carry this time.

— I do wish you well, she bleated as he loaded the van. — Thanks for all your work.

He despised her little-girl pleading voice. She'd be watching to see if he removed anything she'd paid for. Tim was scrupulous in taking only what was legitimately his.

Returning for the remainder of his gear, he realises his ex-employer is out.

Has she changed the lock?

Way back, he located a file with Meredith's bank details, passwords and codes. Memorised them. The numbers pop into his head at night when he's falling asleep. He believes they're fading. He retained one of three keys to the new lock on the filing cabinet, fiddling with it in his trouser pocket from time to time, until one rainy evening his hand plucked it out and, opening of its own volition, dropped the key down a drain. And good riddance. He'll post his door key back through the letter box in due course and that will be that.

Tim grasps his situation more clearly now. A limited loan has been allocated for materials, which cannot be overdrawn. Trivial jobs must supply his grubbing livelihood from now on. Never again — or not for the regulation seven years — can there be another task on a heroic scale.

With Georgie working nights, he often brings their granddaughter along to give his wife a chance to nap. Undoing Non's seat belt, Tim hauls her out, half asleep. — Oops a daisy, Nonni-bird! There we go!

He tries his key. It turns. That was trustful of Meredith, or perhaps she just forgot. She could be a bit gormless, considering she was a schoolteacher. But of course, *chwarae teg,* Tim reminds himself, she'd not long lost her husband.

—We'll go in here for a moment, collect some of Bampi's stuff.

He seats the child, legs dangling, on the Lord's Table. Tim marvels again at the mass and solidity of its timber. The open plan downstairs room glows. Whatever anyone says, I made a damn good job of this, he thinks. The spiral staircase is especially pleasing: whorled like a shell, like the cochlea of an ear. Beyond price, he thinks, and all made with these two botching old hands. He inspects his palms, with a kind of wonder.

Non looks round, wide-eyed. They're in a golden box.

My slate is clean, Tim thinks; my hands are empty. That's it. I know where I am. My feet are on the ground.

Tim's back has been bad, he's suffered colds and flu. For the past month he's been plagued by conjunctivitis, stinging as if the bud of his eye and latterly the whole membrane were stuck full of pins. He tried drops and ointments: useless. Forever rubbing at his eyes, he has wanted to pluck them out.

Now he closes them for comfort and Non asks, — Have you gone bye-byes, Bampi? Is this a sleepyhouse?

Tim posts the key back. I made a very fair job of the restoration, he thinks: learned a lot, gained the experience. Always remember, as Georgie says, we still have each other, a roof over our heads, our granddaughter and our decency.

Mother's Milk

My oldest brother was, at fifteen, in full rebellion: he and his fellow embryo hippies would smoke roll-ups in St Alkmund's Square and plan a Shrewsbury revolution. They spent the Sabbath at St Julian's or St Chad's. As the faithful droned out psalms inside, outside Owen and his pals performed 'Masters of War' and 'The Times They Are A-Changing'.

'Everything's political, Jack,' Owen said to me. 'Our parents, especially Dad, are fascist pigs.'

Especially Dad? A gentler father — insanely mild — I never met. Owen explained our family structure as the rule of a paternalist dictatorship; Mum was just his foot-soldier, Dad held the power. When Mum went on the razzle with Mrs Yeomans in town it was the troops on leave, see. Letting off steam made her more compliant to him and more of a tartar to us.

Mum ambushed Owen at two in the morning as he rolled in sloshed. She demanded to know what he meant by it? His father was dog-tired, didn't Owen appreciate that? Had he been boozing with his fellow louts? Or worse?

Owen yelled, 'Pot and fucking kettle!'

'Language!'

'Language yourself! I've seen you with that blond beast! And why've you locked the bloody kitchen?'

It was Owen's custom to raid the fridge, tipping a pint of full cream milk down his throat. He could sink the whole lot in two glugs. This was one of the few misdeeds capable of angering Dad — for it meant there'd be no milk left if Mum needed a cuppa in the night. She was restless and didn't always sleep well. As for himself, our father wasn't bothered. After the Western Desert, everyday privations didn't register. But he wanted only the best for her.

I wondered what blond beast Owen meant and why Mum didn't query this. Dad appeared on the stairs, his frizz of hair on end. 'What is it, Pammie?'

'Now look what you've done!' Mum shrieked. 'Woken your father — and he has to get up at four-thirty. What if he drove his cab into a wall, where would we be then?'

'Never mind,' Dad yawned. 'The lad's home now safe and sound. Say sorry to your mum, Owen. I know you won't do it again. I promise not to drive into a wall.'

'She's locked the fucking milk up,' Owen informed him.

Dad flinched, condemned to choose between the happiness and health of his angel boy and the rights of the archangelic mother. The black windowpane mirrored a soul in turmoil.

'Oh now, Owen dear. Don't go taking your mum's milk.'

'Mum? What mum? What kind of mum keeps milk

locked up anyway?' My brother unloosed his pony tail, letting the hair flop over his shoulders. 'If it was your sherry I'd siphoned off, OK.'

'Well — what if I pour the lad one small glass, Pammie?' Dad wheedled. 'Strict measure, mind. Leaving enough for tea.'

'No, Teddy, no — how can you undermine me like this?'

'I'm just thinking of you, love.'

Dad and Mum wrangled. Owen stoked their dispute by wondering whether Mum had bothered to breastfeed us as babies. Or did she stick a rubber teat in our gobs, prop us on cushions and slope off with Mrs Farting Yeomans to that den of sin, Sidoli's Coffee Bar?

Tommy, Danny and I hunkered while verbal missiles flew. A jittering thrill corrupted our hearts. Danny achieved armistice by launching himself off the couch and banging his head on the coffee table. Owen absconded through his bedroom window, returning two days later with, Tommy whispered, a *stash of dope* in his jeans pocket. Our eldest brother rested from his labours, curtains closed, listening to Bob Dylan singing that a hard rain's gonna fall — and *wanking in his pit*, said Tommy, with smirking alarm. *It pongs in there.*

It seems to me now that Dad was never quite the same again. His concern for Pam became pathological. It drove her up the wall. Which hurt his feelings. Dad taped cotton wool round the letter box flap and stationed a pillow on the doormat to prevent Mum being awoken by the newspaper. Mum binned it. Dad sorrowfully rescued it. Just don't, she said: stop it, if you want me to stay sane — if I am sane, that is. The next morning the pillow was there again. And he'd taped a sign to the door, asking the paper-boy to insert the newspaper with all possible caution.

★

The juke box blared. Smoke dimmed the alcoves and tarnished Sidoli's dimpled copper table tops. It was the gathering place of the town's mutinous young, as well as a remnant from a generation that had missed out on Peace and Love. We peeped unobserved. Mrs Farting Yeomans, as we'd learned to call her, arrived first, ordering Espresso and sidling into an alcove. Her yellow hair rose in a back-combed hump, with a lacquered fringe across her forehead. Her eyes were caked in mascara and her eyebrows con-veyed pathological surprise. When our mother arrived, they put their heads together and murmured. Mum's face was alight. Her hair tipped up at the ends. We'd helped her with the rollers.

'Hallo, Mum. Can we sit with you? Can we have Coke?' We slid into their booth.

A look we recognised washed over my mother's face. Dismal resignation. Boys would pursue you into any lair. They'd always nose you out. A higher law impelled boys to do it and forbade mothers to object. The Sixties were no use to them: they'd been conscripted according to an earlier code.

'Why aren't you playing football nicely, boys?' she won-dered. 'These are my youngest, Maddie. Tommy and Jack.'

Mrs Yeomans suggested we might like a banana split before we resumed our football.

As we spooned in cream, our antennae quivered: an encrypted conversation occupied the two mothers. In general Mrs Yeomans was the mouth, Mum the ear. We understood that Pam survived on the frugal fare of gossip, which her pal was happy to dish out.

'How was *he*? You know — *him,*' asked our mother.

'Hangdog.'

'Susp-ic-ious?'

'No.'

'What about ... *him?*' mouthed Mum.

A sigh.

'Boys, we're expecting company. Off you trot.'

Was this the company? Surely not. As we left, we bumped into two tall youths in denims, one with hair so blond it was almost white. His skin wasn't good and his jeans were drainpipes. The other was less blond, more stylish, with a flopping quiff. Must be the sons of whoever they were waiting for.

'Jonathan — Bobby — what a surprise!' cooed Mrs Yeomans in a false voice.

As we left, bribes in pockets, I looked back: the two mums were gazing into the faces of the albino and the quiff, as if to suck some juice they craved.

'Nice for Mum to get out now and again,' said Dad, picking us up from Woolworths in his cab. 'We exhaust her with our nonsense. Latitude she needs, darlings.'

Glancing into Dad's face I saw for a moment a man who belonged to the past, with his cufflinks and pipe, his tweed jacket and knitted waistcoat. Dad's gentleness cut me to the heart; yearning seized me to be a little boy again and wrap my arms around him. To hug under his jacket and feel the tender warmth of his body through his shirt, beneath braces and belt — for he wore both, to be on the safe side. His goodness appalled me — something so fragile about him. In the bath Dad's ribs were visible; the veins on his arms stood out like ropes of ivy.

Beside him in the cab, I wondered what Private Teddy Walters might have done in the desert that he'd not told us about. Hard to imagine those slender fingers on the steering wheel holding a gun.

'Did you ever kill anyone, Dad?'

'Whatever made you ask that now, Jackie?'

'Just wondering.'

'Not yet, darling. Joke, by the way.'

'Ha ha. Why does Mum want to go on the razzle?'

'Just a figure of speech. We want her to enjoy herself, don't we?'

'We had banana splits,' said Tommy.

'Lovely. Save any for me?'

'It would've been messy to take out,' Tommy excused himself and Dad chuckled. 'I did want to though. Dad —.'

'Yes, precious.'

'Mum and Mrs Yeomans are meeting boys. One has no eyebrows.'

'Or eyelashes,' I added. 'We call him Bun-the-Bunny.'

'Oh aye? Out you hop then.'

We'd offered perhaps too arcane a clue and could do no more for him.

When Owen slouched in to raid the fridge, I mentioned Bun-the-Bunny. Swigging off cream from two bottles, he ate a sausage roll. He said, 'Yeah, I know the creep. I was exchanged at birth. I'm not really theirs.'

When Mum came home, her face flushed, Dad was getting supper.

'Mmn, smells grand,' she said.

We all relaxed, seeing Mum cuddled up against Dad's back. As he cooked, Dad performed an aria from *Rigoletto*, conducting with the spatula: *La donna è mobile!* We clapped along.

'First the Italian Opera warbles it to Mussolini! Then in 1943 up the boot of Italy marches gallant Private Walters with holes in his underpants and they warble it for him!'

He waltzed Mum round, concluding with the sentiment that no one could be happy who did not on that bosom drink love! *Chi su quel seno – non liba amore!*

*

Our father's need to cosset our mother burst all bounds. He sequestrated not only milk but anything likely to tempt appetite. This elite food was stored in the lumber room, where he installed a miniature fridge for perishables. When boxes of chocolates were seen being spirited in there, rebellion flared. Off-colour as she was, Mum joined in.

'Please stop this, Teddy,' she pleaded. 'I hate keeping food from my children. Goes against the grain, it does really.'

'Your need is more important, love. It won't harm them to respect that.'

'But what's a mother for?'

'To be cherished,' he soothed.

'Please stop fussing me.'

'But I'm doing this for you!'

'Well, don't.'

While they bickered, Owen picked the lock. 'The natural order in this house has been overturned,' he said. 'By the Masters of War.'

The baby fridge sang in a corner. Milk, cream, biscuits, chocolates were revealed. Owen redistributed foodstuffs amongst the four of us. Once each boy was served, he relocked the door.

'Do you have anything you'd like to confess?' Dad enquired.

'No, Dad,' we chorused.

'Are you sure?'

'Yes, Dad.'

'Well, I'm disappointed, dears.' From now on he'd be inventorying all items stored in the lumber room. He purchased a special notebook for this purpose.

Dad would tell a tale of how as a schoolboy he'd attended the Church of St Anthony: Sunday by Sunday skinny orphanage boys in grey uniforms had to rise and chant the *Confiteor*, confessing that they'd sinned 'Through my *fault*, through my *fault*, through my most *grievous* fault,' banging their breasts with their fists. Unloved kiddies they were, never seen to smile. What faults could possibly be imputed to these tragic innocents? It had stuck in his young mind at a peculiar angle, contributing to his later atheism. These boys knew need.

Utter, unmediated need, at a time of life when soul and body must not be starved.

They'd asked for bread and been given a stone.

'Did I ever give *you* a stone, my beauties?' he asked us.

'No, Dad.' I felt remorse but did I regret the chocolates? Never. I'd do it again. He was mothering mother and mother wasn't mothering us.

'Ever?'

'No, Dad. Sorry, Dad. But why do you want Mum to get fat? And not us? It's not fair.'

His face softening, he smiled. 'You don't realise, do you?'

Mum's ankles and hands swelled up terribly in that last, late pregnancy. Uphill work it was, all the way. No more Sidoli's. She lolled on the couch listlessly directing operations.

'It means that Dad and Mum still do — you know,' whispered Tommy. 'That.'

'Yuck, no.'

'Fuck, yes. Probably just once a month. It's conjugal rights.'

Mrs Farting Yeomans visited once before vanishing. Dad was out. Mum and she conferred in low voices. I asked if the two ladies would care for a cup of tea.

'Oh, please. Don't burn your hands. And bring some cakes,' said Mum. 'Here's the key, love. And two jammy doughnuts for each of you boys.'

My heart appeased, I played mother, balancing the laden tray as I nudged open the door.

'Talk about strain,' Mum was murmuring. 'But, bless him, he's so good. Terribly good, and that's the trouble.'

'Do you mean me?' I asked.

'Well, I didn't,' Mum said and laughed. 'But if you grow up into a man half as unselfish as your father, that'll be good enough for me.'

'Jack's making a grand start, though, fair play,' said Mrs Yeomans. She helped me set down the laden tray on the table. Then, turning back to my mother, she said, in that knowing way of theirs, 'Has anyone said anything?'

'Said anything about what? Who to? What are you chatting about, you ladies?'

Mrs Yeomans poured the tea. 'Got him well trained, Pam, haven't you? Catch Anne-Marie lifting a finger. Above *menial tasks* apparently, according to the *Führer*.'

I sat with my doughnuts on the bottom stair. I was learning to crack their codes, or thought I was. The *Führer* meant Hitler and Hitler meant Mr Yeomans, not that there was much visible resemblance. I took one bite from each doughnut; then held them together to compare sizes. Mr Yeomans had a jowly face like a bloodhound, mouth turned down and no toothbrush moustache. His look was heavy with disappointment and reproof. Only his daughter appeared capable of meeting Mr Yeoman's exacting standards. Nibbling round the succulent jam core, I reduced each doughnut to its intense essence.

Leaving, Mrs Yeomans said, 'Ta for the tea. Look after your mum now, Jack.'

That was the last anyone saw of her until this year.

In her wake, Mr Hitler Yeomans and Anne-Marie appeared. She was a subdued, old-fashioned, aloof child, with pigtails pinned round her head, a scientist-in-the-making according to her father. Hunched and speechless, Anne-Marie kept watch on the door behind which the grown-ups were conversing. She wore a blue gingham dress; her lanky legs ended in white ankle socks and cherry red sandals.

We took turns listening at the door. I only remember the words *abandoned* and *young enough to be her blinking son*.

Occasionally I'd glimpse Mr Hitler Yeomans with Anne-Marie, hand-in-hand, in the village — glued together, other bonds having failed. They seemed, as Dad observed, all-in-all to one another. Mr Yeomans took Anne-Marie with him to chemistry conferences in Europe. A pair of prodigies, so my parents said, adding, 'Poor souls'. Dad didn't criticise the mother for eloping with Bun-the-Bunny, observing only that the kiddie would miss her mummy. It was hard work, he commented, being solely responsible for one's father.

Where were Mrs Farting Yeomans and Bun-the-Bunny, we speculated. In a hippy tepee near Carmarthen? In California with flowers in their hair? Or down the road in Much Wenlock?

★

Our baby had tremendous cheeks like a chipmunk's. An easy baby with flaxen hair and speedwell eyes, she cried only for sensible reasons — her feed or a full nappy. We got used to the sight of Mum breast-feeding and would join Andrea in making slurping noises – and were not rebuked. I think Mum accepted her own ageing: Andrea was her harvest and after that comes winter.

One morning I came downstairs to find Owen and his girlfriend Josie bending over Andrea's carrycot and murmuring. Whatever was Josie doing here at this hour? Maybe they were going out on her motorbike. Josie at seventeen did exactly as she pleased. Her hazel hair reached her waist. She was wearing Owen's best shirt over her jeans.

I poured milk and sugar on three Weetabixes. 'Hiya, Josie. What are you doing here?'

'Making babies,' said Owen.

'Shush, idiot.' Josie elbowed him.

'Josie never stayed the night, did she, Ow? Does Mum know?'

'Mum can't object.'

'Why?'

'Pot and kettle.'

'What?'

Mum padded downstairs, her tartan dressing gown flapping open over her slack belly. She looked haggard, her greying hair dishevelled from sleep. Starting at the sight of Josie, she said, 'Didn't realise you were here, dear. Make me a cuppa, Jack, while I feed her.'

Andrea latched on. Mum cooed, 'Oh you're so perfect for your mummy.'

'Looks nothing like Dad though, does she?' asked Owen. 'I wonder why.'

No reply.

'I said, she doesn't ...'

'Are you talking to me, Owen?'

'Well, which part of her is like Dad?'

The silence in the room was horrible.

Josie muttered, 'We should go, Ow. We'll be late.'

'I'm asking,' said Owen. 'I have a right to know.'

Our father was in the doorway. He walked up to Owen and hauled him to his feet.

Owen towered over Dad, to all appearances the cuckoo dwarfing the wren. And yet I would say that my father towered *under* my brother. He brought forth his power. Owen went to mush, as I'd have done in his place.

'Don't ever let me hear you speak like that again. In my house. Or it will no longer be your home. Apologise *now*, Owen.'

It was another man who spoke; not the clement Dad we all walked over like the soft hills of a gentle Shropshire landscape. This was the man I'd once heard trounce a Tory candidate on our doorstep — Private Walters who marched up through Italy.

Owen quailed and, unbelievably, his lip quivered. Mum shrugged: Owen was on his own. No one was going to intervene to shield my brother. I thought, as I sometimes did when offering Andrea my little finger, to pacify her, *He has a powerful suck on him.*

When Owen and Josie had left, Dad walked into the garden. I hovered behind him. He swung the fork, slamming its prongs in the soil; again, again, again. Laying it aside, he stooped to clear weeds. Without looking round, Dad asked, 'What is it now, Jackie love?'

'Nothing.'

I pondered his bent back and the fork. It would be easy to kill a man. This thought visited me as if from a distant battlefield and blew away with the breeze.

'It's all right, darling,' he said. 'Your brother just needed setting right. We all need that from time to time, I do myself.'

I'd been holding my breath; I could release it. Mum brought Andrea out and perched on the rusty old swing. Nobody referred to what had passed.

Dazzled by daffodils flicking around in the breeze, Andrea waggled her bare feet and squealed. I was allowed a taste of Mum's coffee. Later, passing the lumber room, I tried the door, out of habit. It was open. I didn't go in. I wasn't tempted. Nobody was. After a while the fridge disappeared and the hoarding ceased.

★

The family gathers for Mum's eightieth. She looks resplendent in a grey silk blouse, a cameo brooch at the neck, her hair a snow white cloud. Lunch on the lawn is rustled up by my brother Dannie, the chef. Owen, always starving-hungry, finishes wolfing a second plate of salmon and walnut soda bread, before the rest of us are ready to progress to the torte. It's hard to associate his stay-at-home middle age with his teenage delinquencies. Moving in with Mum after decades of footsore wandering, he has somehow never left her side.

The orange-haired pensioner who used to be Mrs Farting Yeomans and is now Mrs Matthew Lightfoot is visiting from Australia. A plumply affable presence, she and her Fourth enjoy an ocean view at Christies Beach near Adelaide.

'I wrote to Anne-Marie — faithfully — birthdays and Christmas,' she confides to Mum, in a pleading, childish voice. 'I did. But ... ah well.'

'We rarely see Anne-Marie, Maddie. She's done very well for herself, hasn't she, in, what is it? — Petrochemicals? She and her father were close.'

'I left them to it.'

'It was a long time ago,' says Mum carefully. 'We all make mistakes, Maddie. And sometimes they turn out well.'

Guilt and shame must have tracked Mrs Yeomans round the world. I can't help but wonder what became of Bun-the-Bunny, the albino she abandoned a daughter for. 'Eaten alive for elevenses,' is what Owen would have said. 'And then spat out.'

'What a charming young person *your* daughter is,' the ex-Mrs Yeomans says to Mam.

'Teddy adored her,' Mum replies. 'And how proud he'd be of her doctorate. Such a pity he didn't live to see it.'

'Did you ever — come across —?'

'No,' says Mum firmly. 'Absolutely not.' She gets up to offer round a plate of fruit tarts.

I look over at Andrea, with her baby-blonde hair, sitting in the shade, shining. Our sister's most flagrant breaches of rules — and Andrea was a rebel — were absorbed into the joyous love our parents had for her.

'I was sorry to hear about Ted,' Mrs Yeomans says. 'So sorry. He had such kindness.'

Mum says, 'Too much.'

'Can you have too much?'

'He remembered standing at his mother's graveside

— Teddy was seven and wiggling a loose tooth with his tongue. The priest intoned. Dirt hit the coffin. It sounded empty but he knew his mummy was inside. Teddy looked up at his father and saw his face contorted. His heart went out to his dad. I don't think it ever came back in. He had to live with a heart out of its cage. With a sympathy so intense and universal that it undid him, there was no centre, you see — and it made for an insane clemency to others. Branded he was.'

'Yes,' reflects Owen and reaches for the wine. 'He was no saint, that's for sure.'

'Don't you ever say that, Owen,' Andrea flares up. 'About my dad. Don't you dare. It's a pity you're not more like him.'

Oud, 1942

Lalage and Delia lounge on the window seat of their classy Gezira apartment, discussing Delia's soldier-boys. She appraises Lal's prosaic face, burnished and glamorised by the late sunlight. In Cairo expat women enjoy the kind of luxury no shorthand typist could command at home. Delia's latest human find is standing outside on the pavement, smoking. She looks down on Rich's flaxen head with a qualm she prefers not to investigate.

Next week the lads will be drafted from Cairo to Cyrenaica; a day later they may be dead, lying face-downwards (if they still have faces) in the sands of the Western Desert. Before they've tasted life. So let them live now! The least you can do is relieve them of their virginity. Perhaps they'll remember your face while they're dying. 'Well, that's my excuse!' Delia cries in a tinny voice. 'What's yours?'

Lal calls Delia's boys her 'waifs and strays', culled from the multitudes on leave or in transit: 'Delia's so philanthropic — a one-woman pet-rescuer!' The capital teems with young Englishmen, lobster-faced, pale-chested, hair beginning to bleach, shining with sweat and naïveté. The plainest girl can pick and choose amongst males.

Frightfully fond of Rich Delia's become, since scooping him off the Cairo street. It scares Delia stiff. The back of his head's so touching, the vulnerable nape where sunburn meets private skin. Rich's eyebrows are so light they all but vanish in the tanned beauty of his face. His hair's like wheat. He's glorious and doesn't know it.

Outside Shepheards Hotel she barged into a youth in officer's uniform, hunkering beside an Arab beggar pluck-ing a stringed instrument. Europeans passed by in evening dress, with toppers and canes. Boys blacked shoes. The beggar had pus in the bud of a sightless eye. Cars hooted, hawkers bawled, wirelesses blared. Beyond or below this uproar, the shock-headed, serious and (she realised with a pang) adorable young man she'd collided with was bending to listen. Delia inclined her own ear to incomprehensible twangings.

'Delia Masson.'

'Neil Richards, call me Rich. Isn't this remarkable?' He straightened up, shirt collar open, skin transparent. They shook hands. He offered the beggar *baksheesh:* far too much, as she advised him. Straight off the troop ship: green as grass.

'It's called an oud. An Arab lute,' Rich explained after-wards. He wanted to learn while he was here in the Middle East, drink it all in — study Arabic. An important lan-guage in world history, the boy said: we can learn so much from its great intellectual traditions. This was a god-sent opportunity to broaden his mind — help build a better world, when all this violence was done. Sitting together on the veranda, they sipped wine as flights of ibis coasted their reflections in the Nile across a ruby sunset. Since then Rich has been her shadow.

★

Delia draws a suspect nylon stocking over her forearm like an evening glove and, swivelling the arm, inspects it for snags. She catches Rich's gaze. Always so shyly intense. Straight from grammar school into the army, promoted within months to the dizzy rank of Captain. Knew nothing, when he came to her. Knows more now, bless him.

Rich ponders her sheathed arm in the window light, as if something were being shown more nakedly for being veiled — and so little time available to witness and worship. Delia leans over to kiss his frown. Nineteen years old. Compared with Rich, she feels herself to be, at twenty-six, set like yesterday's blancmange. In the golden light you decipher minute hairs stuck in the stocking's mesh, flecks of bright dust falling from the weave. Atoms of oneself flaking away. She flicks at what might be an eyelash with her nail.

'Pass the varnish, angel.'

Rich pads over to her dressing table where he sorts through the mess of bottles. What colour does she want?

'You choose for me.'

Delia unrolls the stocking over calf, knee and thigh, standing to fasten her suspenders. The boy studies her every move; settles to painting her nails, perched on a low stool, legs apart. His tongue tip separates his lips as he works. Done: he paints his own thumbnail.

'When all this is over, what'll you do?'

'I've a place at Oxford. Although whether I ...'

Lalage bursts in: 'I say! Randolph's here! Him and the carrot-bearded gnome!'

Delia scrambles her face on. Scribbles scarlet on to her lip; piles her hair in a messy topknot. Rich pins it, bobby pins held between compressed lips like a lady's maid. What kind of warrior will you make, Rich? She pauses a moment to ponder his intent face with compassion.

Rich dresses slowly, his face dreamy, drugged-looking. He's a poet at heart, she's told him: that or a hairdresser.

The apartment floods with Special Operations high-ups. Including the Prime Minister's loutish son. 'Ghastly type, braying ass,' she's heard Freya, the BBC reporter, say in a breathy whisper: 'as harmful to the Allied cause as a roomful of *Waffen-SS*.' Randolph Churchill parks his two mistresses at either end of the couch. His loud-mouthed retinue fills the apartment with smoke and fatuity. Life and soul of the party is Mr Waugh, the carrot-bearded gnome, author of novels no one has read. The gnome spends his time, by his own account, slipping in and out of the priest's confessional, sinning and being shriven. How many Hail Marys for a party at Delia's, she wonders? Who cares? Everyone's having a whale of a time in Cairo: no Blitz, no rationing, no wives. *Autres moeurs* entirely.

The Kemp brothers, absolute twerps but rather a lark,

pour bubbly into a row of beakers. Raymond has a *lech* on Delia, so the younger brother informs her. 'Poor bloke's pining: have a heart.'

Ray is part of the doughy and yeastless bureaucracy of General Headquarters, where personnel take things as easily as they know how. He's a soak: they all are. Ray now sweeps Delia up in his arms, carrying her way off the ground like a ballerina. The nail varnish on her stocking will show — but what the hell?

'Put me down, beast!' she squeals, beating on his oiled head with her little fists.

Delia's young poet leans against the wall looking on. His face is flushed, brooding, sorrowful. When he turns away, something in her twinges.

★

He was weighing our hearts, she thinks a year later, and finding them rotten.

Tobruk has fallen. The Navy has quit Alex. White women and children are fleeing.

Ray calls out, 'Better get out while you can, Pussy.'

He's shaving with his cut-throat razor, a frightful affectation. Still yacking. To himself now, as, drifting into the living room, Delia throws up the sash. The snarling street chokes with traffic funnelling out of Cairo before the city's bombed flat and overrun by Panzermen. Egyptians, nakedly parading their preference for the Master Race over the British 'gentlemen fascists', affect toothbrush moustaches. Herr Hitler's a Moslem, they've heard. He prays five times a day and hates Jews. Allah has sent him to cleanse their land of the infidel.

Delia looks down on a mattress strapped to the roof of a car whose boot's wedged open with the household gods of the Anglo-Saxon race. The car bonnet steams. The exodus has been named The Flap. Stiff upper lips quiver. But we'll be back! From a pyre in the Citadel ascend clouds of stinking smoke: we're burning secret documents. The charred flakes of secrets settle on awnings, on the heads of the anxious mob queuing outside the bank. Arab paupers scavenge classified pages from the pavement. There must be a use for British rubbish: there always is.

It's the judgment upon us, Delia thinks. Ray and Jack, being Jews, should leave before Rommel arrives. She won't leave with them, whatever they say.

For what if Rich escapes from the theatre of war and comes looking for her? He returned once, out of the blue, lean and sombre and tender.

Rich explained that the Arabic lute had no frets. That meant you could slide your finger up and down the stem, no boundaries between notes, no taboos, and make these sensuous slides, *glissando*s and vibratos. Like this, sweetheart. He was so interested in the Egyptians: never demeaned them as wogs, gyppos, darkies. He wanted to return, he said, after this was all over; study the language, the culture. Would Delia consider accompanying him? He'd seen things in the desert that had grown him up, he explained. *Lacrymae rerum*: the tears of things. He didn't specify.

Rich's hands were palm to palm in an attitude of prayer between her warm thighs; his relaxed breathing at her breast stirred on her skin. She'd taught her pupil the arcana of touch; he'd passed to Delia something more, she found. When his leave was up, she walked him to the station, palm glued to hot palm, zigzagging through bellowing traffic.

How she cried that night. The storm didn't subside until Ray fetched up on her doorstep and made her laugh. She let him sleep on her sofa but denied him her bed. He interpreted that as a ploy to get him to marry her. Think what you like, she thought, but don't leave me alone with this — what was it? — grief?

Delia closes the window. 'I'm not running away, Ray, and that's that. Don't keep on. I'm sitting it out.'

Ray pleads, soft-soaps, sulks, commands. He weeps surprising tears and says: 'Anything, anything you want, Dee, what are your terms?'

After he's gone, an explosion rattles the panes. Has Rommel arrived already? No, just a car backfiring. The bedlam in the street persists.

Dusk falls. Dust falls.

Dido mews on the balcony, pressing her lynx-flank against the pane, glaring in at Delia. Milk there is none. 'Give me, give me,' Dido's warm body says, slinking forcefully round her legs in an orgy of cupboard love. 'What have you got for me?' Leaping on to Delia's lap, Dido mews in her mistress's face.

'Oh all right.' Delia stirs herself to visit the pantry. That should do. The last of yesterday's steak and kidney in a bowl of blood. Delia fries it with an onion. Her stomach heaves. She dunks a biscuit in a cup of tea while the cat gorges on offal.

*

The bonfire's out at the Citadel. Rommel, the Desert Fox, has turned tail and is loping back towards Tripoli. The British, Flap over, shuffle shamefaced back to Cairo. Any minute now, the expatriate party will liven up again.

Flopping down on the sofa, Lalage accepts a cup of tea. She's brought some simply thrilling dresses back from Palestine, picked up for a song at a refugees' jumble sale. Couldn't resist. Delia must help her choose which to wear tonight at Madame Badia's. Give Lal Cairo over Jerusalem any day: the Yids loathe us, she reports: 'After all we've done for them! So jolly ungrateful! Well, I wash my hands of them! Whatever's that thing over there?'

Delia explains about the oud, a present for Rich, when he comes back.

'Looks like a tortoise!' Lalage picks it up and the instrument seems to float into the air. 'Fearfully fragile. Pretty — all this inlay.' Reading the expression on Delia's face, Lal observes, not without sympathy, 'You've got it bad for him, haven't you, darling? Any news?'

'Not yet.'

'Well, it's absolute chaos around Alamein, they say. Don't give up, eh?'

Delia holds the lute in her arms. It's the mother of all stringed instruments, she remembers Rich saying, and mellifluous.

She watched it being constructed. The workshop's open to the street in an area known by the Tommies as Deepest Wogtown. They avoid its squalor for fear of assassination.

She sat, in company with the craftsman's relatives, all male — a quiet female anomaly, watching the process through its stages. Thin ribs of wood were glued edge to edge to fashion the instrument's belly.

'As you may or may not be aware, *Madame,* the oud was invented by Lamech,' said the instrument maker's grandfather, who'd acquired a stately command of English in the Great War. 'Lamech, the sixth grandson of Adam. Lamech's son died young. In his sorrow the father hung the body from a tree. When the flesh rotted, exposing the bones, he invented the oud in the shape of his son's bleached skeleton.'

'We had a tortoise once,' Lal prattles. 'Not a tremendously exciting pet — walking to heel wasn't her thing, she snoozed half the year — but I liked her. How's it played?'

'With an eagle's feather.'

'Golly. Can you play it, Dee?'

'No but I'm going to learn.'

'Well, I'm off for a shower — then I'll phone round — see who's back.'

Left alone, Delia cradles the oud. And then it occurs — what she was waiting for — a soft commotion of butterfly wings inside her belly.

Delia listens as the body of the oud picks up the faintest resonance.

Mr Duda

'My name,' said Mr Duda, 'is Polish for bagpipes or bad musician — but I promise not to sing. Are you interested in the Moon Landings? I have TV. I show you room now and bear in mind, Miss Ruth, it is not large but it is tall.'

I was to share kitchen and bathroom with my landlord. Was I a big bather as some girls were? Did I have noisy friends?

'I am a very private person, Mr Duda. Quiet and studious. It is just for the summer till I start teacher training.'

His eyes prowled my figure and he spent some time assessing my hair, that Nico adored and my father the rabbi abhorred as a badge of his ex-daughter's rebellious shame. Straight and shining, down to my waist. Orthodox womenfolk covered theirs with wigs; they deplored jeans.

'Do you leave much hair in the plug holes?' Mr Duda asked.

I reassured him on this point and slid the bolt. Safe. My own space. I could always dodge him. He was a bit lame:

a war wound. Boxes crowded the narrow room which overlooked the house's backside, containing dustbins and a kennel. Despite the summer, it was chilly; I fed the metre with shillings, turning on the electric fire. I hadn't asked Mr Duda for permission to use my kettle in the room in case he said no.

Cross-legged before the fire, I wrapped my hands round a mug of tea. After all it wasn't so very drab and cheerless. I didn't have to share and it was dirt-cheap. Intimately tangled with me in his bed on our last day together, Nico had wept and said he hated to leave me so alone, with nobody behind me. Go back to your family, Ruthie, if you possibly can. Of course his conscience hurt; through these years he'd kept quiet about us to his parents. *I don't need anyone behind me.* Did Nico want me to be fragile and helpless? That wasn't me. I prided myself on being a girl of Sparta. They'd tried to expose me on a mountain side naked to the air — but I'd survived. I would survive, Nico or no Nico.

He didn't even make one last attempt to convert me: if I were a nice Catholic girl, at least formally, Nico's parents would have come round. But Jewish, even though an apostasising Jew, a Jewish atheist? They could never accept such a wife for their eldest son and he couldn't bring himself to do as I'd done, cut free. But if I would nominally convert? What would it matter, he said: it was only words.

And that did it. Only words? That Nico could hold truth — my truth — in such contempt shook me to the core. What had I battled for? Nico never understood that after this I could never have married him, though I loved every bone in his body.

He'd found an enigmatic Chinese poem written a thousand years ago about a candle burning out. *Passion too deep seems like none.* What did that mean? Anything at all? Sadness suffused me but I would not show it. We agreed that this could not continue — and our knowledge of coming sacrifice had added aching tenderness to our lovemaking.

Mr Duda seemed to scent the tea. Here he was, rattling the door.

'Yes, Mr Duda?' I stood in the doorway, the toes of my sandals exactly touching the boundary of my domain.

'Is all to your liking, Miss Ruth? Anything I can do? I could make you nice pot of tea.'

'No thank you. Everything is fine.'

Mr Duda had height. He could see right over my head. As he opened his mouth, ready, I was sure, to forbid the boiling of kettles, I closed the door on him, gently but firmly, for my landlord must accept that this was my space. Not his. He muttered something about astronauts and TV. I slid the bolt and waited. His slippered footsteps faded.

★

Out of the bus we poured, the lasses who worked at the cigarette factory in Droylesden: the banal tedium of our days suited me fine. I was working not only to keep myself over the summer but to pay my debt to Nico. His family owned mansions in three European countries. Their son and heir, sensitive and generous, never bragged his wealth; he eased himself of it whenever a suitable have-not appeared. It had cost him nothing to bail me out of my debts and he didn't want the money repaid. But I intended to refund every penny. Each Friday I added what I could spare to a brown envelope marked with Nico's name. It was getting fatter. After six weeks this hoarding had become my life's secret purpose.

Counting out ten bob notes, I sorted change into piles as bank clerks do. Soon I must swap the notes for the new decimal coins. The threepenny bits Mr Duda collected would have to be exchanged or they'd drop out of currency.

In our shared kitchen my landlord cooked operatically, enticingly, his wooden spoon flourished like a baton. He told me sad stories of past hunger. The fragrance of soup and goulash was out of this world but I steadfastly refused invitations to eat with him. There was something about Mr Duda that unsettled me. A loomingness. A loneliness too like my own. I winced at my own callousness but we have to look out for ourselves in this world, I told myself. I must and so must you, Mr Duda.

A Polish Jew who had taken refuge in Manchester in 1945 must have known suffering. Straight from the camps, no doubt. I noticed however that he lacked friends. Not only that but I'd seen a Polish neighbour, Mr Sawicki, spit as he passed my landlord in the road, causing Mr Duda to skip aside into the gutter, despite his limp. When Mr Sawicki had gone several yards past, Mr Duda turned and also spat. The twin gobs of saliva shone silver for a moment like snail trails. He came back in with a package of meat wrapped in greaseproof, wiped his feet and whistled, murmuring to himself.

Mr Duda conjured feasts from the butcher's poorest cuts. His thrift deplored my extravagance with tea leaves, which he felt reflected poorly not only on my moral character but that of my generation.

'Is a scandal, Ruth,' he said. 'What if war come?'

'I don't honestly think it will, Mr Duda, do you? Unless it's a nuclear war in which case we'll be annihilated anyway.'

'You young people, you do not know nothing about nothing, pardon me for saying.'

Marek let out a howl from the kennel; he'd smelt some foreign cat threatening his domain. Mr Duda shambled out to assess the threat. I thrust bread beneath the grill, hoping to skedaddle before his return. Too late. The Alsatian skittered round the red-tiled floor, shook the rain off his pelt and came to sniff my crotch, snarling.

It occurred to me to wonder whether my landlord inspected my room while I was out. Perhaps he sat on my bed and tested the springs. Rifled through my drawers; read my letters. I looked at him with ashamed disquiet. He was a stranger in a strange land, owning little, an odd bod and loner like myself.

'Try for yourself, Ruth, is all I ask. Tea leaves may be used more than twice. You will not know the difference.'

Many of my father's congregation had kept old soaps on a string and constructed cigarettes from butts. Thrift smelt of the austerity of the immigrants' generation. I offered Mr Duda a cup of my strong tea; shuddering, he affected not to hear.

A knocking. Marek lifted up his voice. Mr Duda's hand went straight to his bulging jacket pocket. Here he kept all that a man might need in extremis, from passport to elastic bands. Marek's ears were pricked, his tail was high, he drooled and he panted.

'Only milkman, Marek.' Mr Duda counted coins. He opened the door on the chain and peered out. 'Oh! For you, Ruth,' he called. As I approached, he whispered, 'Darkie. Says he is close friend. Shouldn't think so myself. Long hair, needs good shave. Marek and I get rid?'

'Ruthie!'Nico breathed short, a melting look in his eyes.'I'm here.'

I gaped.'Yes, but ... what are you doing here? Has something happened?'

'I came as soon as I got it. I couldn't not.'

'Got what?'

'What do you mean, got what?'

He was in my arms; I was in his arms. I smelt the musk of Nico's sweat in the fibres of the pale sweater. As soon as the scent was inside me, I knew I couldn't and wouldn't let go again. My starvation reared and rebelled and would no longer be solaced by pauper rations.

★

We roamed Platt Park, visiting our special places: rowed on the lake and lay on the scorched grass. Couldn't keep our hands off one another. We ordered éclairs in the lakeside cafe, followed by ice creams. My confusion had given way to an elated sense of reprieve.

'I want you to have my baby,' Nico burst out. I sucked sugar off my fingers. 'No, Ruthie, I mean, my *babies*! How many shall we have?'

Into my mind flashed a memory of my sister with a hat covering her wig covering her hair, pushing a pram while a toddler clung round her neck. Throttled, hobbled. Deb at seventeen looked thirty. But Nico's euphoria was contagious. We'd have six children, yes, or seven, why not? We were full to the brim with cream. I tasted chocolate on his lips.

'What brought you back, love?' I asked him.

'Well, your letter, of course.'

'But, Nico — I didn't write you a letter.'

'You did!'

'I really and truly didn't.'

He reached into his pocket.

And, yes, I'd written it: the dreaming girl I'd been eleven months ago. The passionate message seemed to come from another planet. The moon-girl had written it at our old flat one vacation, addressing it to Warrington rather than the sumptuous summer pad his parents had rented for him in Wallingford. It had found him at last. The letter-writer lived in plenty and risked extravagance. And now, belatedly, the message must have touched something in Nico that made him reckless enough to ditch creed, parental prohibitions and inheritance — and whatever marital arrangements might be wished on him in Rome. Just like that.

'It's like a dream,' he said. 'Don't anyone wake me up.'

But was I ready? Time had looped around and tangled

in itself. There was a knot or snag he didn't know about. Two snags really.

'I have something for you at home,' I said. 'It's just an instalment. You'll get the whole lot in due course.'

★

'Come in here, Miss Ruth,' called Mr Duda through the open door of his front room. 'Does *he* wish come in also? The foreign chap. Please wipe dirty feet carefully on mat provided.'

Nico entered, hand extended, wishing my landlord a civil good evening. His posh accent was lost on Mr Duda; his denims disguised his patrician origins. Mr Duda, ignoring the hand, addressed himself solely to me.

'This man comes from where?'

'Oh, from Italy, Mr Duda. He's doing research here. Mechanical engineering. Nico's an old friend.'

Muttering something about spaghetti, my landlord shook his head. 'Ruth, you like to see moon landings on my television, I know.'

The black and white picture fizzed. Two ghostly astronauts struggled to plant the Stars and Stripes in the dust; one came bouncing back to the capsule as if playing hopscotch. Later we went out of doors, all three of us, to gaze at the moon where patriots had taken their flag and their hopscotch. The constellations wheeled around, winking.

'This young Italian chap should be going home now, Ruth?' whispered Mr Duda, cupping his hand under my elbow. 'Time to lock up.'

'No, Mr Duda. Nico is my guest.'

Moonlight silvered the dustbin lids and the kennel roof. Marek growled. Mr Duda said, 'Tenants cannot sublet, Ruth, you know that.'

'Of course not. No question of that.'

'He not pay his keep?'

'Nico is a close friend.'

'Word to the wise. You live to regret this. Save your hard-earned cash, Ruth. As father to child I say this. He is immigrant, though not the worst sort.'

I stared and failed to say: Well, what are you? Weren't you an immigrant when you came to Lancashire? And why advise me to save my money?

Later, as Nico slept like a seraph, looking more beautiful than any man or woman had a right to, I rose and plugged in the kettle. Our candle was only half consumed; its flame stood still in the airless room. The envelope was still in the chemistry textbook — except that it was upside down.

I seemed to see Mr Duda's fingerprints smeared over my possessions. My skin crawled. How many times had he penetrated my space? To what end? Was he stealing? I counted the money: all there.

In ten days' time the halfpenny coin would be withdrawn from currency. It would be worthless. Mr Duda kept a stash in a biscuit tin at the back of the cutlery drawer. I would not remind him.

Nico, propped on one elbow, observed me as I sealed the envelope.

'This is all yours,' I told him. 'I'll pay you by instalments. And the letter — I should have told you — it's a kind of counterfeit — is a year out of date. And I can't have your babies, Nico — all your babies would be lies or half-truths.'

★

A Fallowfield girl had been murdered in Whitworth Park on her way to St Mary's maternity hospital. In broad daylight. Heavily pregnant, she'd been on her way to antenatal class. One moment she was crossing the parched midsummer turf under the trees, the next she was sprawled with her throat cut. All for a lousy three quid. Someone had left flowers against the cherry tree nearest to where she died. Yellow roses wilting in the heat.

I sat down on a bench to think. Safe as houses, she strolled along. And then it was all over for her and her child.

The park did not feel dangerous: it felt soporific. I almost dozed. It was three weeks since Nico had come and gone. The late throb of hope had been moonshine, I'd told him — illusion. He'd left the envelope with my savings under my pillow: OK then, I'd keep it for when my grant came and I could move to a flat. Did my landlord rummage under the pillow? I didn't believe the Americans had got to the moon anyhow: trick photography was all it was, propaganda. I'd curtly refused Mr Duda's invitation six days later to watch the recovery of the space capsule.

My landlord had become wary about his espionage. His antennae had presumably registered the canny arrangement of long brown hairs with which I protected my sanctuary.

And there he went, on the opposite side of the park, walking Malek, his limp slowing him down. That gave me a good half hour unless he took a taxi, which he was too mean to do. I sprinted home. Put the door on the chain. Upstairs. His bedroom. The copied key turned in the lock.

I was in Mr Duda's space.

The curtains were closed. Aged floral wallpaper, peeling. Heavy, dark furniture. I switched on the light: the ceiling was so remote and the bulb so feeble that the room lay in yellowish dusk. I opened the mirrored door of the wardrobe. Rusting cans of rice pudding, corned beef, beans were piled to the roof.

What depths of insecurity still haunted that generation? My stupefied face gaped back from the mirror. Mr Duda was stocked up for a siege, with the kind of food he didn't eat from day to day. How long had it been there? Was it still edible?

You know nothing about nothing.

I was ashamed now to be snooping on my landlord. He had suffered, unspeakably, and if he had come out of that maelstrom not only troubled but warped, who was I to judge? How many had he lost in the ghettos or camps? What was his history?

Nevertheless, my hands pursued their researches. They seemed to suspect something of which I was ignorant. I glanced through Mr Duda's net curtains into the silent cul de sac. A couple of pigeons were poking about in the gutter. The red brick houses kept rigid vigil. Only Mr Sawicki stirred. He left his house carrying his shopping bag, locking and testing the door before taking his usual detour by stepping off the pavement past our house, as if something within offended him with its unsavoury smell. Our world was populated by lonely displaced old men, surviving in the concussive aftermath of universal disaster. Hurry up, I told myself: he'll be back. I'd just glance under the bed before leaving.

The biscuit tin was phenomenally heavy. I pulled off the lid: wrapped in tissue paper, a trove of coins. Not surprising in a way that he'd stashed his cash where he could keep an eye on it rather than lodging it in a bank. My grandmother had done the same. A small fortune distributed between small hiding places had been collected when she died. If Mr Duda wasn't careful, I thought, his coins would all go out of currency. But, hang on, they were foreign coins. Extracting a silver coin, I weighed it in my palm: an eagle with open wings was perched on a crown of oak leaves. *Deutsches Reich 1939. 2 Reichsmark.* Within the crown was a swastika. My first thought was: worthless. Perhaps these were souvenirs. Keepsakes from Hell.

And here was another collection of coins — no, medals and military insignia.

The tissue paper whispered as I pulled out a cloth badge embroidered with twin lightning bolts.

It was only when I saw the photographs that I understood. Fast, fast, I bundled it all back. Mr Sawicki's loathing was explained. I stuffed the tins back under the bed. Go. Where? Anywhere. To Nico? Home to Father? The longing for home came rushing upon me, as if I'd been searching for a bricked-up door all this while in my disquiet exile

from the faces of the people who'd bred and fed and loved
and secured me.

For I'd seen too much. Just leave. How shall I have to
pay for this? Out. What will be done to me? *'Raus.* Hei-
nous knowledge.

But no. I was no longer my father's daughter. To Nico
then. Ring him. Tell him you're between tenancies. Just go.

Was that Marek barking, out there in the street? Terror
pitched me back into my own room. I gathered up documents, clothes, books; crammed them in a case. The dog
was on the stairs. Everything I could not carry would have
to be abandoned.

Piano

'Why choose to live in a ghetto, Suzanne?' Dad bleated. I'd caught him in a ratty mood on account of the Footsie 100 Index. 'You're a graduate now. You should be out in the marketplace, not fooling around doing another footling course with a Mickey Mouse name. Dawdling in a prolonged childhood. You could follow your sister into television. I'm sure BBC Manchester needs tea girls — and work your way up.'

It wasn't a ghetto, I snarled. If we were talking about ghettos, my parents lived in a Surrey ghetto, full of toxic plutocratic racists and bankers and other parasites. And I liked Longsight, it was a place to grow.

'To grow anything in particular?' he wondered. 'Bedbugs? Crime? Marijuana? I'm no racist, as you well know, but the only people in this road who aren't blacks are Irish. High time you found a respectable job like your sister and wore a skirt like your sister. As for growing, quite honestly, growing up might be a first step.'

'Anyway,' Mum intervened before he could launch into rant about immigrants and Welfare spongers. 'Have some lemon cake, both of you. Don't bicker. Suzie, we are equally proud of you both, you know that.'

★

A rough and tumble of joyous Caribbean kiddies played in the road. At evening, their dads would scoop them up squealing and fetch them indoors. I'd wave from my window and they'd wave back.

Laurie arrived from time to time in his vintage car, on his way home from the firm where he was doing his articles. Corinne's boyfriend. I loved my sister so I loved Laurie too, tall and willowy, with an unfinished face. He'd lounge with his latest affectation, a baby cigar. Smoke rings by candle light wobbled into the air: I put my ring finger through one as it neared vanishing point.

'However will you get the piano in?' he asked.

'Oh, I'll manage. I can't bear to live without a piano, Laurie. A piano is better value than a lover.'

'Do you think so?' He appeared to consider how this might apply to his own world. 'But then you are an artist, Suzie. It's different. If you need help, say the word.'

The students in the ground floor flat, Nettle and Paula, shared the phone in the downstairs hall with me. Laurie was kissing me goodbye when it rang: Corinne.

'Oh hi Cory — all right? — no, not seen him. Has he gone missing?'

Laurie, finger on lips, sidled out. Corinne and I talked

for nearly an hour, discussing her hairstyle aspirations. She was thinking of extensions but might they look unserious to her viewers? They would be made from real human hair, ultimate double deluxe. People recognised her in the street, Corinne said: she wanted to look her best for them, not let them down. Lucky you, Suze — you don't have the same responsibilities, she said. Meanwhile I opened and closed the front door to the students who came and went from the downstairs flat. Nettle and Paula lived squalid lives even by my standards. Their sink was offensive, our landlord Mr Marshall pointed out, always threatening to evict them.

'But I am naturally blonde,' said Paula, who was by any standards a peerless beauty and could be charming when it suited her. 'And he never in practice has the nerve.'

Paula's boyfriend Thomas, a Chemistry student, was more or less a fixture in the flux, although it seemed a tempestuous, on-off affair, the tempest being all on Paula's side. She had no obvious aptitude for the quiet life. Paula acknowledged that Tom was good with his hands and a genius at Thai red curry. Chemists made the best cooks, Tom held, for cookery is a science, not an art, right? Narrowing his eyes and inhaling a spliff, Tom confided that he was playing a long game in the certainty that Paula would settle for him in the end.

'Do you want to be settled for?'

'Yeah, I don't mind.'

'Second best is crap.'

'It's not ideal. But still. We do the best with what we have,' he philosophised. 'Don't we?'

Not wanting to admit that I knew the feeling, I kept quiet.

Later, wafts of curry streamed up the stairs. 'Come 'n' eat, Suze,' yelled Nettle. 'Tom's made a bucketful. Got any bottles?'

Nettle's dad owned a pub, The Peacock Inn on the Welsh border, where drinking went on round the clock. We'd visited. Slow on his feet and heavy of speech, Mr Price lived a blissfully pickled life. On the third day, arising from our coma, we'd staggered into the fields to breathe sweet air. Laurie had come along for the ride; Corinne not. Tom had driven us home to Manchester in his van, with Laurie and I lying in the back in one another's arms, as friends do.

Nettle complained to me that it was all right for gorgeous Paula, she could have any man she wanted, but what about herself? It was no joke being dumpy and having lousy teeth. When I tried to comfort her, she objected that I wouldn't know: not only was I an intellectual and a feminist and a Neo-Marxist and an artist but I had a famous sister.

'She just reads the news, she doesn't write it. Anyway, since you ask, one thing you could do, Nettle — if you really want advice — is get some decent shampoo.'

She raised one offended hand to her greasy scalp and went quiet. I mentioned toothbrushes and dentists: in the end they were the only answer. Nettle said it was perfectly all right, she'd asked for a tip and, *chwarae teg,* she'd been fucking well given one. She sloped off with a bottle of cider. She'd have lovely hair if she'd only take care of it.

That phrase echoed: it was what Cory used to say to me.

The walls began to spin; the floor tilted; the air stank of hash. Fourteen young men were passing round roll-ups. In the morning I awoke on a mattress alongside a guy never knowingly seen before. Fair, curly hair and a broken nose. He said his name was Ellis and that I had a lissom body, the body of an angel. What had happened in the night? Oh nothing at all, he said, don't worry. I explained that I was due to take delivery of a piano and he had to go.

The second-hand piano was delivered and abandoned in the downstairs hall. Opening the lid, I ran my fingers over the keys. It was the most beautiful object I'd ever owned. And it was mine, bought with a surreptitious loan from Mum. The frame was scored and scratched: but that was good too. My piano had a life; it had suffered; it carried its history into my world.

Young men lay on floors and couches as if slain where they'd stood. With Tom, never drunk and an early riser, I debated how to shift the instrument. Two snags: the bend in the staircase and banisters at the top. It'd be a near thing, said Tom. Paula came and advised. Then she swept him off to buy ice creams.

Nettle appeared with a towel on her head.

'Really sorry if I was rude last night,' I said.

'Were you? — don't remember.'

'Who was that blondish guy with the broken nose, Minette?'

'Oh, that would be Jerry Ellis. It's not broken — he says it's aquiline, a Roman nose.'

'Is he ... all right?'

'Yeah, why?'

'Just wondering.'

'Word to the wise though, Suze. Jerry only likes other boys. He's not into girls.'

It was a relief. Sort of. And an enigma.

'So what are you doing with that piano, *bach*?'

Not a lot. The instrument sat there all the next day, wedged in the hall. Nobody was bothered: time functioned differently on the ground floor. For long stretches Nettle and Paula and their hangers-on knew no time; then the clock hands might whirl as an essay became due. But Friday was rent day. Mr Marshall always appeared at the front door to collect it and though he never intruded and was unfailingly courteous, I couldn't imagine he'd greet the piano with enthusiasm. Nor could its presence be effectively hidden under a sheet.

'Why not knock next door?' Nettle suggested, going off to dry her hair. 'There are dozens of lads in there who could give a hand.'

*

A venerable lady in black hesitantly answered. Keeping her door on the chain, she peered with one eye between its edge and the jamb. A delicious scent of spices wafted out.

'*Salaam aleikum.*' I greeted her.

'*Aleikum salaam.* Yes, and?' Her eye travelled my t-shirt and jeans.

'Hi, I'm Suzanne from next door. I was just wondering if I could borrow your grandsons? To help me shift a piano?'

Shaking her head, she gently closed the door. Beyond the stained glass pane, a dark form melted away into deep, impenetrable privacy.

Later I sat at the window. Twilight had not yet fallen; the kiddies went in to supper and bed; Mrs Hussein's menfolk arrived home from work. Summer was with us; the close air smelled of petrol and blossom. A three-quarters moon rose. There was the sound of thunder. I leafed through a tattered Mozart score picked up at Blood's second hand shop in Rusholme, a solitary Bohemian pursuing her art by lamplight.

No, not thunder, something menacingly human.

*

Laurie rang. Before I could tell him about the furore in the night, he was off into an account of Corinne's displeasure with him.

'She says I'm an amoeba. Or a hydra, I'm not sure which. No shape and many heads. Going nowhere. She says I hanker after second best. Can I come over?'

'Yeah, but be warned. There are police in our street interviewing everyone.'

Laurie was round like a shot. He stared at the piano wedged at the bend in the staircase. It had shed some of its keys and the back had come unstuck. You could squeeze past if you held your breath.

The young Husseins, after what were being hailed as my heroic actions of last night, had manhandled the instrument up the stairs for me. I'd basked in their admiration though in all honesty, running out banging a dustbin lid and shrieking *Fuck off, you Nazi gits!* was less than heroic. Now I possessed a legion of helpers. Unfortunately there was no obvious way to coax the piano round the bend. Paula's languid suitors stood around with rolled-up sleeves to show willing. Best thing to do was: leave it there and give it some thought.

'Good girl!' Mrs Hussein had cried, shaking my hand in a frenzy of gratitude. 'You were so brave with the dustbin lid! My lovely grandsons will get that piano upstairs if it is last thing they do.'

'It was nothing,' I insisted, glowing. 'Truly.'

Pakis! Pakis! the local thugs had bawled as they lobbed a brick through my neighbours' window. No sooner was I out of my front gate than I was joined by Mr Shanka with his cricket bat. The yobs legged it. The Hussein boys excused themselves from our celebratory party in the downstairs flat. Whatever did the poor souls hear through our walls that witnessed to our depravity? Now however there was firm league between them and us. They'd come back tomorrow, they vowed, and finish the piano job.

Laurie and I settled down with Newcastle Brown Ale. The gas fire rustled like a living fire. Laurie, cherishing a new and flattering view of me, took my socked feet into his lap and caressed them.

'Would you ever like children, Suzie?' he asked.

It was then that Corinne arrived. Tom had let her in and she'd climbed the stairs soundlessly.

'This is nice. Fucking cosy. No, I don't want some

fucking brown ale. It would choke me. What's *he* doing here?' she demanded.

'I do have a name,' Laurie remonstrated mildly.

'*Do* you? What is it? — Frodo Fucking Baggins?'

In her indignation, Corinne looked more arresting than I'd ever seen her even on TV. Laurie explained that he was comforting me. Suzie'd got caught up in a fight with some drunks in the street and she'd rung in tears. He didn't hesitate, Laurie said. He rushed over. He hoped he'd done the right thing, hadn't paused to consider.

'Tell,' said Corinne, clearing my feet off Laurie's lap and flopping down between us. 'Hold nothing back.'

She'd plaited her long pale hair and wound it round her head in a crown like a milkmaid. She was wearing a tiny skirt and high suede boots, very expensive and probably quite warm for summer. Her legs were lean and long. She looked like a film star passing time amongst her public. Laurie would never leave Corinne, that was for sure. How could he? How could anyone? I couldn't myself. I'd rededicate myself to politics and art.

★

Nazis! Nazis! Weirdly hung-over, my body seemed to list. A ball of pain in my temple indicated that I'd been shot on some forgotten occasion. The BNP leaders shuffled from the meeting hall into the drizzle between a double line of policemen. As we charged, each comrade met the same fate: I landed on my shoulder on the opposite pavement. How could I have been thrown so far? I limped off down Deansgate.

I'd played my part. Home now. Letting myself in, I lurched upstairs, clasping my injured arm. Did I need a doctor? Had something been dislocated or broken? Why had I given Laurie and Corinne my bed last night and slept on the settee? Was it drink or guilt? Only at the bend in the stairs did I twig that something was missing.

No piano. No banisters.

Swaying above the unguarded stairwell, I crouched to examine the banister stumps. Scrolls of wood shavings lay around but someone had clearly been busy with a vacuum cleaner. One thing was sure: couldn't have been Corinne. And as for Laurie, he might have managed a dustpan but it was hard to imagine him sawing through banisters. He hadn't that kind of initiative. I called their names but they were long gone.

'Come in, Suze,' called Paula cheerfully, when I knocked. 'Nettle's gone to a lecture.'

'What? Really?'

'She thought it was about time. Just me and boring old Tom.'

And there they lay, glued like coupled foxes in what is called the tie. Tom, on top, was covered by a sheet.

'Whoops, sorry. Didn't realise.' I started to back out.

'Nah, that's fine. We don't mind, do we, Tom?'

No reply.

'Right, well, I just wondered what happened to the banisters.'

'One of the lads next door — Mo — is an engineer,' Paula explained. 'The tall one with the smile, I fancy him rotten. He said the only way to tackle the situation would be to extend the space. He brought his saw. Once the banisters were off, it was a doddle to move the piano into your sitting room. What's happened to your arm, Suze? Want a bag of peas on it? Tom will get you some.'

'But what about the banisters? What will Mr Marshall say? No, I don't want any peas.' I felt, suddenly, older than them all.

'Mo's coming back with his toolbox, don't worry. Luscious guy.'

'You know what, Paula?' said Tom.

'No. What?' She pouted a kiss at him.

'I'm sick of it — sick — you use me — that's all I am to you, a fucking vibrator on legs — I've had enough!'

'Bugger off then, Tom. Plenty of guys are gagging to take your place.'

'No, I won't get off.'

'I said, get the fuck off.'

'No, I fucking won't get the fuck off.' Tom held her wrists beside her head. She grinned. I flinched. Was this part of their love play or should I be anxious for Paula and angry with Tom?

'Tom,' I said quietly. 'Do as Paula says. Now.'

He withdrew. Scarlet, I made myself scarce; groaned my way upstairs and into the kitchen. Hardly had I brewed coffee than I heard Paula calling from the hall: 'Hey, guess what, Suze? Tom and me are engaged! We're gonna have six children! Wish us luck!'

Luck would be needed, especially by offspring of their union.

My head hurt. My shoulder hurt. The piano could wait.

Filling a hot water bottle and swallowing codeine, I crept into the bedroom. Nobody there: the bed had been made, after a fashion. I slipped into Corinne's and Laurie's sheets. There was a smell of sex. Not mine. Of grubbiness. Mine. Must do a big wash. Hours later I surfaced; an ashy twilight had fallen. The hall smelled of fresh paint. And something was different: that was it — my banisters were reinstated. You couldn't see the join unless you got down to floor level. Mohammed Hussein had been and gone with his tool box.

From the front room came a Mozarty kind of music. Someone was playing a record. Laurie would be waiting, as he sometimes did. Had he looked in as I slept and decided to let me have my sleep out? Comforting to imagine him watching over me. I soaked in the bath for a while. Time was ripe. The season had come for me to say to Laurie (or preferably Laurie to me): *It was you all the time, dearest.*

Corinne looked up from my piano and smiled like a seraph but her hands continued to play. She'd passed Grade Eight before giving up: money had been poured without stint into her lessons. The music brimmed, suffusing the room in golden sadness. It was a correct rendering of the Adagio — a little more than that, to be fair. The performance had something beyond technique: it possessed a soul. It fell on my heart like a benediction, one not meant for me.

She concluded.

A moment's silence, then — through the open sash from the dark street — we heard clapping and calls of 'Bravo, Suzanne!' The Hussein brothers had gathered beneath the street lamp. They greeted me as the spirits must have greeted Orpheus.

I waved, tacitly acknowledging the applause, and thanked Mo for his excellent carpentry. Would he come in for coffee or something stronger? He wouldn't.

'Your turn, Suzie,' said the pianist, sliding off the stool.

'Oh. Well. I don't actually play. Yet. You know perfectly well, Cory, you were the one they could afford piano lessons for.'

Laurie was lounging on the settee. 'She said Chopsticks was about your limit, Suzie,' he said. 'I thought maybe you'd bought the piano for Corinne to practise on when she comes round.'

'No,' I said, not meeting his dangerous eyes, not meeting my sister's. I closed the lid. 'I'm going to learn. It's my piano. Come back in a year's time. And not before.'

Lark Fell

My sixteen-year-old spine was pliant as a gymnast's. I could mould to all sorts of contours, as if the clay of me hadn't fully dried.

I'd been tumbling around since I could walk. I was a parlous, all-over-the-place, look-where-you're-going kid, forever in a trance, with a kneeful of picked scabs. But what holds a faller-down suspended high above the Cuerdon Valley when she nods off in a tree? Perhaps fearlessness itself protects you. Or I'd gleaned from Lark a touch of her perfection when she took me under her wing. This was my third or fourth go at running away from home and the Dongas in the protest camp asked no questions. If they had, I'd probably have mumbled that my parents, decent, conscientious people, were *bourgeois conformists* and *carnivores*. My gentle dad liked steak — and liked it bloody.

When I opened my eyes there was a full moon, creaming every surface. And I had failed to fall. Smoke rose from the Dongas' fire through the stillness of the evening. The stars were profuse. I could hear the River Ribblesworth surging. Cradled in the boughs of the beech, I guessed for the first time why people worship.

I hadn't lost my balance. I was immune. But later, Lark fell. Don't think of that. Rowan wrung his hands. She was just there, he said, she was her usual self, and then suddenly she was gone.

I'd never seen anyone wring their hands before. I made a mental note. This is what grief looks like. Tears poured down his face, his long-lashed eyes were almost closed, he was consumed by salt. He wiped his cheeks with his long, soiled hair.

I only looked at her, he said. I just looked and suddenly she wasn't there.

★

Lark's stretcher was winched up into the underbelly of the helicopter. She hadn't regained consciousness. It was not your fault, everyone assured Rowan, huddling round. No way. How could it have been? We're all hazarding our lives here. That's what it's all about. We fight the loggers and the bulldozers and the security guards and the police for the life of every precious tree. We do this every day. Lark is a hero of the forest. We have to go on for her sake.

Rowan, out of his mind, stated that his dark side must have tripped her. He threatened to denounce himself.

— Aye, you do that, growled Michelangelo. — I saw the way you were with her. I think you've got it about right, Buster.

— Shush, said Nessa. — It wasn't his fault. Obviously. You're being cruel, Mick.

— Truth is fucking cruel, was all he said. Mick's hands were gnarled and paint-ingrained. He walked with a stoop. With his cowboy hat and boots, he was a relic of the sixties, an ageing stag amongst the bucks. Whatever did he mean? I puzzled. Was he saying that looks could kill?

I was so upset that I turned for home when the camp dispersed. Stowing my little all in a backpack, I hitched to Gloucester.

My corduroy dad was weeding in the front garden, kneeling on a mat like a man in prayer. He straightened up and looked through me.

— Daddy. It's me. Freya.

He peered. — Good grief. What's happened to your hair?

— You're so thin, my mother said. Taking a deep breath, she held it and me. — You're skin and bone.

I bounded upstairs for a pee. As I came downstairs, I heard Dad say, — She smells like a drain.

— I know. If she's coming back —

— Yes, she'll need to —

— She will. Absolutely.

Hot soup. Warm rolls. Baby tomatoes from Dad's greenhouse. It was comforting to fill my belly with goodness. There was the same old view of the manicured lawn and the beech tree. I'd dropped in on my own childhood, still apparently going on despite my absence. At this table Dad had kept me for a whole afternoon until I ate up my lamb chop. I can't eat lambs, I'd said, and I'm not going to. Lamb's just another word for mutton, he'd insisted.

Our dispute about reality and language began with the lambs. I used the time to fill Dad in on slaughterhouses.

My parents' faces repressed shame at the sight and smell of me, even as they smilingly ladled out rhubarb and soya custard. They were wondering, I knew, whether the neighbours had seen the state of their unwholesome daughter. How can you live like that? their pained eyes asked. Up trees like a chimp? Underground like a rat? Look at you! Clogs to clogs in three generations. Clogs? You've got no clogs! Flipflops and disgraceful feet, filthy and splayed.

— Well, Dad observed. — At least she won't get bunions.

Looking down, I saw what they saw. Two brown, leathery animals naked on the wool carpet they'd scrimped for. I felt sad for my parents. They'd only had the one child and look how she'd turned out.

— Freya, dear, said my mother carefully. – What about a nice hot bath?

The human stain, ripe and gamey: it has honesty. Layers of dried sweat sheathe you in a protective crust. If I met the young me now, I'd peg my nose and run.

I rinsed the forest out of my hair. My mirrored face looked flushed and softened and I thought: hey, I can sleep now, I'm safe here. Nothing bad can happen, only boredom and the narrow outlook from my bedroom window. The ordinary luxury seemed to go to my head. A small ecstasy of relaxation overcame me as I snuggled into the single bed of my childhood.

Lark was not falling in my dream. She and I were lodged, so it seemed, in the one grave.

It's years now since we lived underground in Lark's

tunnel beneath the road-to-be. Lark could read me like a book from that time when we nearly died together. In the tunnel we shared a space so cramped that it could have doubled as a luxury tomb for two. You felt the weight of earth bearing down. Soil in your eyes, mouth, hair. Lark said we had fellowship with rabbits now, and moles, and the roots of trees that open the earth to oxygen and worms. She wasn't prey to the paroxysms of trembling that put me in a cold sweat. But she understood my qualms and said, You're a brave one, Little Frey — have to hand it to you. We lay in one another's arms in solid dark, broken only by the torch's eye.

It had all been real but now I dreamed it and woke in terror.

— Feeling better for your snooze? asked Mum, embracing the sweeter-smelling me. — Has something happened, she asked hesitantly, — to bring you home?

— No, I lied. — I just wanted to see how you were. Sorry not to have kept in touch properly. I will from now on.

No way could I stay: the tedium made me itch. What is home anyway? It's where you feel most alive, surely? A new camp opened at Elmleigh. The group had taken over an old stable next to the bypass-endangered woodland. Nessa was there already, and Rowan, and Michelangelo, who'd already begun a mural — a woodland canopy — on the ceiling.

Dad handed me a wad of cash. — Put it in your jacket pocket, the one that zips up. Don't give it away. And remember, we will come. Just say the word. Buy some strong boots and *wear* them.

—You are my baby, said my mum. —You'll always be that.

— I want a better, greener world, you see, I explained, imploringly. — I want that for you. For everyone.

— Darling, we just want you to be safe.

— I want you to be safe too, Mummy. That's why we do what we do.

They'd seen the news item obviously — but were unprepared to broach it head-on unless I did. Once they heard the details, that knowledge would be forever in their heads. I'd be crashing to earth with Lark every minute of every day. I didn't want that torment for them.

— And don't be a stranger! Dad yelled after me.

When I looked round, my father seemed to have shrunk. My heart flinched, to think that they were ageing and would have to do so without me.

★

Back in that passionate world of shared conviction, there were so many guys a seventeen-year-old might covet, beautiful and idealistic, tender as saplings, or raw and raunchy like Al or Bertie, and for that reason glamorous. For a while the guys passed me round like a spliff.

I'd lost something, I'm unsure what. Not just Lark and her wings over me. Some part of myself. I dreadlocked and hennaed my hair. I tried acid but it disliked me. I clung on to Nessa and half strangled her. She'd a degree in zoology; had studied the fox in its earth, the badger in its sett and how they went about their earthmoving activities. They are engineers, she said. They put us to shame. Some of us are burrowers, others are flightless birds. What am I? I asked. You're needy, Nessa said, you're a bit unborn. Can't tell yet what species you are. You might be an amphibian.

Was amphibian good or bad? I decided not to ask in case I found out.

— Poor Lark, Al said once. — Mick's right. She got herself landed with a fucking parasite, didn't she? Fatally weakened her.

— What do you mean? I asked. — About a parasite? You don't mean me?

– Nah. A tick. A prick.

Michelangelo mumbled about leeches. — They sucker on to open wounds. If you put salt on their tails or light them with a match, they detach but they vomit into the wound and infect you. You die. They have their uses but steer clear of leeches, young Freya.

Mick, in charity shop collar and tie, attended Lark's cremation in Ipswich. Her parents allowed just the one ecowarrior to attend. Lark would have wanted a willow coffin and a woodland burial: what she got was the eternal pollution of an incinerator.

— Lark's true memorial, Rowan said, — is us. Saving the earth in her name. Us and the trees.

Round the fire, we all confessed some intimate source of regret. Rowan — rather proudly — recalled his shameful blooding. He'd hunted deer in his teens and could track soundlessly. The bastard hunters get the viscera of the kill and smear it on a boy's forehead. The blood runs in your eyes. You're now a man, you're initiated.

Rowan, twice my age, had knocked about a bit, he acknowledged. I never knew when he'd appear beside me. He carried a sinister, brooding melancholy. He'd never get over Lark. — Frankly, it finished me, he said.

Nessa stirred the embers and sparks went up. She said, — Correction. It finished her.

— Yeah, Rowan said, — that's what I mean. Compassion hurts. Every man's death diminishes me. I *am* Lark now, he whispered to me, tears in his eyes, smoke on his breath. The pupils were so dilated that his eyes seemed completely black. — I'm what's left of Lark.

I thought those were wonderful words. Reaching out, I placed my hand over his and felt it quiver. This is what grief is, I thought. This darkness. The nightmares began then, but also their antidote: the dream of Rowan.

— I know you miss her, he murmured. I felt he read me; that I could keep no secrets from Rowan. — Lark was scared, he said.

— But what of? I never saw her frightened.

— Emptiness, growing older, living without perfection. Of loving too intensely. Age, mainly. She was twenty-eight, you see.

— That's young though, I objected. The elms around us creaked and soughed. — Twenty-eight is nothing.

He laughed. — So how old are you, little girl?

— Eighteen. Nearly. Old enough to know that twenty-eight is young.

— Maybe subconsciously Lark wanted to go, Rowan said. — I used to think I drove her to it. But I think it was just, you know, her time. You know the song? — To

everything turn turn turn — there is a season. That idea.
A time to be born, a time to die. It was Lark's season. But,
hey, — he swerved in mid-thought and lifted my chin with
his forefinger. — Why the fuck have you cut your arms? It's
stupid, it's attention-seeking. If you're in earnest, slash your
wrists properly and be done with it.

I flinched. That was a vile thing to say. I insisted I didn't
do it any more.

— Yeah, right, Rowan said. Hooking his little finger
under my sleeve, he twitched it up, exposing my wounds
to the firelight. He put his lips to the ridged scar tissue and
I shuddered and he looked up with sly eyes that floated
beads of firelight on their pupils. And oddly enough I don't
think I did it again. That was his magic, or his effrontery. Or
my embarrassment. His stare seemed able to forge its way
into a privacy beyond nakedness.

Rowan dwarfed me, he drowned me out. I liked that.
Except when I didn't. Releasing his hair from its ponytail, he spread it over my face. I lay under him, paralysed.
— Now you're in the dark. My dark. Our dark. He told
me tales of saving the great redwood trees of California.
— Redwoods are the tallest trees and the oldest living
things on our earth. Two thousand years old, some of
them.

He could talk, he was eloquent and had lived nine, or
nineteen, lives.

— I climbed the redwood called Lauralyn, he said. —
Lauralyn is one of the greatest girls in the world. I knew
Judi Bari. Not heard of Judi Bari? Man, but you are one
blank canvas, Little Frey. Pipe-bombed Judi was by Nazis

and the fucking FBI tried to pin it on her. Judi was my soul mate.

And after that Lark was his soul mate. And was I his soul mate too? Sometimes I fell asleep to the sound of Rowan's voice, extolling his serial soul mates. When I woke, he was still going on. Or round.

Had I ever really known Lark? She'd been a person of few words and careful of smiling. When she laughed, you saw that a tooth was missing. My feet were never quite steady again after her death and the effortlessness of climbing was compromised. In the face of that, and for the love I had for Lark, I made a rule for myself to dare the hardest climbs. You're a bold one, that's for sure, she'd said: it had been a milk and honey moment. All Lark had taught me I would bring into the battle. I wouldn't let her down.

All of us were passionately bonded in the tight-knit fight for the forest. Love and trust stretched between us like the wires linking the tree houses. The group's affection secured and composed me.

Rowan saw that and didn't much care for it. — Licence my roving hands, Freya, and let them go … Behind, before, above, behind, below, he'd murmur, and his hands would swarm like a colony of termites searching out habitat. I was abraded from too much touching. — Set me as a seal upon thine heart, Freya … for love is stronger than death, jealousy is as cruel as the grave …

I preferred the poetry to the fucking. Whenever Rowan was arrested and spent a couple of nights in a cell, sleep brought dreams of intoxicating freedom.

We were migrant creatures, transients: we had our

seasons like the swift and swallow — but the Oak Squat, our headquarters, felt like home. People came and went, like Juliet who looked all of twelve but claimed to be sixteen. Everyone babied her. Rowan said she was innocent as a newborn babe and therefore had everything to teach us. His learning sometimes lasted all night. Was Juliet his soulmate now? I was ready to hand over the mantle and its responsibilities. We served tea to the Nimbies, who brought casseroles and cakes and were naively astounded at the violence of police and security guards. They admired Michelangelo's murals and thought it a shame that his art works would be abandoned when we left. We explained our commitment to passing on beauty to strangers: that's what we were for. But the place was magical. I too wanted to stay.

Michelangelo painted as if life depended on it. *Trompe l'oeil*, he said, *sotto in su*, after Mantegna. No wonder he wasn't eager to move on — although up to now he'd always shrugged and said there's plenty more where these works came from. But Mick was sixty-two; his neck hurt and his spine. A grey-bearded hippie from an earlier age, he was a veteran of every cause in his lifetime. But nowadays he felt his roots tingling: they were trying to bed down. You looked up to what Mick had created on the ceiling where blackbirds and finches sang. You went outside and peered into the beech canopy and heard the woodpecker hammering his heart out. It was all one.

Mick made no attempt to touch me and he wouldn't. He mothered me, is how it seems, looking back. And I began to flourish.

— Want to be my apprentice? he asked.

— Please, Mick. Tell me what to do.

I lay on my back beside Michelangelo on the scaffold. My arm burned with the discipline of wielding the brush. Whole days flashed past, as he instructed me in his art. Rowan's voice had lost its power to bring me down.

— What's in that pot, Mick? I asked.

— It's Lark.

— *What?*

— Her ashes.

— Oh. God. Her real ashes?

— Aye.

He'd begged from her parents, and received, a little ash, in return for a portrait. Now he mixed Lark with gum arabic to bind the residue. Just one drop. A little water. Pigment. He'd been experimenting with wood ash and charcoal, until our friend's true colour disclosed itself. And here she was, resisting gravity on the stable ceiling, in the smoky blue of the sky.

I dipped my brush in the grey-blue paint. It wouldn't last, Mick said. We're not fixing her. We can only pass on a few of her atoms. Essentially she's already free. Of us and our claims and representations.

Painting into the night, we fell asleep up there on the platform, to the ocarina hoo-hooing of owls. The next morning I clambered down the ladder and stumbled out to pee. The endangered forest was a remnant of the wild-wood that invaded after the last Ice Age: many of its trees had been coppiced and pollarded for centuries and rare orchids bedded at their mossy base. It was too early for the clearance men to be around. The bulldozers and cherryp-ickers stood idle. The whine of the electric saw was silent and there was a bittersweet delirium of birdsong. In the tree houses no one stirred.

Ten thousand trees the vandals had in their sights.

A woodpecker chick was poking its head out of its nest-hole. Here came the dad with a grub. The ravenous chick popped right out — and stayed there, exposed for the first time in its life, clinging to ivy. I held my breath. Was it ready to fledge? Surely not. It slipped; gathered itself. And then it flapped its wings. It was away. And another. A third. They perched in a beech nearby, the lone dad fussing round them. Where was the mother? No mother. Why were they making such a racket? Are you all right? the frantic dad was asking, over and over. Here, have another grub! eat up! another little grub! you'll need all your strength! The uproar of their exchange would draw the goshawk: here we are! — here we are! — come and get us! Shush, I thought, keep a low profile: the goshawk will dart from the larches and farm you, picking off the tribe of you one by one, easy as that.

★

—They're going for the Cockspur Oak, Bertie yelled. — I just heard.

There's more life in a dead tree than a living one and this oak, to judge from the fungus fruits, decay holes and beetle colonies, was well on its way to this vital death. Its heart was rotting from the parasitic oak bracket that sucked its massive base and left behind a white powder of death. At the same time, the Cockspur, for all its barren branches and lesions weeping sap, was still putting forth leaves. In the hollow of its belly, local cockfighters centuries back had stowed living roosters in baskets before the bloodshed. It must have been a loud tree, alive with terror and violence. The Cockspur had been routinely pollarded and its cloven girth, twenty feet around, supported elephantine boughs, extending at right angles. However did gravity permit that? So powerful was the Cockspur that it could sustain a multitude of dead branches. How they'd hold out when climbed was anyone's guess.

I didn't give it a thought. I was Lark's child, I told myself. It was time for my blooding.

★

— We fought for every single one, I tell my father, who, after several years' remission, is hoarse and dying.

His eyes, now that he has no further investment in life at ground level, gleam with a distant, morphine-calmed curiosity. He's flown free of his mortgage, his alarm clock and the Sabbath polishing of the Fiesta. The strimmer lies beached in the garage and the lawn is a haven for poppies and love-in-a-mist.

— You giddy girls in the trees! What's it like up there with the birds, thirty, forty, seventy metres off the ground? Tell me about the Village in the Sky! How exactly did you fix those high tension cables to connect the tree houses?

I'm no engineer, but I tell him what I know.

— And what about the pitch battles with the police and guards? Weren't you afraid? he asks. — We were. For you. Every mortal day.

— I'm sorry, Dad. Yes, I was afraid. But not of the tree. Or the guards.

What do we have to rely on? A strong bough, a stout rope. Intuition, know-how, a calm and purposeful mind.

And perhaps, as Lark had said: X-ray eyes.

Inspect your tree, I remembered her saying as I stood planted beneath the Cockspur, the vile whine of the electric saws drowning out voices and birdsong. Use your eyes, Lark reminded me: consider this individual's growth, Freya. How did it come to be in this position, how is it feeling, what is threatening it, what steps is it taking to balance out its problems? Trees are wise, they have resources. When I'm climbing, Lark told me, I'm in a trance. A wakeful trance.

My rope held convincingly. As I climbed the scaly ridges of bark, barefoot, bare-handed, I listened to the oak, estimating which limbs would support and which betray me. The boughs seemed to twist and coil. Time had warped them in curious convolutions so that, where they forked, they also turned around.

Twenty metres up, I approached a difficult phase, like a passage in music for a virtuoso player. Although you've never played this passage before in your life, you are required to succeed first time.

My left foot had a hopeful intuition about the dubious bough. Shit, that felt spongy. Decay had digested the sapwood; flakes of bark sifted off. Trust it moderately, I advised myself, and calmly offered it more weight, which the tree accepted.

When you awaken from a dream of love, the illusion tarnishes. Just like that. It's almost embarrassing. You were seventeen yesterday and anyone's fool. Fearful of loss, brimming with need. Today you're eighteen and enlightened and ruthless; you're charting your own course and you haven't a clue what you saw in the guy. You're lighter without him and more supple and focused.

— So what *were* you afraid of, Freya? asks my dad's husky voice. He moves very little, husbanding his remaining strength. The thumb of his diminished hand strokes the back of my hand.

— Nothing really, Dad, at the time. Once I'd reached a pad to perch, it was beautiful up there. I found the place of greater stillness, I tell him. — And that's a good place to be, Dad, isn't it? We don't need to fear that good place.

My climb made the national news. And that was how my parents, on the day of diagnosis, when they might have been fully occupied wringing their hands and abandoning hope, located their daughter. They broke the speed limit. They forced their way through the barriers. When they found the Cockspur, the police had forced the loggers to withdraw. I'd been up there all night, higher than I'd ever been in my life; it didn't rain, there was hardly a breath of wind. The air was clear and cold, with a three quarters moon whose light tricked a robin into staying awake singing. In any case, at that season it never gets completely dark, there's a grey-green gloaming all night long.

Chained to the tree, I couldn't fall unless the tree fell. But you get chilled, your eyelids droop, there's confusion and blur. A beating of wings, was it? Or a revving of engines? I snapped awake, faint and clammy. Men with hydraulic metal cutters were being lifted in the cherrypicker and Rowan was yelling, — Don't give in, Frey, fight the bastards, do it for Lark!

But she was down there too and her voice over the loud hailer was telling me, – Calm now, my darling, the men are coming up in the ladder tower and they'll bring you down, breathe now, come on down to us, you've made your point.

★

Mum calls, — Come on downstairs now, Freya. Eat something. Your father needs to sleep.

She calls again. I go to the top of the stairs. – I'll come when he drops off, Mum.

— OK. I'll have mine. Then I'll be up.

Dad's eyelids close; his grip slackens. His forehead and hand are in a cold sweat. It can't be long now.

— We have to look after ourselves too, says Mum, taking my place. — Soup's in the pan. Go down.

Later, when the nurse has visited to give another injection, Mum and I get a breath of fresh air in the garden.

— In the end, she says, the best thing you can do is to defer the bad thing. But then again, there comes a time. Doesn't there? For letting go, because the bad thing is not the worst. He's very proud of you, Freya. In his quiet way.

My mother's eyes swim with tears. — And so am I, she admits. — You and Mick, painting the world to rights. Don't you miss that forest way of life? Did you ever find what happened to your friend?

★

They built the roads, of course; the stable was flattened; eight hundred were arrested, charged, cautioned, tried, mostly released. Mick and I left for Bristol to set up the studio. Once I bumped into Juliet at an anti-war demo. She was with the Quakers. — Rowan, she said. — What a sad guy. He fed off suffering. Bit of a fantasist. He'd never been to California, of course. Still, he also spoke truth to power. In his way. That is not nothing, Freya. No idea where he is now.

I still ponder the fall of Lark who could not fall. She'd been climbing since early childhood; she could scale a pine without a rope. Lark was more than an athlete, she was an acrobat. Dare-devil? Not really. She thought her way into a tree. Lark was the one they sent up really dodgy trees. Not just because she was agile, for this, to her, was secondary — but that she understood their deep structure; Lark's eyes knew and her foot anticipated when a bough might prove dangerous. We were apes once, this is how we were originally, she'd say, when we had prehensile tails and hung out in the treetops. Look at my hands, Freya: eighty million years swinging from branch to branch formed these long fingers.

It was magical to see her in action. She was off her guard. It only takes a split second.

Lark Fell

Some trees, like the lovely old beech at the end of my parents' garden, with its domed crown, want climbing. They implore you: Come up, Freya, into my arms. I'm so much more careful these days — and that's a loss.

Woman Recumbent

After a day and a night of lying on bare tiles, shafts of cold penetrating her pelvis, hooping her chest, if human warmth ever came, it would strike like a grenade. Libby set rock-hard, puzzled at her rigidity when she inclined to move. Pain was glaciated, fear glazed. In the old days, the clemency of pneumonia would long ago have commuted her sentence: 'the old man's friend'. That friend had several times tapped lightly at her door, dithered and been turned away by the authorities.

Prone on the kitchen floor, Libby spasmodically caught (as an eye twitched open) the wink of house keys hung high on a ring. Through the open door to the sitting room her glance angled the faint cream glow of a wall-mounted phone. Once, waking, she thought, *It is never wholly dark. All night round light wanes but never succeeds in failing.*

Otherwise how could the remote keys, the phone hanging as it seemed in space, remain discernible? Men had space-walked on umbilical ropes. They'd floated out where there was no height or depth, neither up nor down. In this cold, and with a cracked hip or thigh, which she had heard snap like distant twigs, the kinesis had failed that might power an effortful raising of head, torso, belly, from the tiles. At first there was a dimming, then suspense, now fractional intimation of renewal: on the point of extinction, light rallied, to tip dull mist on to dusty surfaces. Her immediate world was bounded by the edge of a dingy mat, inches from her face. How frayed it was, rimmed with hairs like lashes, or a centipede's legs, grease-clogged. For years her soles had worn themselves thriftily thin on this mat, a squalid object if you thought about it, but its proximity now brought a tinge of dark comfort, like some pet, mangy and disgraceful, but known.

She was numb to time. The long pauses between pulse beats stretched away untenably until the heartbeat (unexpected by now) came with a soft explosive startle of her whole body. There was no horror, none. Only the icy abstraction of waiting in death's antechamber, so near to this familiar mat, with pearls of light dewing the pane of the living room window (for the door was open, ready to walk through with a tray of tea). An idea distilled. *Pull down the drying up cloth, lay your head on that.* It dangled above her, and so did the idea, but though she urged herself to claw, hook, flip, drag it somehow down, she could perform this only in imagination: her body withheld assent. Such baffling impotence impelled Libby to try again and again, enacting her project solely on the mental plane, whilst her hands maintained inertia and her head continued unpillowed. Her skull might have cracked open like an egg, and all her yolk slopped out, so concussively hard had she come down.

It dawned on Libby, hearing the sough of early commuting traffic on the Glasgow Road, that she must have spent her last or penultimate night on earth. They would all carry on threshing in and out of a city that had long been less of a memory than a rumour in her solitude; and she would be out of it. Well out of it. Yet some spasmodic instinct still thrust up towards warmth and life: the quickening sap of hope hurt mortally. Tresses of light wavered on the carpet and against the armchair in the living room, so comfy, so ordinary, holding the shape of Libby's light frame. The curtains remained apart like wide eyelids: there'd been no time to close them before being caught short by this whatever-it-was, this seizure.

Or had she tripped on something? A ruck of mat? Had someone got in and assaulted her, how could you know? All around her consciousness the house was open to the light of day. Nakedly open. Strange shame confounded Libby, lying here on the tiles, at the prospect of being found, her body putrefied perhaps, beyond recognition. How ghastly for them: she hoped it would not be Cheryl, her young neighbour, great granddaughter of Libby's decades-dead childhood friend, also a Cheryl. *I'm just popping in, Mrs Muir. Brought you some baked rice with a cinnamon skin, I know how you like it.*

They would blame Danny for not coming regularly to check on her. For always having excuses: *I've got work to go to, a living to make, I can't be round there all the time, it's just not on, sorry.* Poppers-in twisted the knife in Danny's sullen back. *Ah,* they cooed, in unsubtle rebuke, *she's such a spry soul, isn't she, you must be proud to have such an alert, intelligent mother, 94 years of age, and all her wits about her!*

And he made that face, that (to Elizabeth) highly legible face which had first appeared when he went away to school, a stricken guilty-angry scowl, bending his grey head like a schoolboy and mumbling. He'd been the unintended child of her middle age, his debilitating presence in her belly mistaken for the onset of menopause until he could no longer be ignored as a human burden. Sholto had died when his son was twelve and she'd raised the lad as best she could, which was not good enough.

Danny wouldn't come. Why should he? She did not blame him. Not a whit. She should beg his pardon for knocking him down.

Had she indeed knocked him down? On her motor bike? In the war she had sped through bombed-out Glasgow bearing letters as a courier but could not recall knocking anyone down, let alone her one son. But he had come a cropper: of that there was no doubt. It was a conundrum and she let it go. Light washed on the green settee; it must be breezy out there. When you peed yourself lying here, the sensation was warm and comforting, then colder than before. Danny had been a bed-wetter: she had smacked, they endorsed violence to children in those days. And you, criminally, obeyed. A rapture of black impatience quivered through Libby: why couldn't it be over, the punishment? Why be put on this earth, to rot like this, at tedious length? To suffer interminable resurrections. It is unnecessary, she

thought. It contributes and amounts to nothing whatever. It is uneconomic.

Uncle Logan with his healthy brutality, his sense of
timing, had given equal weight to economy and mercy.
With one clean wring of the neck Logan would slaughter chickens. He shot the tired and gallant mare through
the temple. Libby had looked Jenny-Jill in the eye before
uncle despatched her. Trustfully she'd clopped along to her
death between uncle and niece, the tumour in her belly
pendant as though she were in foal. Elizabeth, gazing into
the patience of Jenny-Jill's eye, had fingered her velvety
muzzle, the tapering bone so solidly defined; rushed away
into the farmhouse at uncle's bidding and left Jenny-Jill to
his canny mercy.

Crack went the pistol shot. And your hip, which was
friable as a dead twig, porous, its vital juices and calcium
leeched, cracked one evening, once, twice. No one came
to offer the clemency of a bullet, nor had you means to
make an honourable end of it. The long freeze perpetuated
itself. Libby shut her eyes, to seal out the fringe on the
mat, dust-puffs and decaying crumbs, the wanton bloom
of light on the couch through the door. Everything drifted
down in a fine silt, the leavings, skin-flakes, coffee-particles,
dust powdering surfaces like a pall of ash.

In this extremity appeared the most minor of miracles.
A creaturely presence. The ant had scurried from somewhere into Elizabeth's field of vision, where it now paused.
Her jaw and cheek burned with the atrocity of cold as if
her face were one giant toothache, while her eyes took
in the visitation. The insect had roamed far from its nest:

perhaps the community sent out scouts, to reconnoitre territory. And doubtless the ant, with its superior senses, intuited as foreign the presence of the mountain range of skeletal flesh that was Elizabeth, the foothills of her skirts, and waited irresolute, so near to her milky-blue eyes. She was herself terrain now.

Libby pondered the ant. The habit of intelligence was tenacious. She felt bound to take the ant into consideration. It was a life after all. A creature at eye level. Nothing to do with her, and what a relief. Inhabiting its own proximate world. You put down poison for the colony. This seldom worked, in her experience. A puddle of bleach sometimes did the trick. A cluster of brethren drowned, alerting the corporate mind. Then they'd all decamp. They'd disappear from the cracks in the tiled sill which was the entrance to their nether kingdom, pouring out to forage, pouring in with supplies, only to reappear on the counter by the bread bin. She didn't much mind them. But she had never before been glad of one. She kept her eye on the ant, until it no longer seemed as minuscule, but a companionate presence which she tacitly saluted.

And there beside it, one human hair. White, curved, single. How come she had not perceived it before? It lay in an arc, curving toward the mat with its eyelash-fringe. One of her own hairs, for certain; yet it seemed alien, not pertaining to her as she essentially was, despite the fact that she'd been grey for decades — or rather, pure white, and sparse, so that the scalp showed through a fluffy cloud. But that this should be *her* hair, detritus of *her* head, and not her mother's or grandmother's, puzzled Libby, as if a system had slipped.

Detached, the hair lay there, next to the ant. Presumably as she'd pushed her hair back from her forehead yesterday or the day before, this individual had detached, hanging by a follicle to her sweater, then slipped away into these reaches she had never imagined. Indeed, why should she? What would be the utility? The schoolmistressy riposte rapped out in her head like a ruler on a desk (what attitudinising piffle it had all been, though, the geography and Scripture, the gold stars and the black marks, considering the finality of this perspective, getting down to it, level with this ant, that hair). Perhaps now, soon, she could be quit, make her quietus.

★

A face — youthful — appeared at the window, craning. Consternation seized the face. Not Daniel, because of course Daniel was grizzled now, on the cusp of middle age. The young face was jabbering but she failed to make out the words. His eyebrows worked, his hands flapped. Her heart's sap surged, with painful warmth. If she could have moved, Elizabeth would have shooed Jason the milk-boy away. Now it was all up, they would resuscitate her. Having got so far, the deathly cold having seized her feet and calves in such a vice that she could not longer feel them at all, certain bones having snapped, her mind having pitched down this cliff, they would abort her journey. They would importune her: *You must rise again, so that you can die again.*

Like all acts of public benevolence, this alienation of her rights would be reinforced by violence.

'It's all right, Mrs Muir, my lass, don't you be scared, I'm coming through the window. Only way, see.'

A fountain of glass smithereened; the morning imploded; but its shock was delayed until the warm male hand cupped her head, lifting it from the tiles on to her sheepskin. Then she was shaken with grief at the sight of Jason's tears as he stammered into his mobile phone, hastened for a blanket, covered her and chafed her hands with their great knots of vein, so that warmth prickled into her slow-sliding blood.

'Don't you worry now, darling, ambulance is on its way. Thank goodness it's one of your milk days.'

A slight, fair-skinned boy, crew-cut, a ring in one ear-lobe. Observing the gleaming lobe in the sun-slant, Libby despaired. You ran the egg and spoon race, ran it for safety not for speed, loping on your long legs, plaits bouncing on your shoulder blades, balancing the egg carefully: and though you came in last and all the other lasses had vanished, vanished long ago (because you excelled in caution and stamina, longevity was in your maternal genes, frugality and a spartan diet in your traditions, a brainy, resourceful, bookish lass) — despite all this, you had the tape in sight. And now just within reach, you dropped your egg.

'What was that, Mrs Muir?' The earring bent to her mouth.

'Humpty.'

'Don't you worry now, be here any minute.'

He treated her like a child. Thought she'd gone off her rocker, when in point off fact she had never known such luminous clarity. For (it burst upon her now, with Jason's hand cradling both hers) she never should have had a child. Even the one. Too bony, too hawkish, cerebral, opinionated. She had done wrong by Daniel from the first. Reading Sophocles — Sophocles! — while she fed her baby in the night. *Not to be born is best.* Oh yes, a very nice lullaby when you are hesitantly sucking your rubber teat, a lovely welcome to this world. Closing her ears when he cried. Banishing him to the Siberia of school at the earliest opportunity.

Life means life. When the judge imposed his sentence, he stipulated: *in this woman's case, life must mean life.*

She was raised on the stretcher by men in yellow coats, wheeled out into the mouth of the morning. Her lips gaped apart and she lapsed asleep.

*

The intuition reared that Danny had died: that he had lain prone on a cold floor coiled foetally to hug his head, with people kicking him. She'd sent him into this zone of violence, driven him out. For every time he had to go away, Danny had wrung his hands at the station, at which she betrayed him, saying, *You'll be all right, Daniel. Soon as you get there.* And he had begged, every time: *But.* She spoke over his *but* and drowned it out. They both did. She and Sholto, who'd crammed Dan's blazer pockets with sweets till they bulged, avoided those brimming eyes. She had driven her son off, out, away, go, shoo. The train pulled in with roars, hisses, shocks of smoke and the stink of sulphur. Her fingertips poked into the boy's back as he mounted the steep steps. Up he must go, up; stand tall, like the other boys. She waited, desperate for the whistle to blow. And he said: *But mum please*. Now he had fallen. Under the train? She wanted to ask the man in the yellow coat but a plastic beak over her mouth and nose, with oxygen flowing through it, impeded speech. No, she grasped the recognition, the reassurance, as it flashed through her brain, it was not Danny who had fallen, thank God, but herself who had been lying on the kitchen floor with the cold kicking up into her slack belly, her pouched cheek.

★

'Come to see your mum? We were becoming quite concerned, Mr Muir, we couldn't get hold of you. She'll be so relieved to see you, thinks you've had an accident. Ah, a lovely lady, your mum. Don't worry, she's doing just great.'

His shoulders sagged. His eloquent eyebrows drooped.

Yes, Elizabeth seemed to hear her son say. *I sometimes think she's immortal.*

'Well, of course, she took a nasty fall. But she came through the operation *lovely*.'

'Good.'

'Be a relief to you, I know. Mrs Muir, here's your son to see his mum. Doesn't say much at present, there's always an element of trauma.'

'Yes, I know.'

Danny. You needn't have come, I'm quite all right, I didn't want you to fall, you know that. But I should have kept you safe. You should have had an alarm, one of those gadgets with a bleep, it's connected to a carer, you didn't even have a phone, did you, and if you had, how could you have reached, darling, being such a little boy for your age? Actually of course we didn't have a phone either in those days, and if we had, would I have answered? They say my hearing's acute, but is it? I sometimes think I'm congenitally deaf. I was preoccupied, it was my books, you see, but what excuse is that? I don't ask your forgiveness, no, for letting you fall under the train, it was sheer negligence, I can see that now, and you never got over it, never, I can see that too just from the way your shoulders hunch and you duck your head to one side as if someone were going to cuff you. You should have had home helps, you should have had more than just someone popping in to check up on you and breezing out and then I'm convinced you would *not* have fallen.

Inwardly Libby spoke her mind with her usual crackling asperity, holding his eyes. Daniel was leaning forward and appeared to be listening intently. His breath came fast and shallow as his hand crept toward hers across the starched linen.

But Mum, he said, and couldn't go on.

Star Nursery

I've a skin-tingle like flu or guilt and the key quivers in my hand. In point of fact I'm not trespassing, I tell myself: I've every right to be here. Mair gave me that right.

Or did you swindle it out of her with your sly, fey ways, as her nephews maintain? Did you spy a crafty chance to cadge your way indoors from the cold? Apparently you accosted her in a supermarket queue last year, her family said. You were down on your luck. And you took advantage, seeing that her mind was wandering. You saw the main chance and turned her against us. You'll hear from our lawyer.

Hang on a minute: there was no cold to come in from, or at least, there was, but I'm a hardy animal. Never fancied a cage of my own, not really, a coop to cluck in. An eternal squatter, in digs, on friends' couches, I've aspired to live outside the frame; to go lightly on the earth. What's the point otherwise? And isn't it better for minds to wander than to circle the loop of yesterday's stale thoughts?

It was your fathoming look that held me, Mair said. You looked at me as a person. I noticed that your teeth were not good — but the smile was. I admired your topknot and your patchwork outfit. You seemed to have put your-self together from scraps; you were a wholly recycled lass. I got on with unloading my trolley. I'd just heard a mam telling her son to mind out and not bump into that little old lady. Me!

Little. Old. Lady.

Each word an assault on Mair's dignity.

Where do you suppose we keep our dignity? Mair wondered, turning to me again, holding a bag of spinach. The checkout guy was asking did Madam have a loyalty card? He yelled in case Madam was deaf. I knew she was about to object to the word loyalty, and she did. And the word Madam.

Well, I said, pondering, unloading my own basket. I think I keep my dignity in my gut. Though sometimes I lose it. It kind-of comes and goes. You don't always want or need it, do you? Where do you keep yours?

Good answer! Mine is in my forehead, probably. Just here. And perhaps I'm too often *on* my dignity, Mair observed. I am five foot six and a half, she added as she waited for the guy to check her out. Well, that was my height before I shrank. *Little!* And then there's *old!* In my mind I am approximately thirty-five. How old are you? Thirty-two, going on seventeen, I said, and Mair grinned. I liked the wild cloud of her white hair and her bright red scarf. Her eyes were mint-green and feline and sad and challenging. Once Mair's shopping was checked out, she turned to me and said: But you know, it's that word *Lady* that really rankles. Do you consider yourself to be a lady? Look at me, I replied, do I look like a lady? Can't say you do. I think it was in the two-way laugh that the electric charge passed between us. I'm Mair, she said. And you are? Well then, Pearl, she said: have you got time for coffee?

No, she said, I will pay. Put that away. You are my guest.

The key finally consents to turn and as I push, the door wedges on junk mail. A fug escapes from the hall into the freshness of the day.

Mair is not here; never will be here again. The heart insists that she must be elsewhere. And elsewhere is somewhere. Non-being: who can credit it? I've been out hunting her along the sea front at night. Stargazing. I'm thinking: your atoms have gone back into all this and you're answerable now only to the laws of physics. Bellatrix and Betelgeuse and the Orion Nebula, the nursery of the stars: you showed me that.

You were born in this narrow old house on three storeys and here you died. Your mother before you. And before that, your grandparents. Naturally the nephews thought it was owed to them and theirs. They were counting on it. It was a singular trust, to leave me your entire world. How do I qualify for that? Perhaps it was because I was the only friend lacking not only possessions but the hankering after them.

How did I not know how mortal you were? You didn't grumble when the truly bad thing came along. You kept the irony going. Your life, you said, had been unusually rich in mistakes and false trails, often repetitions of the same error. That is quite useful for a teacher, you explained. You'd at last, in your sixth decade, gleaned a kind of contentment, the capacity for calm and wakeful delight. You felt the trembling of the compass needle on the magnet of the Pole; the power that draws the geese north and the starlings south. The beckoning stars beguiled your eyes.

Mair's world seemed to her with every day more fresh and novel; she found herself surrounded by beauty and interest, so she often said. And the buds of new friendships. Perhaps it was the hormones declining. She no longer felt tempted to borrow people's husbands or elbow rivals out of the way or get up to any other ruffianly stunts.

I stared. Yes, you'd be surprised, she said. I was perfidious. But that was then.

If, in her final days, joyous expectation drained away and the lustre of her life dulled, Mair remained, in a shadowy way, herself.

She met Andreas just the once at the squat and turned on him her listening eyes. I was aware that Mair heard rather more than was said. Invisible antennae waved. She didn't judge me, though her default mode was caustic. Perhaps I was Mair's avatar, adventuring on her behalf. There was something Mair wanted to tell me about Andreas. She never got round to saying it before he bolted, which was his way of telling me. Mair was a prophet who could hold her peace.

She had me ration her family's visits — and no wonder they detest me. I haven't time, Mair said. For twaddling conventionalities.

But they are your nephews, I said.

So they keep telling me. But I met my kin, as it happens, at Aldi's over the baked beans. And we got into conversation. This conversation.

I didn't know what to reply. With late friendship comes no entitlement.

Those final moments: I can't blink them off my inner eye. I held her hands and said something like: *It's all right, Mair, I'm with you.* I don't think she saw or heard, not consciously, she was rocketing back along a passage, away, away, a black corridor, the oxygen was consumed and she sped towards the brilliance at the mouth of the tunnel.

Let every door and window stand open. The house can breathe. And all the while I'm answering her brother's children: Listen, I promise you I didn't prey on her, I've lived as an outsider for years, an odd-job person, a rolling stone. It has felt good except when it felt bad. But Mair beckoned: come in now, Pearl, out of the cold, you and your child. How could she possibly have divined the presence of the baby before I was sure myself?

Should I or shouldn't I accept Mair's gift?

Of course you should, replies the baby. How can you be such a dope? You need to shelve your so-called ideals now. And please listen when I counsel you — pay proper attention. You seem to have lived in La La Land. Look round with me in mind: my needs and rights. I could play skittles in this hall. It would be great. By the way, I'll need safety gates on the stairs. What is there in Mair's building society account? There will be expenses. Oh and there's a cellar. Can we play table tennis there? Can I have a den?

Knowing nothing, the child is already wiser than the

mother. Cup of tea, I think. It's a large kitchen. Everything you need. The fridge purrs. I peep in the freezer: it's still stocked with home-made soups and stews, labelled and dated.

I yank up the sash window. The garden has gone mad in Mair's absence — and a wilderness it will probably remain. Where are you now? The dead don't haunt us. They can't be bothered. Why would they? Intimate preoccupation flies away as they quit the time zone and our radar. Well, that's what she might say.

This has been my fastness, my sanctuary, Mair explained, propped against pillows. It's where I've been most myself. And it will be yours. You will be all right. It is a grow-ing season. Where is the baby's father, Pearl dear, where is Andreas? If I may ask. You don't have to say.

No idea, I had to reply. There are things you can't com-municate: a balance of knowing and not-knowing that must be held as long as possible. But don't worry about me, darling, I begged her. Promise not to worry. Mair knew in her life unspecified affliction. I didn't want her to suffer on my account. I'll be fine, I reassured her, hearing my voice like a pigeon's cooing that would deceive no one.

Aye, said Mair and looked at me shrewdly. I think you will. You're a law unto yourself, Pearl, after all.

It takes one to see one.

★

Mair tumbles out of a book. It is a shock.

The books are where you found yourself and left traces

of yourself. All contain a vestige of you. Between the leaves of this old leather-bound volume, which I've taken down at random, Mair has left a pressed anemone. The purple has blanched to violet, the petals to a whisper of tissue paper; the book's pages have leeched twin stains of colour, ghost anemones. I blow, it lifts and I snare it; weigh its lightness on my palm and restore it to the book's long sleep. In ten years' time the anemone may glide out again, like a dream. My daughter or my son will ask, what's this, Mami? — and perhaps grab and crush it, but I'll remember.

I'm forever famished. The leaping babe steers me towards the kitchen cupboard crammed with jam, honey and ... that's it, peanut butter. Dig in a spoon and scoff it straight from the jar. Important protein for you, baby.

I'd never have said I was maternal. Who'd have thought that sorrow and confusion would lead home to this strange, astringent joy?

★

We walked at night along the coast path before she got ill, and Mair said, taking my hand: There are so many kinds of love, Pearl, I never realised.

Yes, I said, suddenly wise. There's no template for love, is there?

Mair pointed out Orion in the south-east. Look for his belt first, that's it. There was frost on the path. Betelgeuse, Bellatrix, Rigel, the Orion nebula, she said. The nebula is a cradle, a nursery, it's where stars are being born. Thousands of light years away.

The mortal two of us stood tiptoe on the edge of the world and gazed.

That was the moment.

I thought then, incredulously: this is love. This has to be love. But not love as I ever conceived it. Because I want nothing of Mair. Really, nothing. Just to be here with her in this moment.

Can one fall in friendship, I wondered. And if so, what follows from that? What can friendship give birth to?

Hot chocolate, I suggested — as being a homely and reassuring thing. Cake?

Cake, said Mair: hot chocolate. You read my mind.

Acknowledgments

'Pod' and 'Woman Recumbent' were runners-up in the Rhys Davies Prize 2001: they were republished in *Story II: The Library of Wales Short Story Anthology,* ed. Dai Smith, Parthian/ The Library of Wales, Cardigan 2013. Both 'Pod' and 'Pips' initially belonged to a short story cycle which was the basis for a radio play, *Pips,* broadcast as a Radio 4 Afternoon Play, produced by Kate McAll at BBC Cardiff, on February 10th 2006.

'Eclipse' was published in the *New Welsh Review,* December 2013; 'Inside Out' in *The Gift: New Writing for the NHS,* pp. 36-9, ed. David Morley, Stride, in association with Birmingham Health Authority, 2002. A version of 'Mr Duda' was shortlisted for the Rhys Davies Prize, 2012; 'Oud' is published in *When Young Dodos Meet Young Dragons: An Anthology of Mauritian and Welsh Writing,* ed. Alan Parry et al, *L'Atelier d'écriture,* Port Louis, 2015; 'Piano' in the *Swansea Review* 2013. 'Red Earth, Cyrenaica' was longlisted for the Bath Short Story Prize, 2013; 'The Old

Gower Swimmers' was published as 'Sea-Path' in *Planet: The Welsh Internationalist,* as part of Wales Coastal Path series, Summer 2013; 'Tuner of Llangyfelach' was published in *Wales Review Online*, January 2014, and reproduced in the *Wales Arts Review's A Fictional Map of Wales,* ed. John Lavin (H'mm, Swansea 2014). 'Ground-Nester' was published in the *Seren Short Story Anthology* in 2015, ed. Penny Thomas and Francesca Rhydderch. 'Star Nursery' was published in *Planet: The Welsh Internationalist,* Summer, 2017.

I thank Professor Ceri Davies, who read an early version of 'Arrest Me, For I Have Run Away', for tactfully pointing out its more notable absurdities. Richard Davies of Parthian has been an insightful editor.

I am grateful to the late Nigel Jenkins for introducing me to the Roman remains at Caerwent and Caerleon. My thanks go to Wynn Thomas, Glyn Pursglove and Neil Reeve for wisdom salted with laughter; Rosalie Wilkins, for a life-time's friendship; Helen Williams, for sharing her paintings and insight. I thank poet Andrew Howdle, for our years of writerly conversation, and novelist Anne Lauppe-Dunbar for star-gazing with me. Thank you to Emily Davies, for telling me about the lambs; to Robin Brooks-Davies, for his thoughtful sensitivity; to Grace Foster, for every imaginable reason.